DEJA BREW ALL OVER AGAIN

A RUNAWAY BRIDE ROMANCE

LOVE ON TAP
BOOK 3

SYLVIE STEWART

ROLLING HEARTS PRESS

Edited by My Brother's Editor

Print ISBN 978-1-947853-70-6

Ebook ISBN 978-1-947853-69-0

ALSO BY SYLVIE STEWART

Ale's Fair in Love and War, *Love on Tap,* Book 1

Smooth Hoperator, *Love on Tap,* Book 2

Asheville Collection, (Standalone Stories from the *Love on Tap* World)

Full-On Clinger, (*Love on Tap* Prequel - Denny and Rosie) *FREE ebook for a limited time at sylviestewartauthor.com*

* * *

Hot Flashes and Hockey Slashes, *Hot Flash Hookups,* Book 1

Mood Swings and Hockey Flings*, Hot Flash Hookups,* Book 2

Poppy & the Beast

* * *

Between a Rock and a Royal, *Kings of Carolina,* #1

Blue Bloods and Backroads, *Kings of Carolina,* #2

Stealing Kisses With a King, *Kings of Carolina,* #3

* * *

The Fix, *Carolina Connections,* Book 1

The Spark, *Carolina Connections,* Book 2

The Lucky One, *Carolina Connections,* Book 3

The Game, *Carolina Connections,* Book 4

The Way You Are, *Carolina Connections,* Book 5

The Runaround, *Carolina Connections,* Book 6

* * *

The Nerd Next Door, *Carolina Kisses,* Book 1

New Jerk in Town, *Carolina Kisses,* Book 2

The Last Good Liar, *Carolina Kisses,* Book 3

* * *

Then Again

Happy New You

Shorts and Novellas:

About That

Nuts About You

Booby Trapped

Crushing on Casanova

Playing by Heart

The Switch-Up

Taunted

to my dad, the original bad boy

CHARACTER MAP

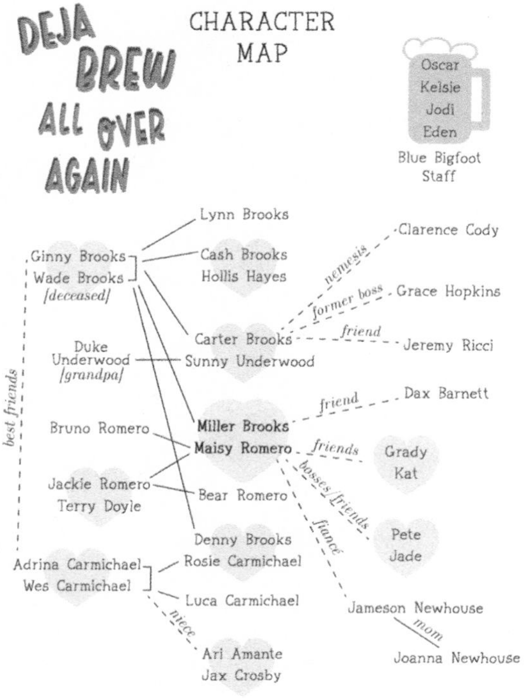

CHAPTER ONE

BEST. CARJACKING. EVER.

MILLER

"If I see you in my courtroom again, we'll be having a very different conversation, you hear me?"

"Yes, Your Honor," I respond in my most solemn tone. Does she think I enjoy being here?

The judge's attention thankfully shifts to the next poor fuck-up. "Next case!"

I waste no time hauling ass out of the courtroom, Luca on my heels.

"Good call on the jacket, man." His voice echoes off the stone walls and ornate ceiling of the cavernous hall. "The dude up next is wearing a shirt that says, 'Juices keep my beard soft.' I'm guessing he'll be out in twenty to life."

Luca and my best friend, Dax, are the only ones I even told about my hearing today, and for good reason. Had the judge sent me to jail, there's no possible way I could have handled the disappointment on my family's faces. Classic Miller, fucking shit up again.

"It always feels good to know you're not the biggest

shithead in the room." I glance around, trying to remember which door I came in earlier. My nerves were so jacked I'm surprised I was able to drive.

"We should celebrate—tell your brothers you got off." Luca Carmichael is not my brother, technically speaking, but he may as well be. I've known him all my life and lived next door to him until he got his own place a few years back. But there's a reason I asked him—and not anyone else in my family—to come today; Luca is always chill, no matter what. And, hey, I needed somebody to pass my mama's car keys off to if I was sent to the clink.

I let out a breath it feels like I've been holding for a month. "Nah, I'm good." I shoot him a lift of my chin. "Thanks for comin', man."

He nods, his messy dark hair falling into his eyes. Physically, Luca is a male carbon copy of his Italian mom, Adrina. She's got the same dark hair and eyes with a semi-permanent tan. In all other aspects, he's the polar opposite. "No sweat." See, totally chill. We do a bro hug with the obligatory back thump, and he takes off to an exit at the side of the main hall. I glance around again, finally orienting myself.

Damn, I could use a smoke right now, but like an idiot, I quit. Even Dax's sticky-finger-discount cigarettes cut into my bike fund, and I'm not getting careless now—especially with this $1000 fine I've just been handed.

A $1000 fine and sixty hours of community service, all because of that fuckwad, Driscoll. The guy was following *me,* and *I'm* the one who gets arrested? The system sucks.

Okay, fine, so I ran from the police, which wasn't the wisest thing to do. But I've already got a record, and I didn't need to court the attention of the cops—or have to explain what I was doing on Ian Driscoll's property. Turns dioxide, and the next there's a vise around my larynx telling me I'm fucked.

"Thank you," she says, but I barely hear her. "Do you think you can drop me a few blocks down so I have a good head start?"

I only nod because it's difficult to talk when you can't breathe. We'll be lucky if I can keep us from crashing into a tree with how distracting her beauty is.

"What the hell did I do?" She settles forward in the passenger seat, covering her face with her hands. I'm somewhat relieved to find I'm not the only one talking to myself today.

Knowing I won't do her any good if I keel over dead at the wheel, I suck in a lungful of air and shift my eyes to the car in front of me. I never get tongue-tied around hot women—I mean *never*. Mama says I was a flirt from the womb, just like my old man, so I'm determined to snap out of it, if for no other reason than me flirting with a girl in a wedding dress would undoubtedly have my dad laughing his ass off.

She continues her one-woman monologue. "I'll tell you what I did. I screwed myself; that's what I did." I see her hands flapping around in my peripheral vision. "It was two words. *Two. Words.* And I couldn't even say them. *I do.* See? Easy, right?"

Since I don't appear to be a necessary factor in her conversation, I keep my mouth shut.

"Right?" she asks again, and I automatically turn to her. She's fucking gorgeous. Long almost-black hair spilling over her shoulders, captivating eyes so dark they match her hair, and lips so plump and perfect that they'd be the envy of any Hollywood starlet out there. The dress has a modest neckline, and there's so much white fabric, it billows up to her chin, so her face is all I can see, but I'd bet my ass her body is banging.

I realize she's still waiting for my answer, so I respond. "The words might be short, though I'd say they're anything but easy."

She blinks at me for a second before exhaling and collapsing back into the seat. I keep on driving. Maybe the groom cheated on her, or he was abusive, or he's just a boring motherfucker. Any way you slice it, she doesn't want to marry him, so she shouldn't have to.

"I can get out here," the girl says when we come to a red light, beginning to gather up the yards of fabric spilling over her lap and the center console.

"I'm not dropping you off on a street corner in that dress. Just tell me where you wanna go, and I'll take you." I may be a fuck-up, but I'd like to think I'm not a *complete* degenerate.

Her eyes move to me again, and it's as if she's only just now realized she's in a car with a complete stranger. She scans my face first before her gaze drops to take in my dress shirt and pressed trousers. I bite my cheek to keep from laughing because God is definitely screwing with me. On a good day, my duds consist of ripped jeans, dirty Converse, and whatever T-shirt doesn't smell like ass. She just happened to catch me on the only day I combed my hair and wore real clothes in the last five years.

"You don't look dangerous. And *I* was the one who broke into *your* car, after all."

She bites her lip again, and I can feel it in my dick, but I'm doing my best to ignore it.

"I promise I'm not a felon," I reassure her, telling the truth. Of course, I leave out the part where I have more than one misdemeanor conviction, and it's been only a month since I was tackled to the ground by two police officers. I consider it an omission more than a lie.

She must be in dire straits because she sighs and lets her dress poof out again. "Thank you. That's really nice of you. I'm Maisy." Her lips finally curve up into a small smile, and I know right then and there that my life is about to get a hell of a lot messier than it already is.

CHAPTER TWO

GETAWAY DRIVER

MAISY

"Miller," he responds with a lift of his chin, his brown eyes studying me like he might be asked to ID me in a lineup later today.

He's cute. Scratch that. He's *hot*.

His dirty-blond hair sweeps over his forehead and curls up just a bit at his collar like he can't be bothered to keep up with trimming it. Pair that with the multiple ear piercings and the tattoo snaking up his neck from beneath his button-down, and he's a fascinating juxtaposition of clean-cut and dirty bad boy.

But what the hell am I doing checking out this random guy when not ten minutes ago I was about to marry Jameson?

Jameson. *Oh, god*. What did I do?

I'm officially *that girl*, the wishy-washy bitch who can't make up her mind and leaves nothing but rubble in her wake. And I've seriously screwed not only Jameson but myself this time.

"Nice to meet you," I mutter as I try to formulate a new plan. When my mom finds out I skipped out on Jameson, she's going to throw the fit to end all fits.

"So, where to, Maisy?" Miller asks in a husky voice, one hand resting casually on the steering wheel like he picks up crazy women in wedding dresses every day. He's likely a true baritone, although it's possible he could drop to a bass if the mood struck him. I'll bet the mood strikes him a lot.

I look at the dash to see that it's one forty. There's still time before Mom gets home from her lunch shift, so when the light turns green, I make a decision. "Tunnel Road toward East Asheville. Please," I tack on.

I really, *really* hope this guy is not a serial killer. I promised Bear I'd never leave him, and I'm pretty sure getting murdered by a serial killer would still qualify as leaving in his mind.

We turn a few times in silence, but I can feel Miller looking at me. I suppose I owe him some kind of explanation, so I go for light and say, "Nice day for a wedding, huh?"

The corner of his mouth lifts slowly in a grin as he glances over. "Nice day for a run is more like it." Is that a dimple in his cheek? Lord, help me.

I choke out a laugh; I can't help it. "I guess I deserve that."

He steers us onto Tunnel Road, and we merge with traffic. "In my experience, people rarely deserve the bad shit that happens to them."

I consider his profile, taking in his strong jaw and straight nose. "So, you're a philosopher, are you? Any words of wisdom for someone who's just royally screwed herself?"

"Again, speaking from experience, my answer is usually weed." His grin is aimed at the windshield this time. "But I've never run from the county courthouse in a wedding dress, so I might not be the best person to ask."

He can't know how much I appreciate his calm, non-judgmental demeanor right now, so maybe I should congratulate myself on choosing the right car to hijack. Instead, I direct him through the next couple turns until we pull into Redwood Mobile Home Oasis. Whoever dreamed up that name was either drunk or delusional.

"Last row, second on the right." My eyes flick over the familiar trailer homes, and I try viewing the park through this stranger's eyes. Miller's car is clean and fairly new, and his clothes are nothing to sneeze at, so I imagine he lives in a nice place far from this shithole. "This one." I point to my mother's trailer, noticing the weeds climbing out from under the unit and the crushed beer cans her deadbeat boyfriend probably smashed against his forehead before dumping them there. I doubt any blow to the head could make Terry any dumber than he already is.

We don't belong here, I think for the millionth time. But a new voice chimes in to contradict me this time. *Maybe you do, Maisy. You should have married Jameson.*

Crap.

I muster a smile as I gather the piles of white tulle around me and unfold myself from the passenger seat. It would have been a lot easier to run in the simple, boho chic dress I'd initially chosen instead of this giant wearable cupcake Jameson's mother foisted on me, but I suppose it doesn't matter now.

"Well, thanks for the ride, Miller. You're an incredibly decent person." I have the sudden impulse to jump back in, slam the door, and tell him to take me anywhere but here. Just drive toward the horizon and never stop.

"Not really," he replies, but his words are accompanied by a smile, so I think he's joking. His eyes flick to the trailer. "Will the dress fit through the door?"

I can't tell if he's poking fun or if it's an innocent comment, but again, I probably deserve it. Before I can decide for sure, the storm door creaks open, and Bear stands in the doorway dressed in the same shorts and dirty tee as yesterday. Why the hell isn't he at school? "Mae? What are you wearing?"

I paste a smile onto my lips and strike a pose. "You don't like it? Oh well, I guess I'll change into something fancier."

The storm door slams behind him, and he descends the three stairs leading to the dirt below. "Who's this?" He points to the Hyundai, where the passenger door still stands open, Miller peering out at us from the driver's seat.

"This is my friend Miller."

"Yo." Miller shoots my brother a two-finger salute, and I swear my nipples get hard.

"I'm Bear." He copies the gesture as if trying it out. "Did you just marry my sister?"

"Not today."

I smooth a hand over Bear's sandy brown hair. "You feeling okay?"

His eyes remain on Miller, giving him a thorough inspection and probably committing everything down to his eyebrow piercing to memory so he can mimic it later. Bear is on an early trajectory to be the king of cool. "I'm good." Knowing why I'm asking, he continues, "Mom got up late, so I missed the bus."

"Is Terry around?" I'm going to ring that lazy asshole's neck. All I can do is thank God he's not Bear's dad. I choose to believe his real dad is some brilliant, kind-hearted guy who had one night of bad judgment when he slept with my mom and came to his senses in the morning before taking off. I don't blame him.

Bear shakes his head, eyes still on Miller. "He said he was going out for smokes, but that was a couple hours ago."

My teeth grit behind my next words as I try hiding my annoyance. "Do me a favor, okay? Run inside and pack a backpack." While Terry's current absence helps my situation, I hate what Bear's casual delivery of the news tells me. This territory is way too familiar.

His blue eyes finally flash to me, brows drawn together, giving him the appearance of a boy older than his nine years. "Where are we going?"

"It's a surprise," I tell him instead of the truth, which is that I don't have any idea where we're going. We just need to get out of here before anyone in my family shows up. That's explanation enough for my brother, though, because he immediately turns tail and hurries up the stairs again. "Don't forget your toothbrush!" I call after him.

I duck my head back down for a last glimpse of my rescuer before I close the car door. "Thanks again, Miller. I really appreciate it."

His brilliant eyes aren't on me, though; they're glancing around my mom's trailer. "I don't see a car."

"What?" I lean in closer, gripping the hot metal of the doorframe. It's got to be ninety out here, and I can feel the sweat beading at the small of my back. There's no way I'll be able to return this dress and repay Jameson's mom, Joanna, if it's covered in sweat stains and trailer park dust.

Miller returns his gaze to me. "I don't see a car, so how are you and your brother getting to wherever it is you're going?"

I shrug. "I was gonna take the bus—or call a friend." In this heat, the walk to the nearest bus stop will be unpleasant at best. It occurs to me that this guy has probably never had to take the bus in his life.

"You just told him *I'm* your friend. And my car's already here." I *knew* he had that bass in him, dammit! His tone is mildly teasing, though, and it's accompanied by a smirk that I'm sure gets him his way ninety-nine percent of the time he uses it. This guy spells T-R-O-U-B-L-E, and I've already got enough of that in my life.

"Miller…" I begin to protest but then remember I can't call Grady if I don't have a freakin' phone. And my phone—along with my driver's license and debit card—are currently at the county courthouse tucked in a ridiculously expensive sequin clutch Joanna Newhouse declared I couldn't *possibly* do without. Crap!

"No pressure. But I don't have to work for another hour, so it's not an inconvenience."

Bear jumps from the top step this time, his lopsided grin growing when he sticks the landing. "Ready in record time. Let's go!"

"Um…" I come to a decision. "Come back in with me, and lemme change real quick, B. I'll be done in sixty seconds, and we'll ride with Miller. You can time me."

If I didn't think my dad and Jameson's family would be on their way here right now, I would refuse the ride, but I need to get Bear and myself somewhere where I can think—where I can figure out my next steps.

Bear starts his countdown with the oversized watch strapped to his skinny arm, and I have no choice but to abandon the white monstrosity on a hanger in Mom and Terry's room before throwing on some short cutoffs, my black Harley Davidson tank, and a pair of red Converse. I shove my toiletries and a few stray articles of clothing into my own backpack and hoist it up on my shoulder.

I've been crashing here for a couple weeks between letting my lease go and officially moving in with Jameson. Mostly to keep an eye on Bear—and probably because deep down, I knew I wouldn't go through with the wedding.

At least I got Jameson to back me on my insistence on a quickie courthouse ceremony so nobody was out too much cash (apart from Joanna with the dress and purse—who knows how much those cost). But he's got to be mad, no matter how cold he knew my feet were.

I can't think about Jameson yet, though. My first priority is getting Bear out of here since Mom will no doubt kick me out as soon as she hears about my runaway bride sitch. I'm unsure how she got it into her head that me marrying into money meant a payday for her, but she's never been entirely rational. And I let her think it since the lure of money meant she and Terry stopped talking about moving away—and taking Bear with them. There is no way in hell they are taking my brother anywhere; I just need to come up with a new plan to prevent it.

I meet Bear at the door just as he yells, "Sixty!" and I put my hand out for a high five. He misses, but I don't care.

"Let's go," I urge with a smile, taking his backpack in one hand while hiking mine up higher on my shoulder as he opens the door for us.

Miller stands waiting, his ass and hands to the hood of his car and his ankles crossed, looking hot as can be. He's rolled up the sleeves of his dress shirt, exposing sinewy forearms and another tattoo peeking out from beneath the fabric at his right elbow. I don't miss the head-to-toe sweep of his eyes over my frame or the appreciative grin coming at me.

He's got player written all over him. I swallow, briefly reconsidering the wisdom of accepting a ride as my belly dips.

But the crunch of gravel under tires catches my attention, and I turn to see Terry rolling toward us in his beat-up Buick.

"Oh, shit!" I shuffle us to Miller's ride and tear open the back door for Bear before tossing our bags inside.

"Oh, shit!" Bear echoes me, but there's no time to scold him.

Miller catches on in no time, and he's back in his seat, pulling forward before any of us even have our seatbelts fastened.

"Keep going!" I command as I twist in my seat to see Terry pulling to a stop in front of the trailer. "It's a big circle, so we can get out this way." When Terry's car stays put, I look to my brother. "Get that belt fastened."

His little fingers work on the clip, so I face forward again and relax back into the seat.

"Lemme guess... next stop is the bank?" Miller inexplicably asks.

I eye him quizzically.

He tears around the corner, spitting gravel and racing back to the trailer park entrance, only then enlightening me. "I've clearly missed my calling as a getaway driver."

And, despite my crazy day and the problems piling up to the sky, I laugh.

CHAPTER THREE

BLOWING SMOKE

MILLER

"Did you know my friend Jordan's got an uncle with six toes?" Bear asks from the back seat.

When Maisy doesn't reply, I glance over to see both her and Bear aiming expectant eyes my way, Maisy doing so with unmasked amusement. "Uh, considering I have no idea who Jordan is, no."

Bear continues as if he didn't hear me. "He's got a pool and an air hockey table and a TV that takes up an entire side of his house."

Now I'm intrigued. "Jordan or the uncle?"

"Jordan."

"B, I think Jordan is blowing smoke up your patoot."

"I got nothin' up my patoot, Mae. That's no lie. Jordan's legit."

I smile at the windshield and decide to mind my own business. "Where am I taking you guys?" I ask now that we've cleared the trailer park and are cruising back toward downtown.

"River Arts District, Roberts Street," Maisy says, and I turn my smile her way, again taking in her shiny dark chocolate hair falling in sheets over her kick-ass tank top that molds to her breasts. This outfit is way better than the wedding dress, and I was right about her body—absolutely bangin'.

"I work less than a half mile from there," I tell her. "Do you live there?" I can't quite believe my luck. Clearly, I'm ignoring pesky details like her apparent engagement to another man.

She bites her lip as she stares back at me, but Bear answers for her. "She works there. She sells T-shirts and coffee—and dish towels with dirty words on them. I ain't supposed to know what they mean, but I totally do."

"No you don't!" Maisy releases her lip and turns to send him a playful glare, but I'm still focused on her mouth.

"Do too! I know the one that says, 'I rub my own meat' ain't about hamburgers."

Maisy gasps, and I can't help the guffaw that escapes my throat. A glance in the rearview shows Bear's self-satisfied smile as he rests back into the seat and crosses his arms over his tiny kid chest.

"That's it. You're not allowed at Jade's shop anymore. You're taking a seat at Pete's from now on."

"Fine by me. His smoothies are fire."

I'm pretty sure I want this kid to be my new best friend.

"Are you talking about Pete's Café?" I ask, remembering that the coffee shop up the street from Blue Bigfoot has a screen print shop right next to it.

"Yeah, you know it? I work at both the café and

Midnight Print Shop. Pete's girlfriend, Jade, owns the shop."

"Small world," I confirm.

She considers me, and I don't hate having her look me over. "Minuscule," she murmurs in a quiet tone I'd love to hear more of—say, while her head rests on the pillow next to mine.

Hey, we've already established I don't always make the best decisions.

I take us on 240 past downtown proper toward the River Arts District. The entire drive takes fifteen minutes, tops, and we spend the majority of it listening to Bear chattering over the sounds of an alt-rock radio station.

"So, what do you do, Miller?" Maisy asks as I exit the highway and maneuver toward Haywood Street.

No sense in lying or making myself seem more important than I am. It's not like she wouldn't find out anyway if we hung out again, and I'm not in the habit of apologizing for myself, even if I probably should sometimes. "I'm a server and busser at my brothers' brewery." She glances at my clothes again, and I know what she's thinking. May as well go all in. "The clothes are purely for show —I had to appear in court today. Luckily, they worked."

Her eyebrows spike, but other than that, she doesn't call 9-1-1 or attempt to fling herself from the car. Although, I get the feeling she'd never dream of ditching her brother in my back seat if she thought I was a threat.

Instead, she grins at me. "Maybe we should take a detour to the bank after all."

My chest shakes with a chuckle at the same time it gets hot. Maybe I'm getting heatstroke.

"Considering I'm driving my mama's car, I'd rather not push my luck and get her hauled in for questioning." I let it all hang out with that confession, maybe because Maisy is too good to be true so far, and I can't trust it. Or maybe just because this day hasn't turned out nearly as shitty as it could have, and I'm feeling optimistic.

"Pity," she responds with a grin, and there's that heat in my chest again.

"Just so you know, I might have been arrested, but it was for a good cause." One I can't think about right now, or this high I'm enjoying will turn to shit.

"I'm totally calling Jordan when I get home," Bear chimes in from the back seat again. "Hanging with someone who got arrested is way more dope than having a giant TV—or a six-toed uncle."

"It ain't all it's cracked up to be, kid," I say over my shoulder. Then to Maisy I ask, "You ever been to Blue Bigfoot?" We're pulling up to the curb in front of Pete's Café, and I'm desperate for any excuse to see her again.

"That's your brothers' place?" When I nod, she continues. "I've never been—not twenty-one yet."

Jesus. No wonder she ditched her wedding.

"Even if you can't drink, we've started doing some killer food on Fridays. We might extend it to other nights too." I shift into park and turn in my seat.

"You got pretzel dogs?" Bear asks.

"No, but now I'm thinking we should," I reply with a grin.

Maisy stops with a hand on the door handle. "Thanks again for the ride—and for helping me earlier." Her smile doesn't reach her eyes, but I send one back anyway. I want to ask for her number, but the timing is shit.

"Anytime." I give her a chin lift and turn to Bear again. "Later, big man."

He mimics my chin lift, and it takes effort to hold back

a laugh. Then they're both on the sidewalk with their bags, walking toward the café door without a backward glance.

Probably just as well, but at least I know where to find her if I'm ever feeling lucky.

"YOU WANNA TELL me why I had to give Mama a ride to work today?" My brother's voice has me jumping out of my skin.

I turn to see him lurking against the wall just inside the back door of the brewery. "Jesus. You scared the *shit* out of me!"

Cash's familiar scowl doesn't budge, which is expected considering I'm pretty certain he was born wearing it. He's sporting several days' dark beard growth and one of his many "Drink Local" tees, this one light blue. He continues to stare me down like he's attempting to read every last sin on my soul. That might take a while.

I try walking past him, but he steps in my way, using his two extra inches in height and twenty pounds in weight to his advantage. "That doesn't answer my question."

"That's because it's none of your business." Christ, I can't wait to get my bike. "She told me I could take her car, so I did." I tell him something I'm sure he already knows. "Now, if you don't mind, I'd like to get to work. My boss is a total dickhead, and I need the paycheck, no matter how measly." That's the damn truth if I'm ever going to move out of Mama's house, not to mention cover that fine from the judge.

I don't miss Cash hiding the quirk to his lips at that. "Well, from one dickhead to another, congrats, little brother." His scowl drops then, and he grins like a lunatic before grabbing me for a bro hug and a back pounding that almost has me choking. "Luca stopped by," he tells me something I already figured out.

"Jackass," I respond, figuring it covers all of my family members and Luca too.

Carter, my oldest brother, ambles in from the brewhouse to join us. He and Cash share the same dark hair and height, although Cart's hair is longer and messier. "Why didn't you tell us your hearing was today? We would have come with. Sunny's gonna be pissed." The part about Sunny is complete bullshit; Carter's girlfriend is the very definition of her name. But considering how tight-lipped I've been about my arrest and potential incarceration, none of them should be surprised I kept it to myself. But it never sucks to have people give a shit about you.

The day I got arrested, my entire family swooped in, creating a crowd in the police station's lobby I doubt they've ever had before or since. It wasn't easy to put my nosy family off after they bailed me out, but I was able to concoct a story along the lines of my past fuck-ups that they bought hook, line, and sinker.

"'Cuz it was no big deal," I lie. They allow it, and all three of us head to the taproom, Carter's hand resting on the back of my neck.

Yeah, having brothers can be okay sometimes.

"Yo, jailbird!" Oscar, one of our bartenders, shouts from behind the bar where he's pouring a pint for a waiting customer. "I'll tell Angie to stop carving that shiv for you now that you got off."

I can only shake my head because I'm sure I deserve all the razzing I'm going to get now that this is behind me. I'm confident they've been storing up all kinds of shit to dole out since the day of my arrest. It's bad form to make big-house jokes when it's a distinct possibility, not so much when it's in the rearview.

Let's just say this wasn't my first foray into crime. I was a shithead teenager with made-up BS to prove and hell to raise—not to mention a dead father whose loss I didn't have the tools to handle all that well—so I was no stranger to cops even then. But a couple years back, I got so drunk and high one night I couldn't tell a park bench from a public toilet and got pulled in for a drunk and disorderly with an indecent exposure rap on top of it. I got community service on that one, and Cash paid my fine. But that shit's not happening again. Nineteen is young enough to fuck up and put it behind you. Twenty-two is a different story.

Not that my arrest this time was due to being young and stupid. The exact opposite, I'd argue, although nobody else would view it that way. Which is why I've kept my trap shut about it. It wasn't hard to allow my family to believe I simply pulled another classic Miller fuck-up.

"I guess that means I should tell Hollis to nix the cake she was baking to hide Angie's shiv," Cash quips.

Assholes. I flip them all off, but they only laugh in my face. Nobody gets a free pass in this family, so I'd better suck it up.

Oscar offers me a celebratory beer, but I turn it down. I've got a shift to work, and I need to get Mama's car back to her at work. There'll be time for celebrating later—once I'm sure we're out of the woods, that is.

Cash claps me on the shoulder. "Seriously, though, we're happy for you. Now you can move on, right?"

I nod because that's what my brothers are expecting.

But I can't move on until I'm sure Driscoll has lost interest. My eyes go to the exposed ductwork under the high ceiling, and I repeat the same promise I've been making for the last six years. *No worries, Dad, I got it covered.*

CHAPTER FOUR

MY KIDNEY IS ALL YOURS

MAISY

"Don't worry about it. It's totally fine," I tell Grady for the third time as I press Jade's phone to my ear.

"I knew we should have made an extra key. They even sell those fake rocks to hide them—not that there's much to steal at our place," my friend says from his end of the line. "If you still need a place next week, we'll be back Tuesday, so don't hesitate, okay?"

"Okay. Promise." He's sweet to worry, but he also knows I can take care of myself. "Have fun, and tell Kat I say hey." There goes my foolproof plan for a place to crash with Bear tonight.

We wrap up the call, and I settle my phone hand on the counter, racking my brain for a solution. Going back to Mom and Terry's is not an option. While they don't normally care when I take Bear, they'll have something to say about it today since Mom will be pissed at me for the wedding. I wouldn't put it past her to make a point by using Bear to punish me.

Dad's place is obviously out too, considering he's likely more pissed than Mom *and* Jameson that I pulled a runner. His thunderous expression as he ran on Jameson's heels out of that courthouse almost had me asking Miller to stop the car so I could go back.

"You grip that phone any tighter, and you'll shatter it," Jade comments from behind me. "I take it Grady and Kat are out of town?"

I nod then turn and muster a smile for my boss, but she's no dummy. She's also not known for being tactful.

"Don't even think about crawling back to your asshole mom or dad, Maisy. I told you, you and Bear can take the pullout at our place. Or I can kick the tenants out of my old place." She's probably not even joking.

I watch her fold a stack of shirts with practiced ease, my eyes catching on the thorny roses tattooed all the way up her arm and disappearing under the short sleeve of her shirt. It has me thinking about Miller's tattoos and wanting to know what they're of—what stories he has inked into his skin.

That's something I've never done—gotten a tattoo. Dad never approved. It wouldn't be proper for a concert pianist to perform Beethoven with ink spilling from her skin. It just isn't done, so I didn't do it.

When I ditched that life, I was tempted, but by then I was too broke to afford it—and smart enough to know a cheap tattoo leads to a lifetime of regret. And I had enough regret, thank you very much. Not looking for the subscription package.

"Girl, you don't even like *pets*; no way am I moving a motor-mouthed nine-year-old into your apartment. You'd murder him before morning. No offense," I add on.

"None taken." She knows I'm right. Jade is a loyal

friend, a kick-ass designer, and a smart businesswoman. A friend to small cuddly things, she is not. Nor is patience one of her virtues.

I'll figure something out.

The bell on the shop's door jingles, and I glance over to see a group of tween girls file in. I'm not certain, but I believe I hear Jade growl from behind the counter. Yeah, kids are most definitely not her strong suit.

"Coffee. STAT," she grunts at me, and I don't even try holding back my grin.

I march through the door connecting the shop to Pete's Café and spot Bear exactly where I left him earlier. He's on his back atop a giant red pouf in the corner, a comic book gripped in his little fists as he holds it above him to read.

"He already suckered Pete into a second smoothie, just FYI," Monica, one of the staff, tells me as she passes by with a tray full of coffee concoctions balanced on one hand. We're not each other's favorite person, so I know she's not telling me for my benefit. My guess? She was the kid who kept a running tally of her schoolmates' transgressions to report back to the principal.

Nodding my acknowledgment, I head behind the counter where Pete is steaming milk.

"You doing okay?" He examines my face, looking for signs I might be ready to hurl myself off a rooftop.

I go for a half smile that communicates my sense of semi-wellbeing and give him a pat on the back. "Yeah." Pete is the sweet yin to Jade's salty yang, making them a perfect match. And they both treat me like the kid sister neither one of them ever had, which works out great for me since I never had an older sibling.

Neither one understood why I was going to marry Jameson—especially at my age—but both having grown up poor and under difficult circumstances, they weren't ones to judge what a person might do for survival. That said, the look of relief on their faces when Bear and I wandered in earlier today didn't go unnoticed.

I whip up Jade's double-shot skim cap and start rounding the counter to check in with Bear when I'm stopped short by the sight of Miller standing across from me. My heart jumps in my chest, pounding like my favorite staccato articulation in ELO's "Mr. Blue Sky." God, I love that song.

"Hey," he greets, but before I can ask him what he's doing here, he holds up Bear's Goomba stuffed toy. "Bear left it in the back seat. I figured it was important."

My eyes widen because he's not wrong. That thing goes anywhere Bear sleeps, and wherever that might be tonight, it could spell disaster not to have it.

"Oh, wow. I thought you were my hero earlier, but now I owe you a kidney." I take the ratty brown toy from Miller, ordering my heart to shut up, and he aims that killer grin at me, complete with the dimple and a raise of his pierced eyebrow. My uterus somersaults inside my pelvis. This is inconvenient. It's also absolutely me. Only I could go from jilting a millionaire in the morning to crushing on a car-less ex-con in the afternoon.

"Not sure I need one, but I'll keep that in mind." Miller holds my eyes like he knows exactly what I'm thinking. He's the same handsome as earlier, but the bad-boy side has taken over now that he's changed into ripped jeans and a black tee. If asked my opinion, I'd say they look way better than the fancier duds from earlier.

"You get a hold of Grady?" Pete materializes beside me, and I startle. Is he *glaring* at Miller?

"Yeah," I answer, moving to subtly box him out.

He stands firm. "He get you squared away?" His stubbled jaw is locked tight, making me want to laugh and smack him in equal measure.

I send Pete a glare of my own. "He and Kat are in Atlanta. And before you offer, I already told Jade we're not taking your pullout. She'd sell Bear on the internet by bedtime."

Knowing he can't argue with that, his lips firm into a thin line to match his tight jaw.

"You lookin' for a place to crash?" Miller interjects, and Pete's expression goes from frustrated to panicked. It takes some serious strength not to laugh now.

I shift my gaze to Miller. "I'll figure it out." The last thing he needs is to do me more favors. The guy just spent half the day in court and the other half driving me around. He's probably anxious to be rid of us.

"I'm sure you will, but just saying, my mama has a house on the east side, and she seriously digs kids." He hooks a thumb over his shoulder toward Bear. All three of us crane our necks to look at my brother, who has switched positions so his belly is on the pouf and the comic book rests on the floor. He's laughing at whatever's on the page and looking as adorable as can be. But I might be biased.

"Who *are* you?" Pete finally asks, not bothering with his usual manners.

Miller's brows arch, and I can see his lips quirk—yeah, he's totally onto Pete's big-brother antics. "Miller Brooks." He holds out a hand for Pete to shake, and I don't even try hiding my smile when Pete relents to take it and share his own name. The inner good guy in him can't bear to be that rude.

"Miller works at that Blue Bigfoot place down the road.

He also helped Bear and me out earlier, so you can back down, killer."

Pete scowls at me, but it breaks halfway through when something occurs to him. His eyes flash back to Miller. "Brooks? You Carter and Cash's brother?"

Miller nods in affirmation but doesn't expand on it.

Pete's frown turns upside down. "I went to school with Carter; we played football together." Then he starts laughing for some reason and tells Miller something he likely already knows. "Your mom is Ginny Brooks."

Even more strange, Miller's eyes close, and he drops his chin to his chest, head shaking. This has Pete laughing harder and throwing an arm around my shoulders.

"Maisy, you should one-hundred percent take the offer of a room at Ginny Brooks's house. Bear will love her." Pete steps over to help a waiting customer, still chuckling as he goes. "Nice to meet you, man," he calls over his shoulder. "Tell Carter we'll stop by again soon."

It takes another ten minutes and a phone call to his mother for Miller to convince me Bear and I won't be an inconvenience if we crash for the night. Since I have no car, he promises to pick us up around seven and deliver us there, but he refuses my offer of gas money. I finally relent when he confesses he's switching out his mom's car for his brother's, and nothing is coming out of his own pocket. There was also something about his brother owing him for traumatizing him this afternoon, but I let that go without further question. Miller leaves with a casual half-wave from his hip and a, "Yo, big man!" to Bear. I decide I like watching him move; he's got a loose-limbed, comfortable-in-his-skin vibe that hits me in all the right places.

At a time that couldn't be more wrong for my own good.

CHAPTER FIVE

JILTED AND JADED

MAISY

My day takes another turn an hour later when Jameson strides through the café doors.

He throws a hand up before I can even get a word out, his shock of tawny hair flipping forward before he smooths it back in place. He's clearly been running his hands through it since I last saw him. "I'm sure I should be giving you more time, but I can't. Our dads have been down my throat for the last four hours, my mother is drunk, and I'm exhausted."

I can feel my face soften at his beaten expression. "Jamie…"

He heaves out a sigh and collapses into an upholstered chair at a two-top table before withdrawing my tiny sparkly purse from somewhere on his being and dropping it on top. I join him there, checking over my shoulder to make sure Bear isn't eavesdropping. But he's busy drawing comic book characters behind the counter now, his tongue trapped between his teeth in concentration.

"I know," Jameson begins again, "You warned me, and I didn't listen."

He's right, but this isn't the kind of thing I have any desire to rub in. "I really did try," I respond, not that it does much good.

Jameson is a lovely person. He can also be a bit shallow and has the rubberiest backbone of anyone I've ever met. Which means he's not at all my type. But I don't know what it's like to be him or to be a part of his sticks-up-their-asses family, so I shouldn't judge. Standing up to my parents didn't exactly work out too well for me, so he might just be a whole lot smarter.

The plan was simple, really. Two birds—no, *three*—with one stone. Jameson's parents won't release his trust fund until he gets married, and I'm in desperate need of both money and a stable home situation to give me at least a fighting chance of wresting Bear from Mom and Terry's grip. The third bird—the bonus—is that my father has been salivating for an entry into the Newhouse family circle since Jameson and I began playing duets when I was five and he was eight. And having Dad in my corner instead of fighting opposite me would make my life far easier—especially given his demonstration of ever-evolving and inventive ways to show his displeasure since I quit playing the part of his organ-grinder monkey three years ago.

But in the end, I couldn't do it. Not even for Bear. I spent the first seventeen years of my life living a lie, and I couldn't go back to that.

Jameson already knows this. I've also expressed that an intimate relationship is not something I'm looking to enter into with him, but I'm unsure if he really believes me. He hasn't made his wishes a secret. And rich people have a way of getting what they want in my experience, even though Jameson is not the kind of person to ever force such a thing. The marriage was his idea, but I still feel like I owe him an apology—and some time to get over his mad. I did just leave him at the altar a few hours ago.

"I'm so sorry, Jamie." I pry the ostentatious diamond ring off my finger and hold it out for him. My hand immediately feels ten pounds lighter. Joanna will definitely be wanting that family heirloom back. "But I really think this will be best for you in the end." He's never going to live a full life or find a relationship hiding behind a sham marriage to me. And I'm not going to just wake up one day and be in love with him.

He takes the ring and frowns at it but doesn't exactly argue. "I'm not good at being poor."

This makes me grin. "Owning your own condo and car doesn't scream destitute, FYI."

"You know what I mean. Passion doesn't pay the bills, Maisy."

"I'm sure Pete would give you a job." I force sunshine into my tone as I eye his outfit. He's changed from his earlier designer suit into slim trousers, a button-down with short sleeves, and what are likely Italian loafers. Not exactly food service attire, but whatever.

Jameson pockets the ring and holds his hands up, long elegant fingers spearing the air. "These hands were not made for brewing coffee." He's not wrong. He's a talented pianist, just not quite good enough to make a living at it in the way he would like. If I could trade with him, I would, but I've yet to find a magic lamp to rub.

"I keep telling you, you could teach." Not that teaching would keep him in Italian leather either.

"Right back 'atcha," he counters with a tap on the table

between us.

I shake my head. I haven't sat at a piano or touched a keyboard since Dad confronted me busking with Grady two years ago and publicly humiliated me. The memory makes my stomach hurt.

"You don't have to *play* to teach," Jameson reminds me, his lips curling like he just smelled a fart. "Although it's a tragedy that you're not playing."

"And you don't have to be *rich* to be happy," I counter with another raised eyebrow.

He leans into the table and props his chin on his fist. "Are you happy?"

I don't answer because we both know I'm not. But that has more to do with Bear right now than anything.

"What did Jackie say?" He's asking about my mom's reaction to today.

"I didn't stick around to find out," I confess with a grimace.

His jaw tenses. "If she tries going through with moving to Puerto Rico, we can be at the courthouse faster than Taylor Swift can do a costume change." Another thing I love about Jameson—he's a Swiftie.

"Like they can afford three plane tickets," I scoff to cover the jitters that blaze down my spine at the very notion of them disappearing with my little brother. We may be half-siblings, but we've got an unshakable bond forged from shitty parents and unfortunate circumstances. "I'll figure something out. Don't worry."

"You know that's impossible, right? I'll always worry." Jamie drops a hand on top of mine, and I want to hug him for being so understanding and loyal. He's the only friend from my old life I've held on to, and there's a reason for that.

And all I can do is give him a tired smile because I know exactly how he feels.

CHAPTER SIX

STIR THAT CAULDRON

MILLER

"Does your mom got a dog?"

A glance in my rearview mirror shows Bear pulling at his seatbelt, remnants of a chocolate dessert lining his lips. "Nope. But she's got a skunk."

"Miller is pulling your leg," Maisy sends me a half-hearted scowl from the passenger seat. She's awfully upbeat for a woman who ditched her own wedding seven hours ago.

I just picked them up from Pete's—after giving my cock a talking to, that is—and we're heading up to the house. I've got the night off, so I can get them settled and see if there's any grub in the fridge. Mama's working late, so it'll likely just be the three of us, but I'm counting on Bear to keep me in check so I don't act my usual impulsive self and lay one on Maisy as soon as I get her in the door.

Cash spends most nights at Hollis's apartment with their three dogs, and Carter moved into his own place so he and Sunny would have privacy to screw as loudly as they want. My sister, Lynnie, is home for the summer from App State, but she's working at the new ballpark and has a social calendar busier than all us Brooks brothers put together.

When Cash and Carter asked why she didn't want a job at Blue Bigfoot, Lynn and I took one look at each other and then laughed our faces off till our voices were hoarse. If she ever hopes to get a date or even flirt with a guy this summer, the last place she's gonna put herself is under the watchful eyes of her four older brothers. Although Denny might not work at Blue Bigfoot, that doesn't mean he doesn't still hang around.

"I'm doing no such thing," I insist. "My mama does, in fact, have a skunk. His name is Mango."

Bear laughs. "Yeah, you're lying for sure. I knew it."

All I can do is shake my head as I steer Cash's POS car onto Tunnel Road. At least he reattached the side mirror that fell off. "We'll just have to see about that, I reckon. Do *you* have a skunk?"

"No. That's preposternus."

Maisy smiles. "Close. Prepost*erous*."

It's hard keeping my eyes on the road with the temptation to watch her, all that hair cascading over her shoulders in a sheet that reflects the evening sun coming through the window. My dick tries rearing his head at the mental image of wrapping my fingers in all that silk. *Stop that shit, you asshole!*

"Darn it. That was my fifty-dollar word this week," Bear grumbles.

I redirect my eyes over my shoulder. "Somebody's paying you for words? I'd like to get in on that gig."

"No. That's just what my tutor at school calls big

words. She says it's good to expand your vocabulary, and she's hot, so I'll do whatever she says."

"Bear!" Our gazes snap to Maisy. "What in the world even makes a woman 'hot' to a nine-year-old?"

"Miller knows."

The kid cups his hands in front of his chest like he's squeezing a big set of boobs. I almost hit my head on the steering wheel from laughing so hard.

Maisy shakes her head but can't help cracking a small smile. "I blame this on Terry," she mumbles, too low for Bear to hear.

By the time we get up the mountain and pull into the gravel drive in front of Mama's house, Maisy and I are all caught up on Amanda, the hot tutor, including how she's dating a teacher at the school and doing a shit job of hiding it. I'm making a mental note to make use of this nine-year-old's talents next time I need dirt on someone.

We park, and I get the urge to rush over to open the car door for Maisy, which is stupid since I've never done that kind of shit before. Instead, I grab Bear's backpack while Maisy gets hers, and we all pile out and head for the bright yellow front door. It opens before we even reach it.

"Hey, *Miller*," three voices sound in tandem, doing that damn sing-song crap girls do, and I find Lynnie standing in the doorway with our neighbor Rosie and her cousin Ari flanking her. It's like my own personal Shakespearean trio of witches. *Yeah, I read. Sometimes.*

My steps immediately grind to a halt, and Maisy plows into me from behind, her hands coming to either side of my torso to balance herself. The skin under my thin T-shirt practically sizzles where she grasps me, and my muscles pull tight at the sensation.

"Hey." My response is wary as hell and accompanied by a healthy glare at our welcoming committee.

"Who are your friends?" Rosie asks, her tone all innocence, as they step aside to allow us entry.

They almost look like triplets, all three of them with long, dark hair and identical shit-eating grins. Ari, however, is built like a brick shithouse, all ass and tits with a sharp tongue that's fortunately kept me from ever developing a crush. That, and the fact that she lives a couple hours away in Greensboro and is married. Rosie was the quintessential nerd next door when we were growing up, until she turned hot and got together with my brother Denny. But she's almost as much a sister to me as Lynn. And Lynn? She plays the part of annoying little sister only too well. All of this meaning I'm in for a world of hurt bringing a pretty girl home—kid in tow or not.

I ignore them and plow on through, looking over my shoulder to make sure Maisy and Bear aren't accosted. But Maisy introduces herself before I get the chance to strategize.

"Hey. I'm Maisy. This is my brother, Bear." She offers a small wave and that stunning smile.

"Whoa." The word whooshes from Bear's mouth, his eyes wide and trained on the trio of shit-stirrers. They aim their huge smiles down at him, and I'm worried for a second the kid might piss his pants. But, in what I'm learning is classic Bear fashion, he pulls it together and gives them all a chin lift and an almost casual, "What's up?"

"He's nine going on nineteen," Maisy supplies, and they all laugh.

I give in and do the introductions, offering no further

explanation. If Maisy wants them to know her business, she can tell them. I've learned better.

But it's partly a moot point when Lynn informs Maisy, "Mama called and said y'all were staying for a while. I made up the attic and Cash's bed. He's hardly ever around."

"No," Maisy interjects. "Please. We don't want to take anyone's bed. We can sleep on the couch—or the floor."

"No way," I butt in. "The attic is vacant—although it's gonna be hot—and Cash prefers staying at his girlfriend's place. It's no imposition, like I told you before."

"Yeah," Rosie volunteers, "they've got plenty of room, and Ginny loves houseguests. She's been pouting since Carter moved out and Cash started staying with Hollis."

"How many of you *are* there?" Bear asks, staring at the three women.

"I'm an extra, slick," Ari explains with a smirk. "Rosie's my cousin, and she grew up next door. I'm just visiting family for the week. But the Brooks crew has Carter, Cash, Denny, Miller, Lynn, and their mom." She counts everyone off on her fingers. "Oh, and Mango."

Bear's eyes widen. "It's true?"

"I told you so." I give his foot a nudge with my Converse, but his attention has shifted to the hallway before us.

"You really have a skunk?" Maisy asks, and we all respond in unison with a "yeah," with only mine having the added unnecessary *duh* to it. That'll teach them to doubt me.

Lynn throws an arm around Bear's narrow shoulders and guides him toward the kitchen. "Let's go find him, and I'll show you your room."

"You should go help," I suggest to the remaining troublemakers.

Ari and Rosie only grin back before Rosie links arms with Maisy and drags her in Lynn's wake. "So, how do you know Miller?"

Ari lingers, only to cackle and punch me in the shoulder before we both follow the crowd in search of my mother's skunk.

What the hell was I thinking bringing Maisy directly into the devil's lair?

CHAPTER SEVEN

A GENTLEMAN'S WORD

MILLER

"You can take your pick," I tell Maisy two hours later as we stand in the upstairs hall at the foot of the pull-down steps to the attic. Mango finally showed up a few minutes ago, so Bear is feeding raisins to him in the den. That skunk has the run of the entire property, so he's good at disappearing.

After their initial nosiness, the girls calmed their shit, and Rosie even put together a quick dinner for all of us. Spaghetti and meatballs with Caesar salad, although we all had to promise not to tell her mom that she used jarred sauce and frozen meatballs. Adrina is from Italy, and it's apparently a mortal sin not to cook your sauce from scratch and let it simmer for six hours.

Maisy didn't appear discomfited by their curiosity, but I wasn't about to let her get pinned under the microscope. Unfortunately, this resulted in the attention being transferred to me.

"Congrats, by the way." Lynn shoved my shoulder

from her seat next to me at the big kitchen table. It takes up most of the room, bordered by mismatched chairs to complement the homey nature of the entire house. "Thanks for telling us about your hearing."

"It was no big deal," I repeated the same lie I'd told my brothers earlier.

"What did you end up with?" Ari asked, popping a crouton in her mouth. Yeah, every-fuckin'-body knew my business, it seemed.

"Just a fine and some community service. Like I said, no big deal."

"I still don't understand what happened. I mean, why did they arrest you in the first place?" This from Rosie.

I'd told everyone an altered version of the truth—that some guy was tailgating me, and I lost my temper, getting out at a stoplight and confronting him. The fact that they all believed it without question said a lot about my role in the family as resident fuck-up.

I didn't look Maisy's way, but I could feel her eyes on me like a physical touch. My focus stayed on my fork as I poked at my salad.

"The cops and I had a difference of opinion, that's all." Still the truth, but not the whole truth. Driscoll had been tailing me for weeks, so I tailed him back (and did a better job of it), parking a few houses down from him before deciding to have a look around his property. It was probably some nosy-ass neighbor who called the police since I doubt Driscoll wanted police attention any more than I did. If I hadn't run from the cops, I could have gotten off. But that would have meant a confrontation with the asshole, and I wasn't going into that blind. "It's over now, so let's just let it go."

Luckily, Bear had my back and decided to share all his

news about Jordan with the ladies, so I got off relatively easy until everyone eventually went their own ways, leaving Maisy, Bear, and me to ourselves. I half expected Maisy to ask about my arrest, but she proved herself just as cool as earlier by avoiding the topic and helping me put the leftovers away.

"Bear and I can share a bed—we do it all the time," she says, toying with the hem of her cutoffs as we stand in the hall. I wonder if our proximity is making her nervous, and though it probably makes me an asshole, I kind of hope it is.

I lean a shoulder into the wall, watching her expression. "You don't have to. I'm happy to sleep in the attic if it's the heat you're worried about." The attic has no air conditioning, but the rest of the place does in one form or another, window units cooling the upstairs bedrooms and a main unit taking care of the downstairs. Word is Dad insisted on all of it the summer Mama was pregnant with Lynnie, and a heat wave the likes of which they'd never seen settled over Asheville and the surrounding mountains. Mama says he took up a side gig to pay for it just so she'd be comfortable, although she never shared what that side gig was.

Maisy's hands drop from her shorts, and her back straightens, bringing her even closer. I can make out a spray of faint freckles dotting the apples of her cheeks from this distance as well as catch a hint of her perfume or maybe her shampoo. It's a light floral scent with something sweet threaded through it, and I want to pull her into me so I can smell her.

That's not creepy at all.

For a second, my brain short circuits and thinks she's

coming in for a kiss, but instead she says, "Wait. You live here too?"

I blink, finally registering her expression of surprise and maybe a little trepidation. It takes effort, but I manage to hold back my smile.

"Yeah. You're standing right outside my room." I've normally got more game than this—staying vague about my living arrangements and circumstances with prospective hookups—but it's different with Maisy. Maybe because I already know she's not mere hookup material.

What the fuck is happening to me? All pretty, unattached girls my age or older—I don't discriminate—are hookup material. At least they usually are. But I know in my bones it's different with Maisy, and I can't explain it.

She's not unattached, you douchebag, I remind myself. That's why she's different. That's all.

Her lips part on a quiet, "Oh." Damn, she's fucking cute. But she's also off-limits, and I need to remember that shit. "Um, that's okay. I promise we don't mind. In fact, Bear will probably feel better if we share."

"Okay." I gesture to Cash's room, which sits directly across the hall from mine.

Maisy tilts her head, all signs of nervousness a memory, making me wonder if I imagined it in the first place. "You know, you're being really cool about all of this. And you haven't even asked for any explanation."

I can only shrug. "I don't exactly love people being up in my shit, so I'm just extending the same courtesy. It's really none of my business." Even if I want it to be.

She bites her lip as if trying to come to a decision. Then she hits me with news that has my mind going in ten directions at once. "I was getting married to keep my mom and her loser boyfriend from moving to Puerto Rico with

Bear. Jameson's family is loaded, and I'm not twenty-one, so I had no hope of pursuing custody without Jameson's help—something that was his idea in the first place. We're just two friends helping each other out. Until I ditched him at the courthouse, that is. Now we're both kind of screwed." She shrugs and musters a halfhearted smile. "But my day would have been much shittier if it hadn't been for you, Miller. So, thanks." Her shoulder lifts again like she didn't just make my fucking day. And when she goes on her tiptoes to drop a kiss on my cheek, it takes everything in me not to turn so it lands on my mouth instead.

Believe me, nobody's more surprised than me that Miller Brooks might just be a gentleman after all.

CHAPTER EIGHT

NEVER TRUST A BEAR WITH YOUR SECRETS

MAISY

It was too much, wasn't it. Dammit, I shouldn't have stressed that part about Jameson only being a friend. It sounded like a come-on. And now I'm all up in his space, smelling him. His scent is hard to pin down—some combination of faint woodsy cologne and a warmth and spiciness I suspect is just Miller. My cheek brushes against the light stubble on his jaw, making me fight a quiver.

When I pull back, his tongue piercing clicks against his teeth as his jaw tenses. "Glad I could be there for you," he murmurs, but it comes out both tense and raspy, like a cello needing tuning. Shit. There I go making dumb decisions again. Time to get back my sanity.

"Bear!" I turn to yell down the stairs. "Time for bed. You've got school in the morning." When I got my phone back from Jameson, I left my mom a voicemail telling her I had Bear and would get him to school tomorrow. She hasn't called back, which wouldn't normally be surprising, but it's not like her to let go of an opportunity to give me an earful regarding my latest perceived failure.

"Can Mango sleep with us?" he shouts back.

"No!" My lip curls. The thing is kind of cute, and I've been assured it doesn't have its stinker or sprayer or whatever anymore, but a girl has to draw the line somewhere. When I chance a glance at Miller, he's wearing that devil-may-care grin once again, his eyebrow piercing glinting in the overhead light as he cocks his head to the side.

"I hate to break it to you, but Mango tends not to ask permission. I've woken up more than once with those black eyes staring into my soul."

"Fabulous," I groan.

"Bathroom's down the hall. I'll let you guys get settled." Miller pushes off the wall and steps toward the stairs, halting at the top. "What time do we need to leave to get Bear to school?"

"Oh, um. I can call an Uber—or a friend." Pete or Jade would come get us.

But Miller pins me with a look I'm coming to understand means he wants me to pay attention. "*I'm* your friend too, Maisy." Then the look is gone, and he's back to his mischievous grin. "Besides, I don't want to miss out on any of Bear's stories." With that, he winks and jogs down the stairs with his patented loose-limbed ease, and I take my ass to his brother's bedroom to wait for Bear—and calm my ovaries.

The bedroom is small with just enough space for a double bed, a nightstand, and a mismatched dresser. It has the same feel as the rest of the house—well-loved and cozy. The stairs leading up to the three bedrooms creak and groan when climbed. Walls are scuffed with what I imagine might be sneaker marks from five kids or the results of countless tussles and horseplay. What fun it must have been growing up in Miller's family with all the noise and chaos and love.

By the time my brother takes a shower and changes into pajamas, he's so wiped he doesn't even try to convince me to invite Mango to bed. He just crawls in, and I settle the covers over him before smoothing my hand over his damp hair from my spot in the bed next to him.

"You been missing a lot of school?" I ask after a few quiet moments. Working at a coffee shop, I was gone before everyone woke up these last couple weeks I've been crashing with them.

"Not too much," he responds through a yawn. "And missing school means more Amanda time." One side of his mouth curves up, and mine matches it.

"I'm gonna have a talk with your teacher tomorrow and make sure you're on track. I promise I won't tell Amanda, though."

"School's over next week anyway." His eyes drift shut. "Love you, Mae."

My heart squeezes in my chest, making me think whoever decided that's where our emotions lie knew exactly what they were talking about. "Love you more."

I wait for his breathing to even out before closing my own eyes and letting sleep take me.

"YOUR MOM'S french toast is sick," Bear declares as Miller lopes into the kitchen the next morning, wavy hair damp from a shower and eyes deliciously drowsy.

Ginny turns from the stove, eyebrows raised. "I'm assuming that's a good thing?" I can see now where Miller got some of his coloring. His hair is a shade lighter than his mom's, and doesn't have the same wild curls, but it's a far cry from his sister's dark chocolate waves. And Miller's pale caramel complexion clearly comes straight from Ginny. I noticed a collection of family photos peppering the walls last night, many of them featuring a handsome man with the same dark hair as Lynn, but I've been afraid to ask about him.

"The best," Bear assures her, mouth full of syrup and toast.

Pete wasn't lying when he suggested we'd like Ginny. When I treaded hesitantly into the kitchen thirty minutes ago in search of caffeine, she welcomed me like I was a long-lost daughter, then started chatting as if some previous conversation between us had been interrupted, and she was simply resuming where we'd left off.

I've even been asked my opinion on when Denny should pop the question to Rosie. I told Ginny I'd only met Rosie the once and had never laid eyes on Denny, yet she appeared to give my opinion on the matter equal weight to her own kin's. This opinion, by the way, is that Rosie is lovely, and Denny would be an idiot to delay if she's indicated she wants to get married soon. Just because it didn't work out for me or anyone in my family doesn't mean I'm mad at the concept for other people.

"Mornin', Mama." Miller crosses the kitchen and shocks the shit out of me by squeezing Ginny's shoulder and dropping a kiss on her hair. My neck heats for some stupid reason. Not that I expected him to kick her or something, but he oozes cool out of every pore, and last time I checked, kissing your mom wasn't in the Dudes' Handbook of Badassery. But *damn*.

He immediately turns and parks his fine ass in the

chair next to Bear and across from me. He's kitted out in gray cutoff sweats and a Van Halen T-shirt today. "You guys sleep okay?" His fingers spear through his damp hair in a move that I'm certain is unconscious, but it plays out in my head in slow motion, complete with its own soundtrack. God, he's pretty.

"Like a rock," I reply, both hands gripping my coffee mug for dear life.

"Mango slept on my head for part of the night." Bear giggles into his glass of milk.

"That must mean you're a smart one, Bear. Big brains radiate heat, and Mango likes to stay toasty." Ginny raises a spatula toward us and sends my brother a warm smile, clearly not bothered that she's throwing all sorts of sunshine.

I hide my smile behind my cup while Ginny transfers hot slices of toast onto a platter and brings it to the table.

"You want some more?" Miller looks at my empty plate, and I wave him off. I already had two pieces, plus a mess of strawberries, and I'll explode if I have more.

I don't miss the sweet smile Ginny sends her son as he loads his plate. An unbidden spike of despair hits me as I imagine what it would be like to grow up with a parent who's so easy to please that a simple exercise of decent manners has them beaming with pride and love. I've experienced the pride in spades, but the cost to earn it was too much.

"So, Bear, what did the three of you get up to yesterday?" Ginny asks as she takes a seat by me and forks a slice of toast onto her own plate.

Miller chokes on his french toast, but Bear and Ginny both ignore his coughing as Bear decides to share all of our business. "Mom forgot to get me up for school, and Terry's lazy so he didn't take me, but that's okay because I got to play video games until Maisy and Miller showed up at lunchtime. And, get this, she was wearing a wedding dress! It was huge! But I could tell she was mad at Mom and Terry because she told me to pack a bag, and she ditched the giant dress—good thing, too, because it hardly fit in the car. We peeled out of there when Terry showed up, and then I told Maisy and Miller about my friend Jordan's six-toed uncle, but I decided Miller is much cooler since he's been to *jail* and everything. Maisy said I didn't have to go to school since there was only gym left, so we were gonna rob a bank, but decided to go to Pete's and have smoothies instead. Then after Miller left, Jameson showed up, and he and Mae talked for forever, and when he left, Miller came back and got us and brought us here where I met three babes and had a ton of spaghetti and got to feed Mango some raisins. Then we went to bed. Can you please pass the syrup, Mrs. Brooks?"

Ginny's fork froze halfway to her mouth by the time he finished the second sentence of his monologue, and I had to fight the urge to leap over the table and clamp a hand over his mouth. Miller finally stopped choking by the end, but it was too late by then.

Ginny regains her composure first, passing the syrup to my brother as her lips spread in a seemingly genuine smile. "Well, that sounds like an exciting day to me!"

Needing to say something but entirely clueless as to what, I choose, "The bank thing was a joke."

This sends Miller choking on his food again. Ginny inexplicably throws her head back and laughs. And Bear is right there with her.

Thirty minutes later, we're parked in Ginny's car again watching Bear disappear through the elementary school doors. "Your mom is super sweet," I tell Miller something he already knows.

"She's nuts is what she is." His comment has zero sting since he smiles through it. He glances Bear's way again, but my brother is out of sight now. "Can I ask you a question?"

"Sock it to me," I respond. I'll tell him anything he wants to know at this point. Well, almost anything.

His mouth stretches into a smile that has his dimple popping and my breath catching. "Sock it to you? How old are you, eighty?"

"I'm an old soul." I go for a casual dismissal to cover my absolute dorkiness.

"Okay, Gladys." My face flames at the embarrassing nickname, but he continues by asking, "Why doesn't Bear live with your dad?"

Happy to focus on something besides my red cheeks, I explain, "We have different dads."

"Oh." His eyes hit mine. "And *his* dad?"

I shake my head and shrug. "The only thing I know about his dad is he's blond, his name is either Jason or Mason, and he's loyal to Marriot. At least that's where he was staying when my mom banged him during some trip to Charlotte in June of 2014. Oh, and he probably has blue eyes because everyone on my mom's side of the family has been dark, and Bear's eyes are blue."

Miller tilts his head. "That's both oddly specific and completely vague."

This has me smiling. "I quizzed my mom when I got a wild hair to find the guy a couple years ago."

"No luck?"

I only laugh at that, and he joins me. Damn, he has a great laugh—like he uses his whole body and feels it everywhere. I don't think this guy is very good at half measures, and I'm finding the notion more attractive than is wise.

Sensing my need to stay light, Miller props both hands on the steering wheel. "Where to now?"

"Do you think you can drop me at Jameson's so I can get my scooter?"

"You ride a scooter?" I can't tell if he's confirming so he can make fun of me or not.

"It's all I can afford." I don't know why I feel the need to defend my choices.

"No, it's cool. I like the image of you on a sweet little ride like that. It fits."

"Sweet little ride?" I ask on a laugh. "It's no Ducati."

His nod is slow, and it comes with a perusal of my entire frame. "Oh, now that—that's an even better fit." My nipples take this as an invitation to present themselves for his consideration, and it takes all I have not to glance down for a quick bullet check. Miller continues in a casual tone as if he hasn't just thrown down the feel-me-up gauntlet with that eye scan. "I had a Kawasaki until it fell apart earlier this year. It was a real piece of shit. I'm buying a used Triumph next week from a guy in Black Mountain. Soon as he's back from some trip, I'll be done bumming rides."

I decide that if Miller is ignoring my nipples, I may as well too. "I'd love to have a real bike. I don't feel safe taking Bear on the scooter unless I have to, but a proper bike, yeah."

He puts the car in reverse and checks behind us. "Well, a scooter is better than nothing, that's for sure. Which way is Jameson's place?"

Did he just add snark to Jameson's name? I'm clearly

imagining things. "Downtown," I tell him as he backs out. "The condos at 60 North Market."

Miller whistles. "Damn, you weren't lying that he has money. Sure you don't want to rethink that wedding thing?" he teases, and I knock him on the shoulder with a fist.

I don't want to let go of this giddy feeling I have when I'm with him, so I'm determined to hold on to it until we get to Jamie's. Then I'll let myself stew in the reality that he's right. I should marry Jameson and do whatever it takes to get Bear from Mom and Terry before he gets chewed up and spit back into the system.

So why is it the very last thing I want to do?

CHAPTER NINE

DAZED AND CONFUSED

MILLER

Maisy says she'll call later if they still need a place to crash, and I watch her ass sway in those cutoff jeans until she disappears into the swanky building's garage. I know it's stupid, but I appear to have taken up masochism. She may claim she and this Jameson guy are just friends, but being an owner of a dick, I can conclusively say Jameson is a big fucking liar—not that I blame him. Being friend-zoned can't be easy, especially when we're talking about someone as hot as Maisy.

Cursing myself, I swing a left on Woodfin and head for Dax's crib down near Hall Fletcher. His building is one step up from a crack den, but it's an important step—meaning I've never been jumped when hanging out there.

"Yo, man, what's up?" He greets me at the door with a tendon-straining bro handshake. "Thought you were coming by last night?"

I follow him into the dingy living room where the acrid scent of stale cigarettes and beer oozes from every porous surface. "Open a window every now and then, yeah?" I wave a hand in front of my face. Behind the closed door and drawn curtains, it's practically impossible to tell if it's night or day, the place lit only by a single lamp in the corner and flickers from the TV screen.

"And ruin this vampire vibe I've got going on? Never." He grins, reminding me as usual of an extra from *Dazed and Confused*, complete with seventies throw-back hair falling to his shoulders and a T-shirt that's a little too tight to be decent. "So?" His tone is expectant.

"Thousand-dollar fine and sixty hours of CS. Got forty-five days to pay the fine."

He shakes his head. "And the douchebag doc doesn't even have to answer any questions. I *told* you you should have reported him as soon as he started tailing you." Dax is the only one who knows the whole story, which is fair since he played a major part.

"Yeah? What was I gonna say? 'Sorry for running from you, officers, but the dickhead doctor whose house I was casing killed my dad six years ago, and he's been following me for weeks. Why? Oh, funny story: my best friend and I got him busted for drug possession—drugs which, by the way, were provided by my best friend—and the doc just finished serving a nickel, so I dunno, he might be pissed?'"

"Well, when you put it like that..." Dax snatches up a pack of Marlboros from the coffee table and pulls one out before extending the pack my way. "At least you can still afford the Triumph. Smoke?"

"Told you ten times now I quit." I only smoke the occasional weed now—especially when I need to focus or calm my ass down. It's a better solution than the stimulants I was prescribed as a kid. That shit messed with my head.

"Right. Forgot." He collapses onto a couch that's covered in what I can only assume is dirty laundry, and I join him, glancing around at the mess before studying my friend. Dax always has an ease about him, like nothing in the world fazes him—which is why he's good at making friends—but his eyes are red-rimmed this morning, dark shadows hanging in crescent moons beneath.

"You sleep last night?"

"Nope." But he grins, the same disarming one he's used since we were in middle school and he started conning his way out of detention. "Spent about five fuckin' hours tryin' to get into Teyana's pants, then couldn't get rid of my stiffie, so I watched some porn."

I rocket to my feet, afraid to even look down where I was just sitting. I need another shower.

Dax busts out laughing, almost setting the couch on fire with his cigarette, which, let's face it, wouldn't be the worst idea. "Not on the couch, asshole."

"Jesus," I mutter, dropping back down to my ass and getting to the point of my visit. "What you got goin' today?"

"Nothing much. Why?"

"Thought maybe we could play some one-on-one and then drop by the senior center. Mama says they got a job opening—custodian."

Dax ashes the cigarette on a half-full ashtray balanced on the armrest. "Never quite pictured you as a janitor, but I reckon no job is too small." He takes a pull, smiling around the Marlboro.

"No small jobs, just small people, jackass," I correct him, waving a plume of smoke from my eyes before I give into temptation and snag a smoke after all.

"One of Wade Brooks's classics." He stubs his cigarette

out, ash flicking out onto the fabric as he ignores it. "I think my favorite was, 'Always be careful when you follow the masses; sometimes the M is silent.'"

"I'm being fucking serious, Dax." I suck on my tongue post, trying to rein in my annoyance. "And I'm pretty sure Dad got that one from a fortune cookie."

"Hey," he responds, throwing his hands out to indicate his glamorous digs. "I ain't the one still living with my mama."

"Fuck off." He knows why I live there—and why I moved out of the slightly-less-shitty digs he and I used to share after he stopped tempting fate and quit dealing. One condition of Cash bailing me out of my last run-in with the law was that I move back home to give myself a better shot of avoiding future trouble. My brother had a point. Dax is no stranger to the local law enforcement himself, this being the very reason I keep trying to get him to make an honest living. He's got no job right now, as far as I can tell, which makes me suspect he might be back in the game. I don't want my best friend spending the better part of his life behind bars, which is where he's heading if he goes back.

"You know," I remind him, "no way you're ever getting in Teyana's pants if you end up in jail."

"Fuck off," he throws my comment back at me and then changes the subject. "You working tonight?"

"Four to close, so I got all day."

"I guess I could kick your ass in a game or two." He's kidding himself. Back in the day, we were evenly matched, but not so much anymore.

"Keep dreaming. I know for a fact you haven't played in months." Then I flex my bicep just to be a dick. "Some of us make a point to keep in shape." Gyms are for assholes, but I make sure to get in enough cardio and weights on my own.

My comments have their desired effect because Dax is off the couch and headed to his room to change before I even finish. I move to the window and slide the curtains open, letting the sunlight in, even if there's no fresh air to go with it.

One of these days, Dad, I promise, *I'll get through.*

"WHERE'S DAX, DARLIN'?" Mama asks, looking behind me with a hopeful spark in her eye. I just walked through the front doors of the senior center after kicking Dax's ass on the court.

Before I can respond, the old guy standing beside her butts in, "That the kid with hippie hair and an idiot look on his face all the time?"

"Shush, Marvin." Mama shoos him with a hand. "Or I won't seat you next to Patty at poker night."

"Why the hell would I want to sit next to Patty? She cheats, and I'm pretty sure I caught her shoplifting."

I settle in, knowing this might take a while. Marvin, known to all others besides Mama as Duke, is a cranky son-of-a-bitch with a lot of opinions he's not shy about sharing. He's also Sunny's grandfather.

"How many times do I have to tell you the cookies in the common room are free?" Mama snaps back. "And just because she's better at poker than you doesn't mean Patty cheats, you old curmudgeon."

Duke turns to shake his head at me. "She's pulled the wool over your mother's eyes, young hooligan." Not one bit of this encounter is surprising, as Duke is known for not only his grumpiness but his unrelenting paranoia.

But Mama isn't big on being dismissed. "He's set on finding something objectionable about Patty because she's sweet on him and he's scared."

Duke's bushy white eyebrows scrunch together like two fluffy amoebas joining forces to create an exponentially more powerful one. "I ain't scared, woman! She's way too old for me."

"She's five years younger than you, Marvin." We're now drawing an audience, but I reckon the senior set can use the entertainment.

"So she claims. I have yet to see a birth certificate! Don't be so naïve, Ginny." Without another word, Duke huffs and whirls around to stalk off. However, due to his bum hip and reliance on his cane, it's less impactful than I'm guessing he intended. We both watch him shuffle toward the common room, one hand on the cane and the other swatting at the air as if attempting to rid himself of even the memory of this conversation.

"I see Duke is fighting fit as usual."

Mama smiles, completely unaffected by his negativity. "I saw him watching Patty yesterday, and let's just say it wasn't an expression of disinterest on his face."

Not anxious to prolong this dissection of senior citizen love, I fish Mama's keys from my pocket and hand them over. "Dax said to tell you thanks for thinking of him, but he's got something in the works." We both know it's a lie, but Mama nods anyway.

"We'll get him sorted soon." She squeezes my forearm.

"I keep trying to think like Dad, but I'm coming up blank," I confess. Dad had a soft spot for troublemakers, seeing as he was one himself.

"The important thing is to never give up on those you love." Her brilliant blue eyes go soft like they do every time she offers advice.

Seems I'm not the only one trying to channel my father.

She releases my arm and holds the keys up between us. "You sure you don't need the car? I can get a ride with Lizzie later," Mama offers.

"Nah, you take it. I have my ways." I send her the grin she calls my "trouble's comin' smile".

"Don't I know it," she responds, nothing but affection in her tone.

I lean in to kiss her cheek. "See you tomorrow, Mama. I'm working till close." When I turn to go, she halts me.

"Maisy and Bear staying over again?"

"I doubt it—I dropped her off at a friend's place." I don't want to think about her staying with her pseudo-fiancé, Jameson whoever-the-hell. Not that it's my business anyway, I remind myself.

"She's awfully pretty." Mama's tone and accompanying eye-sparkle spell more trouble than any I could dream up.

"Hmm." I'm not talking to her about this, so a vague sound is the wisest response.

"And sweet."

My eyes drop to my shoelaces. "Gotta head out. Later, Mama." I nod at her and haul ass toward the door.

"And I'm guessing she's not into boring frat boys!" She shouts after me, and all I can do is shake my head while fighting a grin as I walk back out into the blazing Carolina summer sun to catch the bus. Damn, I can't wait to get my bike.

CHAPTER TEN

KEEPIN' IT CLASSY

MAISY

"Open this goddamn door, Margarida Jolene!" The pounding on the door repeats.

"Shit, she's pulling out the big guns. She must be *pissed.*" Jameson takes a step back from his door.

"You're not helping," I hiss. Thank God Bear isn't here to witness this display of motherly excellence.

More pounding. "I know you're in there, you little bitch! I saw you on that stupid scooter."

Jameson raises an eyebrow at me, and I relent, knowing his neighbors didn't pay a gazillion dollars for their condos just to have some trashy woman yelling obscenities down the hallways. I trudge the few remaining steps to the door and crack it open.

"Mom, keep your voice down."

She shoves past me, pushing her way through the door, her bad bleach job scraped into a high ponytail so tight it strains the skin at her temples. Her tiny tank top emblazoned with a TJ's Tavern logo complete with a scantily clad cowgirl pushes her boobs out on display for anyone who cares for a gander. She must be on her way to work.

Not bothering with pleasantries, she stalks straight to the living room and into the kitchen. "Where is he?"

"Where is who, Jackie?" Jameson asks, still stationed near the door—probably so he can escape if things turn violent.

Mom's lips pinch. "Bear. Honestly, Jameson, I thought you were the smart one in the relationship."

Ouch.

But talk about smart…

"He's at school," I inform her of something she should already know, my hands propped on my hips now.

"Still?"

"It's barely lunchtime." After Miller dropped me off, I headed to work but agreed to stop by Jameson's over my lunch break to chat. He said he had news, so I rushed over a few minutes ago. Apparently, I acquired a stalker along the way.

Mom only waves me off and scowls at Jamie's braided rug like it offends her. Then her gaze swings to us. "You fix your issues yet?"

I take a breath and try to summon patience. "We don't have issues. We're just not getting married."

"Well, why the hell not?!" She points at me, but her eyes dig into Jameson. "She's got birthing hips. Give you an heir for your family name."

A glance at Jameson shows he's about five seconds from making a break for it. The chances of Jamie procreating with his family's deep-seated dysfunction are about as small as a Benedictine monk's.

"Super classy, Mom."

"Your father said *you're* the one who ran away." My mouth drops open at that—I can't begin to fathom the degree of my father's woefulness if he deigned to reach out to Mom. Now I'm looking forward to our eventual conversation even less than I already was, and my previous anticipation was only one step up from having needles shoved under my fingernails. "What were you thinking?"

I step forward with my palms out. "It's really none of your business. This is between us, and we're not getting married. It's better this way."

Her chin dips to give more power to her glare. "Better for who?" I'm still baffled by her apparent assumption that wealth is transferable through osmosis.

Jesus, she's a piece of work. I don't respond, instead walking to the door and holding it open. "Time to go, Mom. You'll be late for work," I try.

Her glare doesn't falter, only getting stronger as she approaches and stops six inches from my face. She's only forty-four, but the lines radiating out from her lips and eyes tell the story of a hard life—one mostly of her own choosing. She's still holding on to beauty, but only by the tips of her fingers. "Don't matter much. I'll be putting in my notice any day now since we're moving to San Juan."

My pulse bangs in my ears like a kick drum, but I do my damn best to keep my expression blank and not show the panic zipping along every nerve ending. "Last I checked, plane tickets are a little outside your budget. And I doubt Terry's family would want three new houseguests."

Her lips curl up at the corners, reminding me of a

cartoon villain. All she needs is a coat made of adorable puppies to complete the visual. "You think you're so smart, but everybody knows you're nothing but a quitter who can't hack it when things get tough. Don't know how you're my blood." When I don't react or respond to her scathing words, she continues, "Me and Terry got a plan, and if you don't smarten up and get back to that courthouse, Bear'll be on that plane with us before you can blink." She backs up a step so she can encompass both Jameson and me in her wicked glare. "You get me?"

"Get out." Jameson's voice is quiet but ice cold as he stalks to the door and shoves me behind him. "Now."

Mom's freaky grin only deepens, but she doesn't say another word before strolling through the open doorway like she has not one care in the world.

Jameson slams the door behind her and turns to me, one side of his mouth tipping up. "I think I might be turning into a badass."

Despite the dire circumstances, I can't hold back my grin.

Ten minutes later, however, I'm finding nothing amusing.

"They're subletting your condo?! How can they do that? I thought you owned it." His parents appear to be in competition with mine for the Shitty Parents of the Decade Award.

"They co-signed the mortgage. Something about a low-interest loan being more financially sound than paying outright."

Crap. Although it kind of makes sense since Jameson isn't actually wealthy himself, and he'd never get a loan with his employment history—or lack thereof. Playing piano doesn't exactly pay the bills.

"What are you going to do?" I slump back in his leather armchair while I watch him run a frustrated hand through his hair. He's a handsome guy with a head of thick toffee hair, a tall, lean frame, and excellent bone structure. He also dresses better than anyone I know—today's outfit of linen shorts and designer collared shirt being a perfect example.

"Move back in with them. What else can I do?"

I bite my lip because I know exactly what else he could do—marry me and get his trust fund. *Shit!*

"Jamie, I—"

But he cuts me off. "Maisy, I swear, I'm not telling you this so you'll reconsider. You're twenty years old, and you managed to break free from a life you hated, making your own path and working your ass off to do it. Not to mention looking out for Bear along the way. I'm not going to be the one to suck you back into that bullshit. You'll figure something better out."

"And what about you?"

He forces a smile. "I told you I'm turning badass—balls as big as grapefruits, just you wait."

"Jamie." I don't mention that sounds more like an unfortunate medical condition requiring immediate antibiotics than a sign of courage or conviction.

He ignores my gentle tone and continues, "I assume you're good at Grady and Kat's?" Jameson and Grady only know each other through me, but our shared love of music makes it so we all hang out sometimes. Grady and his girlfriend, Kat, do gigs all over town and even go on the road now and then. They're fantastic; however, their tastes go more the way of folk rock as opposed to Jameson's devotion to classical music with maybe some jazz thrown in.

The temptation to lie is strong, but I don't in the end. "They're out of town until Tuesday—but Bear and I are crashing with… a family friend." Okay, so it's sort of a lie —but Jameson doesn't need to worry any more than he already is. When his expression turns skeptical, I quickly tack on, "Her name is Ginny; you haven't met." Then I change the subject. "What about that master's program at UVA? It would mean moving, but maybe that's not a bad thing at this point. At least it comes with a stipend and housing." My avoidance plan doesn't work.

"You're *not* going back to Jackie and Terry's," he orders.

"You're really taking this bossy badass thing seriously, aren't you? And, no, I'm not going to Mom's. She'll probably poison me in my sleep."

"Obviously, you can crash here tonight, but you'll have to help me pack to earn your keep," he teases.

This time, I can only muster a half grin. It's possible Mom is bluffing, but with this latest escalation, I need a smarter strategy to keep Bear out of her and Terry's reach. This is the first place she'll come looking for him. By now she's undoubtedly left instructions for Terry to bar me from taking Bear for the weekend—something I do more often than not so she and Terry can get up to whatever the hell it is they do together.

At least I can take comfort in the knowledge that she'd never call the cops to hunt Bear down. The only thing she hates more than me is CPS.

I'll pick Bear up from school and talk to his teacher, then get my ass online to find a room to rent. Surely, it can't take more than a couple days to secure a new place or convince my previous landlord to let me re-up my lease. I never should have let it go in the first place! We just need a place to hide out for the weekend, during which I'll devise a foolproof long-term strategy. Absolutely.

Welp, looks like I might not be out of Miller Brooks's life like I thought. I ignore the sudden rush of adrenaline and pull my phone from my back pocket to scroll to his contact.

CHAPTER ELEVEN

SEEING GHOSTS

MILLER

"You guys should serve food *every* night. These nachos are delicious." Maisy licks a drop of cheese sauce from the corner of her mouth, and my dick takes that as an invitation to raise his head.

I balance the bus tub on my hip and watch Maisy and Bear suck soda through their straws in perfect synchronicity. "I'll pass the suggestion on to my brothers," I respond over the surrounding chatter and the band warming up by the popcorn machine.

It's a busy Friday night, and I'm on until close, so when Maisy texted asking if she and Bear could crash another couple nights, I told her she was more than welcome. Then I invited them to Blue Bigfoot for some food.

Cash and Carter hired a new girl named Eden about a month ago who's a better grill master and cook than anybody else on staff—even with the limited kitchen resources we've got on site. She's champing at the bit to expand our offerings, so it's just a matter of time. Eden and I switch off bus duty, giving me some server shifts to earn better tips and her some time making grub. My brothers haven't said much about it, but I know they never expected me to last this long in my job, much less graduate to server. I don't exactly have the best employment history so I can't bitch about it too much. But I actually like this job, which is something I couldn't say about many of my past gigs.

There was a carwash job that wasn't so bad, but I lost it when I was late one too many times. Then there was a landscaping gig I got fired from for coming to work high. The fast-food places were all ones I quit—except for the taco place that axed me for flirting too much at the drive-thru window. Let's just say it's been quite the revolving door. But I want this one to stick—and not just so I don't disappoint my brothers.

The place is packed tonight, and it's only seven. Ever since some players from the Asheville Arrows started hanging out here, it's been mayhem on the weekends—even when the players are out of town for away games and customers know not to expect any celebrity faces.

The taproom takes up the front of our unit at the warehouse shops along the French Broad River, with the brewhouse, storage, kitchen shit, and the office occupying the back half. The high ceilings mean lots of wall space, and practically every inch is covered with kitschy, themed décor or random shit that's only loosely related to sasquatches.

My personal favorite is a giant battered wood sign announcing "Warning: Bigfoot Breeding Area—Avoid Eye Contact." But the customer favorite has to be the two-foot carved wood statue that sits by the register and is worth a mint, having been made by a famous sculptor and gifted to our dad years before the guy's work became valuable. The statue's name is Larry, per Dad's proclamation, and its twin, Drunk Larry, graces the brewery sign and logo, carrying a mug of beer.

Our dad was a huge Bigfoot nut, so we all come by it honestly. In fact, the entire business is one big tribute to Wade Brooks, and nobody would have it any other way.

"Don't forget to mention the pretzel dogs," Bear adds when I lean over to grab a couple empty pint glasses from the next table over.

"Hey!" Rosie sidles up to us, her dark hair pulled back in a ponytail and her usual bright smile aimed at my new friends. "You guys should come sit with us." She gestures to a table across the taproom where Denny, Luca, and Ari sit with beers in front of them—except Ari, that is. She somehow has a martini. I have no idea how she managed, seeing as we don't have that kind of liquor license. But that's Ari.

"Um…" Maisy glances down at Bear whose gaze is glued to Rosie. "Okay." She shrugs and gathers their shit. But she turns back to me, allowing Bear and Rosie to weave through the tables ahead of her.

I wait a few seconds for her to speak, but she only bites her lip, giving my dick more ideas. I can usually tell when a girl is into me, but with Maisy, I'm getting mixed signals—even though I know which way I'd prefer reading things. She could be playing me, but that's not the vibe I'm getting.

So I lean in closer than I probably should. Yeah, she does a little inhale just like she did last night in the hall outside my room. "I usually take my break out back around eight. You still gonna be around?" I tilt my head toward the back hall and hold her eyes.

A hint of color rises in her cheeks, but she keeps the contact and nods, finally releasing her lip. Fuck, this girl is going to tie me in knots, I just know it.

I bus tables and wash glasses, periodically glancing over to their table to see everyone laughing and having a good time. The band starts playing, and I glare at Cash so hard he must feel it because he turns to me with an apologetic, "I know! I'll get a new fucking band," as he continues pouring pints.

When eight rolls around, Maisy is already looking my way where I stand behind the bar, so I jerk my head to the back hallway again and watch her ask the crew to keep an eye on Bear before she excuses herself. Although it looks to me like he's holding court with everyone, probably making up shit to impress them.

Maisy's still in her red Converse, but she's changed into faded army green shorts that mold to her hips and ass, paired with a tight white top with super short sleeves and some graphic emblem I don't recognize. I motion for her to go ahead of me, not even trying to kid myself that my reasons are at all gentlemanly. I just want to check out her ass. Then I want to peel those shorts down and take a bite.

I reach an arm out from behind her to push the door open, brushing my chest against her shoulder in the process, and even the light contact has me sucking in oxygen to keep me breathing. Jesus. I feel like I'm fifteen.

"Any more brides hijack you today?" Maisy asks once I position myself against the bricks of the building. She's a few feet away, hands shoved in the pockets of her shorts.

I grin. "Shockingly, no. But that's probably only because I'm avoiding the courthouse."

"Same." She laughs before continuing, "This place is

really cool, but that band…" she trails off, and I'm shaking my head along with her.

"They suck, right?" I groan and drop my head back. "Last time they played, they must have had a different singer or something. I have no idea what happened there."

She joins me against the wall. "I've got some friends who play in lots of bars around town. They're amazing. I can put you in touch if you want."

"Yeah? That would be helpful. Cash has shit taste in music, and after tonight, a good band might get me a promotion."

Her responding smile is dazzling. "I've got to know. What's with the Sasquatch obsession? Even the beers have Bigfoot names. And who's Larry?" Her expression turns adorably confused.

She's not wrong. We've got everything from a cream ale called *Squatch Blossom* to a double IPA named *Hop Squatch* and a wheat *Squatch This*. There's also *Cryptid Chaos* and *Legendary Larry*, among others.

I tell her about the inspiration and my dad, explaining Larry's origin and the fact that customers like rubbing his head for good luck, which has her laughing again. I enjoy the sound too much. It's throaty and rich, yet somehow light, and she closes her eyes whenever she laughs, letting her long lashes brush the tops of her cheeks.

I don't say anything else, wanting to simply bask in her sound and her energy. We watch in shared silence as Tom from the smoke shop a couple doors down hauls his trash to his dumpster and waves.

Maisy's gaze travels between Tom's flat gray dumpster and our bright pink one with ridiculous dogs painted on it. "Umm…"

"Cash's girlfriend, Hollis, owns the pet grooming shop

next door, and let's just say he's pussy whipped—pun entirely intended. Luca painted it to get Cash out of the doghouse."

"You're just full of puns, aren't you."

"People usually say I'm full of shit, so I'll take it."

She smiles. "I don't believe that. You've been nothing but genuine with Bear and me."

I raise an eyebrow. "Or maybe I'm so good at lying I've fooled you into a false sense of security. I may have nefarious intentions." If she only knew.

"Nefarious? I highly doubt it. Any guy who kisses his mom on the head and reunites lost stuffed animals with their owners is a big softie."

Her characterization takes me aback, making me unable to respond with a smart-ass comment. If she notices, though, I can't tell because she moves the conversation in a new direction.

"So, can I ask how long since your dad passed?"

"About six years," I respond immediately. "Surgeon fucked up during a routine gallbladder surgery. Gross negligence." That's an understatement.

"Oh my god." Her hand settles on my arm, and my skin heats where the pads of her fingers press in. "I'm so sorry, Miller. It sounds like he was a great guy."

"The best." I smile at her because a sad Maisy makes my chest tight. "Mama says I take after him in a lot of ways, which is pretty much the best compliment anybody could pay me. But she's my mom so of course she's gonna say shit like that."

"I'm glad you got two awesome parents." Her smile and tone are earnest, almost vehement.

Based on the impression I've gotten of Maisy's mom thus far, I know I should be counting my blessings.

"What about *your* dad? You said he was one of the guys chasing us yesterday?"

"Yeah, the Brazilian one with angry eyebrows." She kicks a tiny stone with her shoe and watches it skitter over the asphalt. "Our relationship is… thorny. We used to be close, but not so much anymore."

"Why not?"

Her nose scrunches, and it's cute as fuck. "Difference of opinion, you could say."

I watch her, making it clear that it's her choice if she wants to share or not. Turns out she does, which pleases me.

"He doesn't approve of the way I live my life or the decisions I've made about what to do with my future and career."

"You're only twenty," I point out. "Hell, I'm two years older, and I have no idea what I want to do with mine."

She doesn't respond to that, instead saying, "He thought marrying Jameson would make me focus more. That, and get *him* some clout."

What the fuck does that mean? "Are Jameson or his family famous or something?" What do I know?

She coughs out a laugh, but it carries zero humor. "In some circles, yes. You don't want to know."

"Sure I do. What? Are they mafia?" I joke.

"Definitely not. They're a big name in music circles. You know the Valley Symphony?"

"Sure. It's not exactly my scene, as you might have figured out, though." I drop a hand down my frame, indicating not only my clothes but my obvious affection for tattoos and body piercings. It has the unintended but not unwelcome effect of her eyes sweeping me from head to toe, and my cock again takes notice. I'm not sure if I can wait till Maisy and Bear move out to take care of some business with my fist at this rate.

Maisy's voice is detached when she continues, "The Newhouse family's name is on the auditorium in Charlotte."

Does she find me as distracting as I find her? God, I hope so. I want to ask if she spent the day with this Jameson guy, but I manage to keep the urge at bay.

That's why it takes a second for her words to register, but when they do, my eyes go wide. "Shit. Seriously?" I've got zero chance going up against this guy if he's that rich. But since it's placed a frown on her lips, I want to know more about this contention between her and her dad. "So your dad's into the symphony? Or the Newhouse money?"

"Both." She shrugs, and I try to picture the Maisy in front of me hanging out at a stuffy symphony. I draw a complete blank.

"I'm pretty sure my dad never listened to anything besides country and classic rock," I tell her.

One side of her mouth tips up. "I think I would have liked your dad."

"I think he would have liked you too."

A silence settles between us again, only the sounds of passing traffic and chatter from the taproom patio breaking through.

"I gotta get back to work," I finally say, my tone communicating my reluctance. I'd like nothing better than to stand here all night with her. "Denny'll drive you guys up the mountain. You can leave your scooter here—either lock it up, or we can pull it inside." When she pushes off the wall, clearly about to object, I cut her off. "It's not safe to take that road with Bear, especially at night." I use Bear as the excuse since she might not take too kindly to me informing her there's no way in hell I'm letting her make that ride even without her brother. I secured a lift with Denny the second she pulled that scooter up to the brewery earlier.

"He doesn't have to do that."

"Yeah, he does. And if you think I'm hard to argue with, good luck with those jackasses in there."

She rolls her eyes but doesn't object again, and I open the door for her to go ahead of me back into the building.

It isn't until about thirty minutes later—when they've all taken off and I'm behind the bar—that the hairs on the back of my neck stand at attention. At first, I wonder if I'm imagining it, but a glance to the front doors has my feet fusing to the floor mat.

"Jesus, Miller!" Cash collides with me, and I throw a hand out to the bar to keep myself from crashing headfirst into it. "What the hell?" He slams the pint glass he was carrying onto the bar and grabs a towel to wipe up the spilled beer.

But I barely hear him because every last micron of my attention is riveted on the guy who just walked in the door like I summoned him through my conversation with Maisy. He glances around the taproom until his eyes lock on mine. It's the clearest view I've gotten of him yet, and even from this distance, I can make out the frown lines around his mouth and the streaks of white threaded through his thinning hair.

My jaw goes tight as a bowstring as I try to fathom what could possibly make Ian Driscoll think he has the right to waltz in here—into a business owned by a family he rendered fatherless through his gross negligence. When his gaze slides to Cash, I instinctively turn to my brother who's scowling at me and still waiting for an explanation.

"Sorry." My voice is strangled, my mind racing. "Can you do the keg switchover? My arm is giving me trouble." I raise my right arm, the same one I broke a couple months back in a car accident—one I'm almost convinced was the work of the asshole at the door. Fuck.

My brother glances at my arm before throwing the sodden bar towel into the sink. "Yeah, I got it. Get a *Cryptid* to Joaquin." He nods toward one of our regulars at the end of the bar by the register.

As soon as he turns to go, I swing back around to locate Driscoll, but he's disappeared. My eyes sweep the room, inspecting every corner before I haul ass out to the patio. But he's nowhere.

If I weren't stone-cold sober, I might wonder if I hallucinated the entire thing. But I know I didn't. And that's a big fucking problem.

CHAPTER TWELVE

DEJA VU

MAISY

It's official.

I have a massive crush on Miller Brooks.

And Bear has an equally massive nine-going-on-nineteen-year-old crush on Rosie, not that I blame him. She's super sweet and has amazing hair.

But Bear isn't faced with the pressure of knowing his crush sleeps twenty feet from him—which is why my brother is fast asleep beside me, and I'm wide awake staring at the ceiling while listening for Miller's footsteps in the hall.

Denny and Rosie dropped Ari and us off around nine, Ari waving goodnight as she sashayed up her aunt and uncle's driveway, and my brother and I headed for Ginny's door. We found Ginny puttering in the kitchen with Mango circling his mistress's legs. Bear wasted no time asking for treats to feed the skunk, an activity that kept him occupied until I finally put him to bed. It may be the weekend, but that kid gets cranky if he doesn't get his sleep.

When I wandered back downstairs, Lynn sat at the kitchen table, having just gotten home from work. I got the sense Ginny didn't often sit still, a notion reinforced by her deciding on a whim to whip up a breakfast casserole for tomorrow morning. I helped myself to a glass of water and sank into the chair across from Lynn Brooks. She has to be about my age, with intelligent caramel eyes and a mischievous smile that I'm guessing has guys lining up to date her.

"Have you got any family around here besides your mama and brother?" Ginny asked over her shoulder as she expertly diced potatoes on a cutting board.

If it were anyone else, I'd wonder if she was asking to get me to cut my stay short, but I'm certain Ginny was just trying to get to know me. "My dad lives near Lake Lure, but my extended family is in Brazil and… I don't even know where my mom's side is. We're obviously not close." I made my tone light to keep things from getting awkward.

"Mama and Dad were originally from out that way," Lynn shared. "They grew up in Mill Spring."

"Miller told me about your dad. I'm really sorry for your loss."

Lynn shot me a sad smile while Ginny replied, "Sweet of you, Maisy."

"What was he like? I heard all about his affection for Bigfoot, which I love, by the way." I find the entire story of a legacy entirely endearing.

Lynn laughed while Ginny shared, "A carbon copy of Miller—not in looks, mind you, but in everything else." She shook her head, raising her knife in the air. "I swear sometimes it's like déjà vu. Wade was the definition of trouble when we met, and what teenage girl doesn't get a big-ole crush on the local bad boy?"

I choked on my water at that but managed to play it off. Although something told me Ginny saw right through me.

"Didn't you say he stole a car or something while he was trying to get you to date him?" Lynn asked, not appearing the least bit scandalized at the idea of her dad engaging in felonious activities.

"Boosted it right off Bartholomew Ott's used car lot—the most unpleasant man you'd ever want to meet, by the way. And not a bright one either since he had a habit of leaving car keys in their ignitions." She turned to face us, eyes twinkling. "Wade pulled right into my parents' driveway in that car and leaned against the hood chatting me up for a good half hour—not that I knew the car was stolen at the time."

Lynn and I shared a smile before looking back at Ginny for the rest of the story.

"While Bart was on the phone reporting it as stolen, Wade parked it right back where he found it. Police got in Bart's face about calling in a false report, but nobody felt bad for him seeing as he saw nothing wrong with ripping strangers off by dialing back odometers and harassing women into buying pieces of junk."

"Sounds like something Miller would do to impress a girl. Only he'd get caught," Lynn crowed, her smile especially naughty this time.

"Oh, your dad didn't always get away with his shenanigans, believe me. In fact, the same day I found out I was pregnant with Carter, your dad spent the night in jail."

"What?! Why?" Lynn asked while I stared at Ginny with wide eyes.

She turned to the fridge to pull out a carton of eggs. "He didn't like how my daddy was speaking to me and made that plain. Mama called the cops when things got physical, and they hauled Wade off." She gesticulated with the egg carton, making me worried for the fate of the casserole for a minute. "I warned him time and time again my parents weren't worth it, but you know your dad. Protectiveness of a lion with the impulsiveness of a squirrel monkey."

I snort laughed at her characterization of her husband.

"And the attention span of a fruit fly," Lynn added. "How many projects did he start and never finish?"

Ginny's hand perched on her denim-covered hip. I was starting to wonder if the Brooks family owned any pants besides jeans. "I didn't care as long as he finished the important ones. Which he did, God love him."

We chatted some more while Ginny finished the casserole, covered it, and stuck it in the fridge. They didn't quiz me about anything but Bear, so I was able to relax and enjoy their company without confiding any more than I was comfortable doing.

Ginny yawned after a spell. "Well, I'm off to bed. Carter and Sunny are taking me to the flower show in the morning, and we're dragging Marvin along to civilize him."

"Carter's going to a flower show?" Lynn's tone was incredulous.

Her mom grinned. "Love does funny things to a man."

"And by 'funny things,' you apparently mean an entire personality transplant. And Duke's going? How'd Sunny maneuver that one?"

I had yet to meet Sunny, but I knew she was Miller's oldest brother's girlfriend. No clue who this Duke-slash-Marvin was, though.

"She might have told him it was a UFO convention," Ginny divulged with a grin.

"Ah." Lynn appeared satisfied with the strange explanation. "'Night, Mama."

"Good night, sugar. Night, Maisy. Holler if you need anything."

"I will, and thanks again for letting us stay." This family really was too good to be true, I thought as I watched Ginny head for the stairs, Mango appearing again to follow her.

"She's right, you know." Lynn drew my attention.

I stood and took my empty glass to get a refill. "About what?"

"Miller and Dad." Her voice was casual as she picked up her phone and ran her thumbs over the screen with practiced ease. "I burned a hole in the kitchen counter one time when I was eight. I wasn't supposed to be using the stove, but I thought everyone was treating me like a baby, so I did it anyway. Got halfway through melting some butter and set the hot pan right on the counter. Seared straight through it. You can still see it right there." She pointed to the stove, and sure enough, a round black circle was etched into the laminate countertop beside it.

I turned and gave her an *eek* face as she continued. "Miller walked into the kitchen thirty seconds before Mama did, saw the look on my face, and snatched the pan out of my hand. I thought he was gonna light into me at first, but instead, he told Mama *he* did it. Got grounded too—well, he already was for something else, but this added onto it. Later, he got in my face telling me I could have hurt myself and made me promise to never do that shit again. He was ten years old and no stranger to fibbing, but he served his sentence and never breathed a word of it to anybody as far as I know."

I returned her grin. "That's sweet. And kind of funny."

"That's Miller." She shrugged.

My throat went dry, but I covered it with what I hoped was a relaxed smile before Lynn's phone rang and she excused herself to her room to answer it.

And now it's one in the morning, and I have to work the early shift at Pete's, which means I need to haul my ass out of bed in five hours. I decide a cup of hot tea is what I need. It always used to settle me when my nerves would hit the night before a performance. I pull the covers back and sit up in bed, careful not to wake Bear even though the kid sleeps like the dead. But just as I rise to my feet, I finally hear the creak of the stairs, and my heartbeat picks up like Seabiscuit racing for the finish line.

I try homing in on Miller's movements, waiting for the click of his bedroom door shutting, but it doesn't come. I wait a while longer, and when I still hear nothing, I figure I missed him closing his door and pad on my bare feet to open ours.

Then I lose a good ten years off my life when I open it to find Miller standing in his bedroom doorway, one arm propped on the top of the doorframe, his long body relaxed against the jamb on one side. I'm tempted to glance around for a camera crew because I'm pretty sure I just walked in on a photo shoot in progress. His thick, messy hair and rumpled shirt give him the look of somebody who just got through giving it good to some lucky girl against the wall instead of a guy who just got off a long shift serving beers.

"You scared the crap out of me," I whisper-hiss at him as I cross my arms over my chest to hide the fact that I'm not wearing a bra.

His expression remains serious, a surprise seeing as he typically delights in messing with me. The broody look has my nipples going tight and a flash of want striking low in my belly. "I heard you shuffling around in there. What are you still doing up?" he asks in a husky whisper that does not help my situation even a little bit. I'm afraid I might need to change my underwear after this conversation.

"Can't sleep. I was going to get some tea."

He gestures to the stairs with his chin before releasing his grip on the door frame and moving into my space. I beat a quick retreat down the stairs with Miller at my heels.

"Bad night?" I ask when we reach the den—arms still crossed over my chest, by the way.

"To be determined." Miller collapses onto the sofa. It's a wild floral print with oversized throw pillows and cushions you could get lost in.

"That sounds cryptic."

His brow furrows. "Had a visitor I wasn't expecting."

"Oh yeah?" My tone is cautious as I imagine a gorgeous ex-girlfriend showing up to reclaim him. "Who was it?"

He's silent for a few moments as he stares at his long fingers while they trace a flower stem at the sofa's arm.

"Sorry, it's none of my business." I finally get over myself and drop my arms, turning to the kitchen to begin my teabag hunt.

"It was the doctor who killed my dad."

CHAPTER THIRTEEN
CONFESSIONS OF A TEENAGE BAD BOY

MILLER

"I'm sorry… what?!" Maisy halts her steps and whips around to face me again, her long ponytail whipping around her.

I bring a finger to my lips, my eyes flashing to the stairs before returning to her. "Shh. I don't need Mama and Lynn in on this conversation."

She smacks a hand over her mouth and moves to take a seat next to me before continuing in a whisper, "What did he want?" Her nearness is a distraction I'd love to take advantage of instead of allowing Driscoll to continue messing with my head. I'd hoped we were free and clear of him, but I'm apparently not that lucky.

"I have no clue." I don't know why I'm telling her this when I took pains to keep it from my brothers just hours ago. My dick is probably to blame, but Maisy and I have a connection I can't explain, given the two days we've known each other.

"So, he just decided to drop by for a beer? Did you guys have to talk to him?"

"I'm the only one who saw him, thank Christ, and he disappeared pretty much immediately."

Her brow creases, and it's cuter than I need right now. "Maybe he didn't know who owns Blue Bigfoot. And when he saw you guys, he took off."

"No. It was intentional." I run a tired hand through my hair and take a surreptitious sniff of my pit to make sure I don't reek. "It's a long story." She doesn't need to deal with my shit on top of her own family trouble.

She folds one leg under her and shifts so she's facing me. I can smell her sweet floral scent again, and I wonder if it's her skin. Whatever it is, I want to bury my face in it. "I'm not exactly sleepy," she invites, her expression open and warm. She's tempting in every way, and I know in my bones I could lose myself in her if she'd let me. After the shock of seeing Driscoll tread on Dad's legacy, I'd love nothing more than to ignore reality and get lost in Maisy Romero.

This entire saga has stayed between Dax and me for five years for a reason, but that reason is hard to remember when Maisy pulls me in with those deep brown eyes and soft expression. I'm the guy who leaps before looking, who goes with my first impulse, who throws caution to the wind. So why not lay it out for her like she's inviting me to? I push away any warning—and likely wise—voices and decide *to hell with it*.

"I was still a teenager when my dad died, and I was pissed as all hell. Carter got a lawyer, and we sued the hospital, but that wasn't going to make anything better. The surgeon who fucked up and killed Dad—a guy named Driscoll—and one of the nurses got a slap on the wrist, and we got a cash settlement. But I wanted my pound of flesh. Carter wanted them to cough up more money. Mama just wanted it over with."

"That's so unfair. They didn't even lose their jobs?"

I shake my head. "Their position was, essentially, *shit happens*." I adjust on the sofa to face her as well. The single dim lamp lighting the room throws shadows onto her features and underscores the intimacy of my confession. "I had all this pent-up rage I didn't know what to do with, so I started following Driscoll, figuring maybe catching him off guard and beating the shit out of him might make me feel better." She raises an eyebrow at that, and I can only shrug. I was a kid, and jumping into fights was pretty much my MO back then—and until embarrassingly recently, I admit. "My friend Dax tagged along one day and shocked the shit out of me when he recognized Driscoll. Dax has always considered himself a businessman, and at the time, his business involved some seriously illegal substances. Substances Dax told me he regularly sold to Driscoll."

"You're kidding?" Her spine straightens, and she grasps my forearm. "Do you think that's why he messed up the surgery? Because he was strung out or something?"

"I reckon that's *exactly* what happened, not that I could ever prove it. But based on Dax's input, he was using both smack and coke at the time of Dad's surgery."

She gasps at that. "So what did you do?"

I pause. Somewhere in the recesses of my mind, I know it's a risk telling her my secrets for a lot of reasons. But her wide dark eyes and the need to finally get it off my chest have me continuing, "We made him pay."

"I don't understand." Maisy's hand drops from my arm, and I immediately miss the contact.

"Next time he came for his fix, Dax threw in a few bonuses. Gave me the heads up when he left the meet, and I used a burner to call in an anonymous tip about witnessing a drug deal. Bad neighborhood, cops were already close, so they busted him on the spot."

Her mouth drops open, but if I expect her to recoil or look disappointed in me, her reaction is far from it. "What about Dax?"

"Even at seventeen, Dax could take care of himself. Driscoll didn't know his real name and only had a burner number for him."

"Did Driscoll go to jail?"

When I nod, her lips spread in a wide smile that has me wanting to laugh—which is really fucking odd considering the topic. "He lawyered up, of course, and he might have gotten off with some bullshit legal gymnastics, except that when he got busted, it made the hospital take a closer look at some pharmaceuticals that were unaccounted for. They called the cops, who got a warrant and searched Driscoll's house. Found the hospital's shit and had him dead to rights. He served just under a nickel and got out a few months ago."

"Wow." Maisy's dark eyes roam my face, and she shakes her head. "I can't believe you did all that when you were just a teenager."

"I did all that for my dad. Could have been ten, and I still would have done it."

Her entire face goes soft then, and she reaches for my hand like it's a reflex more than an intentional act. "I believe it." She squeezes, and I suddenly feel twenty feet tall. Like I could do anything. Be anything. "You felt powerless. You wanted your power back." Her lips curve in a sad smile. "I totally get that."

And it's clear she does. Is that how her mom makes her feel? Her dad? I should quit talking about myself and let her lay her troubles on me instead of the other way around.

I twist her hand in mine until our palms align, and then it's my turn to squeeze hers. "Who took your power, Maisy?"

She opens her mouth but doesn't say anything at first, those plump lips parting in a way that has me groaning internally. Every part of me wants that mouth—in every way it can have it.

But this isn't the time.

Her eyes bore into mine as if trying to determine my trustworthiness. Just because I shared with her, she has no obligation to do the same in return. Not a lot of people bet on me, but I want more than anything for Maisy to do just that. "I want to know everything about you, Maisy," I admit in a whisper. This isn't me playing my usual game to get into a girl's pants. This is a new kind of desire that's entirely foreign. I want her to trust me, to know me, to give me her troubles so I can help shoulder them.

My expression or words must somehow communicate that because she clears her throat and then licks her lips before confessing, "I… I could be rich right now. And famous. But I gave it all up because I hated that life—even though I'd been groomed for it since I was four years old."

I'm silent in response, not having the first clue what she's talking about. The only direction my brain goes is to an insane idea that maybe she's a princess hiding out in Asheville pretending to be a normal American. But that's idiotic, so I stay silent.

Luckily, she continues, "I'm a piano prodigy. I played with the Valley Symphony Orchestra when I was six years old, the Munich Philharmonic at eight, and Carnegie Hall when I was nine. At twelve, I played for the Queen of England."

"I'm sorry, what?" She's entertained the Queen, and she's working in a coffee shop and crashing in my brother's room? Where is her bodyguard and her entourage?

"I know. It's weird."

"It's not weird," I insist, still holding her hand and raising my voice before remembering to keep it down. "It's fucking impressive." I can't imagine being that good at something.

"My dad insists it's a gift that shouldn't be squandered. That I 'owe it to the world' to use what I was given." She does air quotes in place of an eye roll. "He was my manager until I quit three years ago, and he can't forgive me."

"Well, that's bullshit." My response is immediate.

The corner of her mouth quirks. "Which part?"

"All of it." I give her hand another squeeze, and she looks down to our connection. "It's *your* gift, so you should be able to do with it whatever you want. And he's your dad. He's not supposed to judge you like that."

"Ha! Welcome to the Romero family."

I'm getting worked up on her behalf. "Fuck that."

"You know what the worst part is?" She leans in closer. "I *love* music. I breathe it, get lost in it for hours, give my entire body over to it. And Dad loves it just as much. It was always our bond, and for a long time I kept up the grueling schedule, the panic attacks, the aching joints, all to please him. Until I finally stopped long enough to realize it was all *his* dream, not mine. I love playing when it's for me. I hate the stage and all the rules and expectations." She repositions herself, fire in her words now, but she doesn't pull away. "I didn't even go to regular school. I had tutors who traveled with us all over the world. I hardly even knew my brother until I quit playing. The only friends I had were fellow musicians, but it was all one big competition, so none of them were real friends—except Jameson."

"Does he play too?"

She nods. "He's a pianist. We grew up in the same scene, even played together for a while."

"So that's why your dad is so fired up for you to hitch yourself to him." It's all starting to make sense. And if I were this Jameson guy, I'd probably try to lock that up tight too.

She nods again.

Even if it's none of my business. I need to know for sure. "But you don't want to be with Jameson?"

She rubs her lips together, and I bring my other hand around to hold hers in both of mine. Finally, she smiles. "I'm pretty sure carjacking you in a wedding dress answers that question."

I can't stop my grin, which has Maisy's eyes dropping to my mouth. When her tongue pokes out to wet her full bottom lip, I'm a complete and utter goner.

And, once again, I leap before I look, knowing at least I'll enjoy the fall even if I crash and burn on the rocks below.

CHAPTER FOURTEEN

SOMEONES

MAISY

Miller is going to kiss me, and I don't give a single shit if I'm foolish to allow it. It's so happening.

Instead of drawing me in slowly like I expect, however, he yanks my hand, and I tumble into him, completely losing my balance and throwing my free hand out to his chest to break my fall. My mouth pops open in surprise, and he deftly moves to wrap an arm around my waist and drop his chin on a devilish grin.

"Hey," he murmurs before dipping to cover my mouth with his.

On contact, my whole body sighs in contentment. His lips are the perfect combination of hard and soft, and they're so warm I might just curl up here for the winter. But contentment soon gives way to need as he slants his head to caress my lips with his, and I feel the wet brush of his tongue asking for entry.

I do him one better by getting my knees under me and pressing my entire upper body into his hard chest. My nipples constrict as Miller's tongue sweeps into my mouth on a groan, and his hand fists the back of my T-shirt. I give a muffled yelp of surprise when the tip of my tongue encounters the cold metal of his tongue piercing, providing a delicious contrast. I'd forgotten all about it in all the fornication anticipation, I guess.

His other hand circles my back as well, pressing me even tighter against him before it skims up so he can bury his fingers in my hair. He yanks the tie from my ponytail in one pull, and my hair tumbles over my shoulders and onto his chest.

"Fuck," he says into my mouth. "You're so soft everywhere."

I rake my own fingers through his hair in return, responding, "Less talking, more kissing," and I can feel his grin against my lips before he uses his to perform more of their magic.

Somewhere in the next few minutes, I end up with my back to the couch cushions and Miller on top of me, his hips cradled between my thighs as I grind up into him, having clearly lost my mind. My fingertips skate over his cotton-covered back, and I breathe in his faintly woodsy scent while his hand drops from my jaw to my neck.

Then he's skimming down my side, and his hand slips under the hem of my shirt at my waist. The contact sends a bolt of need to my pussy, causing my hips to jerk up again. Miller takes this as a sign of encouragement, brushing the pads of his fingers along my rib cage until they sweep over the underside of my breast.

"Miller." I arch into him this time, and he answers my unspoken demand by strumming his thumb over my hard nipple, his lips tracing the line of my throat now.

With my brain on vacation, there's no one to stop this

train from driving through the tunnel, so to speak, and I can't muster any fucks to give about the wisdom of our actions. I just know I need Miller. I need him like oxygen, like sunlight, like… music.

"Oh, shit! Sorry!" a loud masculine voice breaks through my lust fog, and Miller's entire body locks tight on top of me. Instinct has me rolling to face the back of the sofa while I yank my shirt down, so I don't even get a glimpse of the voice's source.

"Cash? What the fuck?" Miller hisses, moving in front of me and tugging on my shirt as well.

Wow. This isn't an embarrassing way to meet his brother at all. Before I can think of a way to somehow turn this into no big deal and laugh it off, something cold and wet lands on my thigh. I yelp and whirl around to find a brown and white dog sniffing my crotch, and—is it smiling at me?

"Betty! Off!" Cash demands, and my eyes flash to Miller's brother without a thought. He's tall and dark with bright blue eyes and a healthy dose of scruff, but I can still find similarities between him and Miller—they both share the same strong jaw and straight nose. I, of course, saw him from afar earlier tonight, but we haven't been introduced. The dog pushes off the couch and returns to her master's side, tongue lolling, giving her an adorable look that has me forgiving her immediately for the awkward greeting via my lady town.

"Sorry about that," Cash says, sparing me a glance before addressing his brother. "How was I supposed to know you'd be defiling someone on the couch?"

"Why aren't you at Hollis's?" Miller demands, running a frustrated hand through his hair and sending me a pained look of apology.

"I told Mama I'd fix the gutter tomorrow morning, so it made more sense to crash here."

Oh shit.

I scramble to sit, making sure I don't expose myself in the process. "Oh my gosh. I'm so sorry. I think my brother is sleeping in your bed." When I move to stand, Miller bars my way with an arm around my middle, pulling me down so I land on his lap. Hmm.

"And he's staying there." Miller eyes me before shifting a glare to his brother, who throws his palms out.

"No need to get your panties in a wad, little brother. I can crash in the attic—since I can assume you've somehow convinced this poor girl to share your bed?"

"Oh, we're not—" I start, but Miller cuts me off.

"Maisy. Her name is Maisy." Then he turns to me. "Maisy, this is my pain-in-the-ass brother, Cash."

"Nice to meet you, Maisy." It's clear Cash is past his initial surprise and is now trying to hide a smile.

"You too," I manage. When I try standing, I'm again restrained by Miller, having no other choice but to get comfortable on his lap. The hard cock pressing into my backside, however, makes that a little difficult.

"We'll see ourselves out," Cash says, dropping his eyes to Betty—who, apart from the initial greeting, has been a perfect lady throughout this exchange. "Come on, girl. Let's leave your uncle alone to try salvaging this one." The two of them trot to the stairs without another glance. "Nice to meet you, Maisy," Cash calls behind him.

I drop my face into my palm. "Did that really just happen?"

Miller replies strangely, "In hindsight, I should have seen that coming," before he flips me on my back again and hovers over me. His grin makes a return. "Don't give it another thought. I promise Cash won't."

His words are meant to be reassuring, I know, but their implication hits me a second later. Cash is used to witnessing Miller feeling girls up. He's used to Miller with any manner of "someones". It's no big deal. *I'm* no big deal. I'm just one in a line of girls who've probably had their backs to this very couch.

I try pushing up again, and when Miller resists, I bring my eyes to his. Something in them must register because when I push on his chest this time, he lets off and allows me to sit.

"I… should go to bed. I need to be at work really early." Shit, I don't even know how I'm getting there. There's no public transportation out this far. I'm going to spend the entire day's tips on an Uber.

"Oh. Yeah," he responds. "Um, what time do you need to go?"

"You don't have to—" I say at the same time he says, "And don't tell me you don't need a ride."

I force a smile. He's such a great guy. And he doesn't owe me anything, whether it's a ride to work or an apology for banging lots of women. Hell, the last thing I need is to get attached only to be disappointed when shit falls apart like it always does.

"I'm not a good sleeper anyway," he says by way of explanation, clearly trying to get me to stop protesting.

"Um, six forty-five." I grimace.

He raises an eyebrow, but his carefree expression doesn't falter. "Then we should definitely hit the hay."

Relieved, I stand. "Thanks, Miller. I'll find a way to pay you back somehow." And I mean it. Nothing in this life is free, and I don't want to take advantage. I'll figure out a way to pay Miller and his entire crew back for all their kindness.

He scowls, but it has little force behind it, and I take my chance to escape up the stairs and close the bedroom door behind me.

Back to the door, I draw in a deep breath and wait for my eyes to adjust to the darkness. When they do, I find Bear sprawled sideways on the bed, covers strewn every which way and Goomba tucked under his head as a makeshift pillow.

My chest swells. This boy is all that matters; the state of *his* heart is the only one I need to think about. There will be plenty of time to give care to the state of my own down the road. On that thought, I fit myself into the space along-side Bear and pull him into me before dropping off to sleep.

CHAPTER FIFTEEN

HELLO, KARMA

MAISY

"What about that one?" Jade asks, leaning into my back and pointing to an apartment listing on my phone.

My call to my former landlord crashed and burned. Turns out his mother-in-law is moving into the room. It was a sweet deal—a shared kitchen, but otherwise all my own space plus my own bathroom. The options I'm finding online aren't even coming close.

I turn to curl my lip at Jade. "You can actually *see* the mice in the photos."

"Those are mice?" She snatches my phone and brings it closer to her face. "I thought they were doorstops."

"This is stupid anyway." I pull the phone from her hand and lean back into the counter.

Miller took me to retrieve my scooter early this morning, both of us too tired to even attempt conversation, thank God. I woke Bear up before I showered in the hall bathroom, but Miller insisted that since he didn't work until afternoon, he was happy to hang with my brother for the morning. Again, I stupidly took him up on his offer, only putting myself further in his debt.

We're having an unusual late-morning lull at Pete's, so Jade popped over to make out with him in the kitchen but got distracted by my apartment hunt on her way. Sorry, boss.

"I need to find a nice two-bedroom apartment in a safe neighborhood," I declare, refusing to face Jade.

"Uh." She doesn't need to say more. Finding an affordable two-bedroom in a decent area in my price range is like looking for a straight man at a Lady Gaga concert. There are probably a few out there, but they're not advertising.

Despite my exhausted state, I've spent the morning devising my new strategy and have decided to focus on pursuing custody in ten months when I turn twenty-one. I'll just have to keep my fingers crossed that Mom doesn't get the money for airfare and doesn't draw the ire of CPS in the meantime. Which means I have less than a year to establish a healthy income, a secure home with enough space for Bear to have his own bedroom, and a meticulous recording of all of Mom and Terry's transgressions. The last item is already covered; I've been keeping records as best I can since Bear came back from foster care, so at least I've got one out of three.

My phone rings in my hand, and I take it as a middle finger from karma when my dad's contact comes up on the screen. I pull in a deep breath and step away from Jade and into the seating area to answer.

"Hey, Dad."

"Finally! Where have you been? I've been looking for

you all over." His voice is strained, and I can practically hear him pacing in his office.

I glance around, avoiding Jade's eye. "Um, I'm at work."

"At that coffee shop? I went there yesterday, and the guy at the counter pretended not to know you."

I can't help my smile, but I'm careful not to inject it into my voice. I love Pete. "He probably thought you were talking about someone else. Anyway, what's up?" I ask, like this week never happened, and he wasn't chasing after me outside a courthouse the last time I saw him.

"Very funny. Joanna said Jameson is moving back home."

"I know. And?" He's going to have to say what he's thinking if he expects a response.

"And that's not really fair to him."

I cough out an incredulous laugh. "And that's *my* fault? Talk to Joanna and Darian!" They're the ones keeping his trust fund captive.

"You know how they are."

"Yeah." Yes, I do. They're self-important and as tightly strung as a drumhead. It occurs to me that I should sell that dress and purse on eBay and give the money to Jameson.

My dad exhales loudly, making sure to express his annoyance. "People get married for all sorts of reasons, Maisy. Marrying for money is nothing to be ashamed of."

I dip my chin into my chest and want to throw up. What kind of parent wants their kid to get married for money? Oh, right—mine and the Newhouses.

He takes my silence as an invitation to continue. "Why did you agree to marry him in the first place if you're so happy living life as a transient?"

I grit my teeth. He doesn't know about the plan to get Bear. He doesn't need to know, although I'd cave in a second if I thought he'd help.

When I don't respond again, he changes the subject. "Maryanne Baldwin called yesterday."

Shit. Maryanne is the Valley Symphony director of programming.

"One of the artists slated for the summer symphony showcase died. Lee Joong-ki. Violinist," he informs me. I know the name, but we've never met. "It's not particularly prestigious, but it's a foot back in the door."

"I don't play anymore, Dad." This exchange is a broken record. "I don't know why you'd even allow Maryanne to think it's a possibility."

He scoffs. "You're damn lucky she called at all after the way you humiliated us in Boston."

Here we go again. Skip, skip, skip. I'd rather marry Jameson than play another concert hall.

"That was on you. I told you I was done, and as usual, you completely ignored me." It was a huge venue, and I'd just suffered a massive panic attack and met with my therapist who supported my decision to quit.

"Because I'm your manager, and I know what's best."

I want to scream. I want to throw my phone across the room. I want to hang up and never talk to him again. The need for a hug unexpectedly overwhelms me, and I have to brace my hand on the back of an empty chair.

"Best for who?" God, am I echoing my mom?

I can perfectly picture him sitting in his office chair, elbow to the desk, forehead resting in a hand, jaw tight beneath his short beard. "You don't squander talent like yours. Especially when it affords you a good living."

I lift my chin and let my eyes take in the café. Monica

ignores a beckoning customer as she hurries to the counter to serve a hot guy. The place is practically deserted otherwise; just a few regulars hunched over their laptops with cardboard cups of Americano at their sides. Everybody is either out enjoying the summer heat or hiding away from it. Tips will be abysmal today. Just what I need.

"I don't want to be a concert pianist, Dad. I never did. I only did it to please you. To pay you back for taking me on and getting me away from Mom. But I paid my dues, and when I told you I'd had enough you wouldn't listen. *You never listen.*"

He perfectly demonstrates my point by responding, "Do you know how many little girls would kill to have the talent you have in your pinky finger?"

"No, but I have a good guess as to the number of their parents who would." Harsh but true.

"That's not fair. It's all for you, can't you see that?"

"No, Dad, it's never been about me. Until I *chose* to make it that way."

"So what are you going to do? Schlep coffee and obscene T-shirts for the rest of your life. How can that possibly be fulfilling? If that's your choice, maybe I should have left you with your mother."

Ouch. This is the same woman who sees nothing wrong with slapping her kids when they wet the bed. At least with my dad, I know there's love and pride there somewhere, despite our rift. I've never had a single precious thing from Mom, and he knows it.

"I can't believe you said that."

He responds on a heavy exhale, "I didn't mean it. I'm sorry. I'm just frustrated." His anger dissipates. "Why can't you at least marry Jameson?"

"I don't love Jameson. Not like that."

"Who said anything about love?"

He's right. Love only wounds. It doesn't heal. I know that already, so I should avoid it like the plague and marry Jamie.

"I have to get back to work," I say over the frog in my throat.

"Okay, but think about Maryanne's offer, okay? Talk soon." He hangs up, and I just barely refrain from hurling my phone against the opposite wall. But phones are expensive, and I need every penny I can get now, don't I?

CHAPTER SIXTEEN

SASQUATCHES VS. CAVEMEN

MILLER

"We saw Bigfoot!" Bear shouts to the entire café the second we stroll in. "We're going back to set up a trap tonight, and tomorrow we'll be famous!"

"I think she heard you, dude," I tell his back as he changes direction to the counter where Pete is beckoning him over. Maisy watches him race by with a smile on her lips. Her hair is pulled up in a ponytail again, her tan apron hiding some of her figure in another pair of short shorts and a fitted tee.

She tucks a stray lock of hair behind her ear, and I don't miss the faint blush on her cheeks. Is she thinking about last night too? "Sounds like you guys had a big morning."

I reckon we did. After Mama's famous breakfast casserole, Lynn and I took Bear for a hike on one of the old forest trails where Dad used to take us. Without any conspiring beforehand, she and I immediately found ourselves adopting Dad's role and pretending to spot movement in the trees along with traces of giant footprints. It took only minutes to get Bear on our hook, and we spent the next hour on a wild goose chase of our own making. It was a blast. That kid would have stayed out there all day if we'd had the time.

When we got back home, Cash was perched atop a ladder, struggling to hold a new length of gutter while he drilled it in place, so I borrowed the Carmichael's ladder to give him a hand. Bear watched with rapt attention as we replaced the leaky sections, all the while begging to use the drill and climb the ladder. Once we were done boiling like lobsters in the summer heat, I let him hold the drill before we closed up the garage and retreated inside to cool off.

Somewhere in the midst of our activities, I agreed to build a Bigfoot trap. I have no idea how it happened, but it's clear I'm not getting out of it. I can think of worse things.

"He wants a power drill for his birthday, FYI," I tell Maisy. "And I might need your help building a Sasquatch trap." The second part is a lie, but that doesn't mean I don't want her company. Especially after last night.

If Cash hadn't cock blocked me, I honestly don't know how far we would have taken it. It's no secret I want in there, but with the way Maisy backed off as soon as she got a second to breathe, I'm thinking the interruption was a good thing.

I never thought I'd see the day I'd be happy to slow things down with a hot girl, but I've also never met anyone like Maisy. She's got a firm sense of self and strong convictions; I need to pay attention and do whatever's best for her. Even if that means last night is a one-time deal. But Christ, I hope it's not.

Maisy thought me taking on Driscoll at seventeen was impressive, but she's not only been living on her own since eighteen, she's hellbent on taking on parenthood at twenty. That's way beyond setting up a dubious drug deal and making a few calls. I can certainly afford to up my game, especially if I want any chance of her seeing me as more than a friend she can call on for a ride.

"I can't say I know much about catching Sasquatches," she replies on a shrug of her slim shoulders, "but I'm willing to try." After a pause, she asks, "You want a coffee or anything? My treat."

I'm not letting her pay for my fucking coffee. "Sure. I'll take whatever's hot. But I'm paying."

She rolls her eyes, and we both move to the counter where Pete is passing a bright purple smoothie over to Bear.

"Powerberry Avalanche," Pete tells me. "It can change your life, but sadly, it has no caffeine."

Maisy hands me a paper cup of steaming dark coffee with a cardboard sleeve, and I fork a few bucks over to Pete.

"Bigfoot trap will have to wait till tomorrow, Bear. I'm working tonight, but I've got tomorrow night and all of Monday off."

Bear's initial frown at the news changes to a half smile. "That's cool. Can we spend the night in the woods tomorrow?"

I'm giving it serious consideration—Maisy sleeping next to me in a tent?—when Maisy chimes in, "Tomorrow's a school night."

"But the last day of school is this week. We're not doing nothin' but watching movies, and I can take a nap on my desk. Or skip." He snags the straw with a sweep of his tongue and sucks up the purple concoction.

Maisy straightens his light brown hair that's been mussed from our day's activities—and a tussle with Betty. "Your teacher said you're lucky you're even moving on to fourth grade, you've missed so much work this year. You're going, and Bigfoot can wait until later in the week."

Bear rolls his eyes but doesn't talk back, instead continuing to suck on his straw before stomping off to a nearby table.

I pour some sugar into my coffee and stay out of it.

"How about a little coffee with your sugar?" Maisy suggests as I go for one more pour.

"It's just bean water if you don't add sugar." I give my coffee a stir with a stick, my tone unapologetic.

Pete whimpers, and Maisy reaches over to give his arm a reassuring squeeze while fake glaring at me. "Mind the coffee fanatic, will you."

I smile at her in response before giving Pete a nod. "Sorry, man."

A couple minutes later, I'm out the door, making the ten-minute walk to Blue Bigfoot with my perfectly sweetened coffee in hand. Kelsie, another server and part-time bartender, stands outside the back door when I get there.

"I wouldn't go in there if I were you," she warns, her purple-tipped hair swinging around her ears. She's a fan of piercings and body art, like me, and her new matching purple nose stud glitters in the midday sun. I had a septum ring and lip ring until recently, and her new piercing kind of makes me regret letting the septum close up. The lip ring I can do without—that thing was hell on my gums.

"What's going on?" The doors opened a half hour ago, so that's not enough time for drama to build.

"Cart has lost his mind."

I shake my head and open the door, not too bothered by that. My oldest brother is the brewmaster at Blue Bigfoot, and he often gets in a mood when the beer he's working on doesn't turn out precisely as he imagined.

But as soon as I enter the back hall and near the brewhouse door, I know this isn't about beer.

"News flash, Carter Lucien Brooks. I'm a grown-ass woman," Lynn hurls at my brother, her fingers digging into her hips. Bear and I rode in with Cash, but Lynn must not have been far behind, clearly having some reason to drop by before heading to work herself.

"You're a teenager." Carter's working on a good scowl as he shoves his apron over his head.

"*Lucien*? How did I not know your middle name is Lucien?" Sunny, Carter's girlfriend, asks from her position on the sidelines where she sits on a worktable in a bright pink pair of overalls that clashes with her classic red hair.

My siblings ignore her, Lynn countering, "I'm twenty."

"I'm hungry. Is anyone else hungry?" Sunny hops down from the table, clearly trying to calm everyone's asses down. "We should go out and get tacos, Lynn."

I could totally go for tacos. "What's going on?" For some idiotic reason, I enter the fray.

Carter points in Lynn's face, and she smacks his hand away. "I'll tell you what's going on. Your little sister is flirting with a man old enough to be her father."

I feel a sharp pain behind my right eye. "Who? Is he here?" I turn back for the door. "What's this asshole's name?" Yes, we are one giant cliché wrapped in a time capsule and doused in Old Spice aftershave. But I figure that's what happens when you have a baby sister and you all lose your dad.

"Carter." Sunny steps between my brother and sister, only delaying the answers to my questions.

"No." He gives a firm shake of his head. "This is bullshit."

"You're just upset because Jeremy has been talking to *me* instead of *you*," Lynn snarls.

"Who's Jeremy?" I ask, determined to find this guy and rearrange his face.

"His old colleague from DC," Sunny explains. Carter used to be a congressional aide in some bigwig's office in Washington until they all started doing shady shit, and he got them busted. He's better off as a brewmaster, if you ask me.

"That guy?" I ask, studying Lynn for a second. We all met this Jeremy dude a couple months back—definitely a player and dresses like he's got plenty of cash to blow on women. Strikes me as the furthest thing from Lynnie's type.

"There was… maybe a bit of a falling out when everything went down, and some feelings got hurt," Sunny says, her words addressing me but her eyes and hands on Carter. "Anyway, it's not that big of a deal, if you ask me. In fact, I think it's a good thing—this just means he's getting closer to mending fences if you ask me."

"He's a perverted old man if you ask *me*." Carter's expression has dropped to one step below thunderous now.

"You are unbelievable." Lynn shakes her head and yanks her phone from her back pocket. "He's your friend. And we aren't flirting—not that we wouldn't have the right to."

"I saw your text notification from him." Is Cart sweating? "It said, 'Next time I'll be all over you.' What else could that possibly mean?"

My chin jerks back at that. Sounds like more than flirting to me. Is that asshat fucking my little sister?

"Oh, I don't know." Lynn's voice positively oozes sarcasm as she waves her phone in the air. "Maybe that he's sick of me kicking his ass in Words with Friends?"

Oh. Okay, time for tacos.

"What the fuck does that mean?" Carter asks, his stomach clearly not on the same page as Sunny's and mine.

"What the hell is going on in here?" Cash bellows from the doorway. "I can hear you guys over the music in the taproom." He points a finger at me. "You're late."

My eyes flick to the clock on the wall. "No, I'm not. I'm here."

"You're on bussing till Eden gets here at four," he responds like he didn't hear me.

"It's online Scrabble," Sunny explains, and a glance in their direction shows her biting back a smile.

Lynn crosses her arms and scowls back at Carter. Exactly. Not that it's any of your business."

Cart is still frowning, but he's calmed to a tropical rm from the original Category 5 hurricane he'd started Why are you playing Scrabble with Jeremy?"

ash straightens and loses all interest in me. "You're ng Scrabble with Jeremy? Is he here?"

o." Carter, Sunny, Lynn, and I all respond to Cash in His brow creases in confusion.

offers more explanation to Carter. "He reached sk about *you*, you idiot, and I happened to be Vords with Friends when his text came in. It just sort of happened, and now we play sometimes. Not flirting. Not sexting. Scrabble. You need to pick up the phone and call him."

"Sexting?!" Cash lurches forward. "What the fuck!?"

Lynn pins him with her scowl this time. "Just playing Scrabble! And chatting now and then. Not that I don't have every right to *sext*—or *have sex*—with anyone I choose!" Carter and Cash's color rises at that, but I'm finding this hilarious now. "But, honestly, *Jeremy*? He's so not my type."

I knew it! I could really use those tacos now—and maybe a chair to sit and enjoy the show while I eat. What was I thinking by skipping lunch? Egg casserole can't hold a guy over till dinner.

Lynn chooses to poke the bear by adding, "Besides, I'm dating someone."

"Who?" Cash asks on another step closer.

Carter's "How old is he?" is right on its tail.

Sunny drops her chin to her chest, and I choke
laugh. We're only missing Denny, and this would be
star Brooks offspring showdown. My money woul
on Lynn, hands down.

"Oh, for god's sake. Do you hear yoursel
throws her arms out and whirls on her heel, h
door and passing by me. "Forget it! I'm go
work."

"FYI, fucknugget is an excellent Scr
Jeremy's ass," I tell her.

She rolls her eyes, but I don't mis
as she counters with, "Chauvinist i
legal."

"Touché."

Her boyfriend is probably

at the ballpark, not that I'm going to offer my suspicions up to the room. This protective streak isn't new, and I know it's ridiculous in today's world, but love shows itself in fucked-up ways sometimes.

"Welp," I say. "Now that the fun's over, I reckon it's taco time. What are we thinking? White Duck? Grey Eagle? Taco Billy? Whose car can I borrow?"

Cash tosses a bar towel at me and leaves the room. Cart shakes his head and turns back to the fermenter. But Sunny links her arm in mine and whispers, "White Duck. It's Carter's favorite—*and* it works wonders for crankiness."

"I heard that!" Cart shouts over his shoulder, but I notice he doesn't disagree.

CHAPTER SEVENTEEN

TWO BEDROOMS, TWO BATHS

MAISY

MOM:

Your brother needs to come home

The text comes in mid-afternoon, just as I'm clocking out. Bear is getting a basic lesson on milk frothing from Mika while I gather my things. She's a fellow employee I actually like, which means we often commiserate about the pain in the ass that is Monica.

ME:

Why? He's having fun

MOM:

Because he's my kid not yours

ME:

Aren't you working all weekend?

MOM:

Yeah but Terry ain't

Wow. What a bonus.

ME:

And Terry wants to hang out with Bear?

Terry tolerates Bear because he likes getting sex on the regular from Mom, and he likes even more that he doesn't have to pay rent if he doesn't feel like it. He's probably an alcoholic, and he yells a lot, but he's not deliberately mean or anything; he's just lacking basic sensitivity. He's incapable of extrapolating his own experiences to consider the people around him. If it's lunchtime and he's hungry, it never occurs to him that perhaps the child in the next room might be hungry too. Is it so hard to make a kid a sandwich?

MOM:

Bring him home now!

Suddenly, bitch-face Monica doesn't look too bad in comparison.

ME:

He has a playdate

It's not a lie; I'm just not specifying *when* the playdate is. I talked to Jordan's mom this morning to schedule one for tomorrow since Bear shouldn't have to spend so much time hanging out at the café and screen print shop. She's going to pick him up from here tomorrow and take the boys to the splash park while I'm working.

Lord knows what we're going to do once school's out. I know a lot of kids spend all of their summer vacation at home playing video games—not going to camps or taking trips or hanging out with friends. I get it. Working parents with limited resources do what they can. But it's becoming increasingly obvious that Bear is being left alone way too often.

And I'm not okay with that. He's nine, and while he loves to pretend he's older and wiser, he's not. He's a child who needs to be looked after and loved and given every opportunity I can possibly provide.

Pete and Jade will work with me to accommodate Bear's schedule as much as they can during the school year if I need it, but the summer is another story. Something else to add to my list of money woes.

MOM:

Well why didn't you say that in the first place? Have whoever it is drop him here after

I close the message app and shove my phone in the back pocket of my shorts, deliberately not replying.

"Let's go, B!" I beckon my brother.

"Where are we goin'?" He rushes to my side, and I open the door for us. The heat hits us like a brick to the chest.

"To look at a potential new apartment."

He squints up at me, and I make a mental note to get him some sunglasses as I drop mine down on my nose. "What's potential mean?"

"It means possible, as in maybe I'll live there, maybe not."

"What do you need a new apartment for anyway? We're staying with Miller and Mrs. Brooks."

I guide him up the sidewalk toward the bus stop. I'm leaving the scooter in the back of Jade's shop even though I have a helmet for Bear. The bus is a lot safer, which is another reason we need to get out of the Brooks house. No bus. "We can't stay with them forever. They're being super nice and doing us a favor, but you never want to outstay your welcome."

"Mrs. Brooks already said we're welcome, and she don't look like a lady who fibs a whole lot."

"No, I'm sure she doesn't." Teaching etiquette to a third grader is harder than I imagined, so I change tacks. "Don't you think maybe Miller's brothers might want their rooms back at some point?"

"I guess." You'd think I just told him Mario and Luigi split up by the disappointment on his face. He drops his eyes to his shoes as he trudges beside me.

"Hey, guess what. The apartment we're going to see has two bedrooms and two bathrooms. You know what that means?"

"I can poop as long as I want?" The joy has returned at the mere thought of poo.

The trailer has one bathroom, and while Bear does have his own bedroom, it's tiny and cramped. I crashed on the couch while I was staying there, and I'll bet it was more comfortable than his room.

"Uh, sure," I answer—because boys. "You'd get your own bedroom *and* bathroom when you stay with me."

"Tight."

In a stroke of luck, we get to the stop just as the bus pulls up, and I nudge Bear ahead of me, swiping my card when we get to the top of the steps. The air conditioning is struggling to keep up with the heat, that much is written all over every face on the bus. It's going to be a long ride to Haw Creek.

I initially didn't even consider this apartment because it's too close to Mom's for my comfort, but it was literally the only one I could find that I can possibly swing. And if you don't strike fast around here, rentals disappear like fresh chocolate chip cookies on a plate. It would also mean Bear wouldn't have to change schools once I get custody, so there's that.

When. Not if. We're thinking positive here, people.

A seat opens up, and Bear drops his little booty in it while I hold on to the bar above. My feet are sore from running coffees and pastries all day, but in heat like this, it's a mistake to sit on a vinyl bus seat while wearing shorts this small. The backs of my thighs would likely tear right off when I stood.

When we finally reach our destination, we walk the ten minutes to the apartment complex. It's older, with brick and wood siding and a parking lot that could use a refresh. But it's well-kept, there are no shady people hanging around, and the vehicles in the lot aren't trashy. All good signs.

The rental agent meets us outside the second-floor unit, and Bear immediately talks her ear off. I narrowly save her from having to hear the news about unlimited pooping time.

"This is way nicer than your old place, Mae," Bear tells me as he runs to the hall bathroom to check out his possible future domain.

He's right. It's way nicer.

"The current tenant is moving out next week, so it will be available in two weeks," the agent informs me.

The furnishings filling the place are not included, unfortunately. My last place was furnished, so I'll have to buy beds and a couch and all sorts of shit. Damn. I hadn't thought about that.

"And you said the utilities are included?" I ask, taking in the galley kitchen—with a *dishwasher*!

"Only water. The rest is your responsibility."

Shit. I bite my lip as I follow in Bear's footsteps to the hall and check out the two bedrooms. They're both decent-sized, and the master has a roomy shower that's calling to me.

"There's a balcony!" Bear exclaims when we return to the main room. He dodges the couch and end table to get to the sliding glass door. "We never had a balcony before!" His blue eyes dance as he hops out the door and grabs the railing with both hands.

I confirm the rent with the agent and mentally review my bank balance.

"And first and last month's rent, of course."

Shit. My old landlord didn't require that. That's two months of rent plus utilities and furnishings—*and* my normal expenses plus possible care for Bear. There's no way I can swing that.

What am I doing? Bear and I could be tucked in all comfy and safe at Jameson's three-bedroom condo right now if I'd only uttered two words. I close my eyes and envision the three of us kicking back on Jameson's couch eating take-out. That would be fun. Nice.

Then I imagine Bear asleep in bed and Jamie and I alone on the couch. My brain automatically takes that thought and flips it upside down, and now I'm on Ginny's couch with Miller cradled between my thighs. My nipples tingle as I recall the sensation of his thumb strumming one like a tight guitar string. Is the A/C even on in this place? Why am I sweating?

I blink and shake myself out of it before turning back to the agent. I shoot her a weak smile and prepare to back slowly out of the room. "Thanks for taking the time to show us around."

"Of course." She nods and gestures to the door, clearly used to impractical daydreamers wasting her time.

Bear is talking to himself on the balcony. "Bear! Come back inside and lock the door behind you."

He does as I ask. "Are you gonna live here?" His expression holds all hope and happiness.

I force cheerfulness into my tone. "This one's not going to work out, but I'll find an awesome place, don't worry."

He trudges to the front door, and I decide to do all further apartment hunting solo.

Desperate for air conditioning and feeling like shit, I take Bear to the dollar theater—which is a total misnomer because it actually costs four dollars. We sit in the back row and watch an animated movie from last year. Well, Bear watches while I continue my apartment hunt on my phone.

There's absolutely nothing with two bedrooms that I can afford. I switch to one-bedroom searches and it's not much better, considering I'm limited to places near public transportation.

By the time we leave the theater, my mood is bleak, and I've concluded that I only have two real options: marry Jameson or go back to performing. Both make my gut swirl with dread, but I force a smile as Bear recounts the entire movie, and we head back out into the evening sun.

I know it's foolish and a waste of money I don't have, but I call an Uber to take us back to Ginny's, unable to face the prospect of keeping ourselves occupied until someone in Miller's family can give us a lift. One of my friends would have picked us up had I called around, but I just want to lay down and leave this afternoon behind.

Bear is still chattering about cartoon dogs when we

pull up to the house, and the driver takes off with a wave. Ginny's car is in the driveway, so I ring the doorbell.

"What're you doing ringing the bell?" She asks as she swings open the bright yellow door. It bears a wood sign with a Sasquatch and the word "Believe" on it, which normally makes me smile, but not tonight. "You're always welcome to just come on in—everybody does."

And for reasons completely unknown to me, something horrifying happens at her generous words and kind expression. Tears form in my eyes like heavy clouds and spill silently onto my cheeks.

Ginny's face swims in my vision, but I hear her say, "You know, Bear, it's a good thing you're here. Mango is in the kitchen and was just begging for sunflower seeds. They're in the cabinet next to the fridge. Do you think you can find them and give him a handful?"

The squeak of sneakers on the wood floor is my brother's only response.

"Now, come on in darlin', and let's have a chat." Ginny pulls gently on my arm, and I follow her without question or protest.

Maybe this is what it's like to have a real mom.

CHAPTER EIGHTEEN

JOY

MAISY

"The summer before ninth grade, Miller's dad got him this old dirt bike on Craigslist. He rode that thing every chance he got—morning, noon, and night that boy was on that thing." Ginny shares with me like the memory is a treasure no one has had a glimpse of before. We're at the scarred kitchen table again, which I'm coming to learn is the central hub of the Brooks household. My hands wrap around a cup of hot tea, and Bear is lost in the world of Super Mario Brothers on an old PlayStation in the den.

Ginny sets her own mug down and resumes her story. "He was always coming home caked in mud and, more often than not, with a new scrape or bruise. But he got really good. So good, he was entering local races within six months. He always placed too, but it was just a cheap circuit for fun—nothing like the ones you see where parents spend thousands on equipment and big crowds with cash prizes."

She eases back from the table, one hand dropping to pet Mango, who's stomping his front feet so hard on the wood floor I can feel my chair vibrate. We've been stationed here for a good half hour, me spilling my guts to Ginny and her handing me tissues while she listens. I told her all about Jameson and the failed plan to wrest custody of Bear from Mom and about my former life as a concert pianist. I shared about the upcoming summer concert as well, and the futile apartment hunt that acted as the proverbial straw to break the camel's back and send me into my pathetic state at her door. Now she's sharing this story about Miller, probably to distract me—and likely because my crush is not so secret, and everyone knows thinking about your crush is far preferable to wallowing over the pitiful state of your life.

"The next summer, when he won probably his third race in a row, a guy from the bigger circuit was there watching. They got to chatting, and he offered Miller a shot at that fancy circuit. Told him all about the money and sponsors and traveling. Got him all hyped up, as you can imagine." She shakes her head while I listen and sip my tea. "But with the bigger circuit came hefty costs with no guarantee to win it back. It was a big deal. And a big risk. Wade and I talked about it and told him if he was serious about it, we'd figure out a way to try and make it happen. His brothers were almost more excited than he was."

"So did he do it?" I can't believe Miller didn't tell me any of this when we were talking about bikes.

"Nope."

"Why not? I mean, you said he was really good, and I know he loves anything with two wheels and an engine."

"That he does. And that's the reason. His brothers

never understood—and never let him forget it. But I knew exactly where he was coming from. He said riding made him happy, that it let his mind go quiet and the adrenaline take over. Nothing but him, the wind, and his bike. Now, doesn't that sound lovely?" She smiles at me, and I return it with my own because the way she describes Miller is an image I can easily picture. "It was something he liked doing that was just for him. He reckoned if he did it for work, it wouldn't be him doing something he loved for the sake of doing it anymore. It would come with expectations, pressure, disappointment—and he didn't want to suck the joy out of it."

"Ah." I'm feeling like a bit of an idiot that it took me this long to catch on.

In case I missed it, she clarifies, "Sounds to me like the joy got sucked out of playing piano for you."

"Yeah, in a way," I concede. "I told myself I quit playing because it was too hard, but playing wasn't what hurt—it was the schedule and the command performances that tore me to shreds. Maybe not playing at all is only punishing myself."

"Where is your piano now?" Her voice is all kindness, a calming alto with a husky undertone.

"At my dad's."

"You miss it." It's not a question.

"I do. My friend Grady has a keyboard he let me use when we were busking together a couple years back. When I left Dad's, I had a thousand dollars and no job, so I paid cash to rent a room and met Grady at a record shop. He was pulling in decent money busking, so I figured why not? We had the best time. He plays guitar and has an amazing voice—perfect pitch."

Ginny's eyebrows spike. "Does he have a blond partner with blue streaks in her hair?"

"Yeah, Kat. How did you know that?" My expression is incredulous.

"Oh, I know everyone, dear." She reaches over and pats my hand like this isn't the most bizarre thing ever. "I told Kat they should play at Blue Bigfoot."

"Seriously? I just recommended Grady and Kat to Miller last night!" Am I in an alternate universe?

"Great minds." Ginny's smile is conspiratorial. "So, you quit busking when you got your current job and started looking after Bear?"

"Sort of," I admit. "Kat and Grady introduced me to Pete and Jade, my current employers. Pete owns Pete's Café, and Jade owns Midnight Print Shop next door."

"Oh, I love that place. I bought Denny a T-shirt from there last Christmas. It had a cute Santa on it and said, 'Big Nick Energy.' He loved it," she shares. Denny must be one very tolerant son. "Go on," she urges. "Tell me about the busking."

"Well, I quit busking because my dad tracked me down."

"This doesn't sound good." She pushes the plate of cookies closer to me, having pulled them out during my initial meltdown and promising they were a panacea. She wasn't really lying.

"It wasn't. Suffice it to say he didn't approve, and he made that clear. Loudly." The memory is excruciating, starting with him calling Grady a drugged-out nobody—which is the furthest thing from the truth on both counts—and ending with him telling anyone who would listen that I was throwing my life away playing stoner music for their uncultured ears.

I don't share all the gritty details, instead sticking with, "So, then I just… quit."

"If you don't mind me saying, it sounds like maybe you let him win in a manner of speaking," Ginny says, grabbing a cookie from the plate and taking a bite.

I pause and give it thought. "Crap."

This gets a chuckle out of Ginny as she reaches for her mug to wash down the cookie. It's white with the words "Of course I talk to myself—sometimes I need expert advice," printed on it. It seems she spends a lot of time at Jade's. "Well, I'm sure you'll figure it out. But don't forget to do what's best for you, darlin'. Things have a way of working themselves out. And, in the meantime, you and Bear are welcome to stay as long as you want."

The working themselves out thing hasn't exactly been my experience, but I don't dispute her. She's been so freaking lovely. "Thank you so much, Mrs. Brooks."

"Ginny," she insists. Her gaze goes to the clock above the table. "Oh, look at the time. You two must be starving. I've got gazpacho in the fridge and all the fixin's for BLTs."

Oh god, I'm taking a page from Terry's book and not feeding my brother! Oh wait, he ate his weight in popcorn at the movies. Sister of the year right here.

She stands and goes to the sink to wash out her mug. "Oh look! Miller's home."

My heart jumps in my chest, and I shoot up from my chair. Shit! I just know I've got a red nose and a puffy face from all that boohooing. I can't let him see me like this! I do almost a full turn before I remember which direction to go, then I bolt for the stairs.

"I'll be outside planting the new flowers I got at the show today. There's still a couple hours of light left, and it was much too hot to plant them earlier…" She trails off as she heads for the back door off the den. She's clearly plotting to leave me alone with Miller—well, and Bear.

This is supremely embarrassing, but there's nothing I can do to change it. So, I scamper up the stairs with every intent to barricade myself in the bathroom until I look like a normal human again. I might be there till morning.

CHAPTER NINETEEN

ALL THE DIFFERENCE

MILLER

"Maisy?" I call as I walk through the front door. I've texted her three times and called twice trying to find her but never got a response. Cash let me have his car to track her down after my shift since Hollis is hanging out till close anyway. I'm starting to worry Maisy tried coming up here with Bear on the back of her scooter and had an accident. But there was no sign of them on the road as far as I could tell, and the scooter's not parked outside.

"Mama?" I try again with the same result—nothing. But the TV is sounding from the den, so I hurry that way to find Bear parked on his behind on the rug, my old PlayStation controller grasped in his hands. The fist clenching my gut immediately loosens its grip. Thank fuck.

"Yo, B. Where's your sister?"

His response consists entirely of a single shoulder shrug, so I do some investigating of my own, starting with Cash's room. When I come up empty, I check the kitchen then poke my head outside to find Mama kneeling in front of a flower bed, neon pink garden gloves covering her hands and pots of colorful blooms surrounding her.

"Hey, Mama, have you seen Maisy?" Maybe she took off to hang with her friends or something. Maybe she went to Jameson's and left Mama to watch Bear. Dammit.

"Hi, sugar. I think she's upstairs. Good day at work?"

"Yeah, thanks." I reverse course and end up outside the hall bathroom upstairs.

"Maisy, you in there?"

"Um, yeah?" It comes out as a question, which has me smiling for the first time in the last hour. Today was a good day otherwise, with no sign of Driscoll. I'm starting to wonder if Maisy was right, and he happened in without knowing my brothers own the place. Maybe it really is over.

When Maisy says nothing else, I realize I should give her privacy and save the questions till she comes out. But I have to ask, "How'd you get home?"

"Uber."

"Uber? Why? That had to cost a mint. I texted you."

There's a pause, followed by, "Can we talk about this, um, later?"

"Oh, yeah, sorry. I'll wait for you to, uh, finish." Now that I've shut my mouth, I realize how awkward it is—me shouting questions at her while she uses the toilet.

"I'm not…" she begins at almost a shout before trailing off. "I'm just washing my face."

Okay, a little less awkward, but I'm still entering creeper territory hovering over the closed bathroom door. Jesus, how did I get here? I don't care what a girl I'm interested in is doing every minute she's not with me. I don't get invested.

"Oh, right. I'll be in my room," I mumble, trying to get my head straight.

But I'm not going back downstairs because she'll just use Bear or Mama to avoid answering my questions. And, for reasons I don't understand in the least, I need a read on her before I can let go of my worry. It's another five minutes before I hear the door open, and sure enough, she tries sneaking by my door to the stairs.

"What the hell am I doing, Dad?" I ask the ceiling. I don't get an answer.

"Hey!" My voice has her halting in place, and I spring off my bed to intercept her. "Why didn't you call me back?"

"I didn't realize you called." She won't look at me, so I step in front of her and bend at the knees until our gazes are even. Her lips are red like she's been worrying them, and her eyes and nose are nearly a matching shade. Shit. She's been crying.

My hands reflexively go to her upper arms. "Baby, what happened?"

Her red-rimmed eyes snap to mine, and my heart turns over in my chest at the same time my inner caveman demands to discover who made her cry so I can put my fist in their face.

"Nothing." She tries to wave me off. "Just a long day. I'm fine."

"Your face doesn't agree." She scowls at my comment, but I ignore it to wrap a hand along the side of her neck and trace the hinge of her jaw with my thumb. "What happened, Maisy?" I don't recognize my own voice.

For a brief moment, she looks like she's about to argue or pull away, but all the tension in her body melts on a sigh instead. "The story is almost as long as my day, and

I'm worried my stomach might eat itself from the inside, and Bear will fuse with the PlayStation if I don't turn the TV off and make BLTs in the next five minutes." Despite the rawness in her features, she's cute as hell.

I smile and stroke her jaw again, wanting to pull her into me, but I know if I do that, I won't let her go again. "I'll be the bad guy and cut Bear off while you make sandwiches. Make sure to use the real mayo, though, and not that light crap. I promise it makes all the difference."

Twenty minutes later, the three of us are chowing down on crunchy BLTs while Bear tries talking us into squeezing another Bigfoot hike in before dark. While the long June days offer plenty of light, it doesn't change the fact that Maisy and I both worked full shifts today, and the last thing Maisy needs right now is Sasquatch hunting. So, when Mama comes in and coaxes Bear outside to help her finish planting flowers, I can see the relief in Maisy's expression.

I finish my sandwich and grab a cookie while Maisy takes tiny bites of hers and avoids eye contact. *Don't fuck this up, Miller.* "Was I right about the mayo?" I ask.

She fights a grin and finally meets my eyes. "You were right about the mayo."

I send her a smug smile, making her roll her eyes just like I intended. As soon as she finishes eating, I take our plates and put them in the sink before grabbing her by the hand and pulling her up the stairs behind me. When I steer us into my room and close the door, she starts to protest, but I lead her to the bed and sit on the edge of it while she stands in front of me. She's got all the power here. She can talk, or she can walk away, but I know which one I want.

"You're fed. Bear is breathing fresh air. Time for that long story."

"Fine," she says, and it sounds like she's under duress, but she sits on the bed next to me anyway. I reposition myself so I'm facing her. "My dad called today and said he's got an offer for me to play at Valley." I try my best not to let my expression give me away, but I obviously fail because she says, "I know," before exhaling loudly. "And I went apartment shopping only to be reminded that I'm practically destitute and will never be able to afford what I need to eventually get custody of Bear if things stay the way they are."

I want to tell her not to worry, but the words would be empty. So, instead, I reach for her hand again and squeeze it, saying, "That's a lot for one day."

She inhales through her nose and closes her eyes. "I either have to go back to performing or marry Jameson."

"The fuck you do." The words are out of my mouth before I can stop them.

"Miller—" she begins, but I cut her off. Performing literally makes her sick, and she's spent three years putting that life behind her. And the Jameson thing? Nope.

"You can stay here as long as you want and save up to get a place—besides, CPS has got to care more about a loving home than a fancy one, right?"

"It doesn't work like that. And we can't stay here, Miller. You and your family have been super generous already, it's too much. And, besides, I can't keep bumming rides or blowing my paycheck on Ubers. I need to get a place in town."

Before I can think, I blurt, "I can get a car instead of the Triumph." But once it's out, I know I'd do just that if it made her life easier.

She turns to face me, tears welling in her eyes again. "I think you're the sweetest guy I've ever met, Miller Brooks."

Nobody in my life has ever called me sweet—well, besides Mama—because I'm *not* sweet. I've never been sweet. I've been a lot of things—impulsive, careless, arrogant, stubborn—but never sweet.

"You're getting your bike, and I'm taking care of Bear." She brings a hand to my cheek, and I put mine over hers. "But it means the world to me that you want to help."

"I'm *going* to help." It's a promise.

"What are you going to do? Break into the CPS offices and file a fake order of custody?"

I tilt my head and bring her hand down to my lap to hold it. "You know, that might work."

She shakes her head and smiles, tears gone. "I don't know that I could have your incarceration on my conscience, but it's the thought that counts."

"Sunny and I went on the dark web a couple months ago to threaten someone," I offer. Her chin jerks back before I realize how that sounded. "Oh, it was this corrupt guy working for an even more corrupt politician, don't worry."

"I'm not sure how to respond to that."

"It doesn't matter. I'm just saying I know how to play dirty, and I ain't afraid to do it if it means saving you or Bear."

"Nobody's ever offered to break the law for me, you know." She laughs this time.

"Consider me your knight in tainted armor." It does have me thinking about possible ways to help out. Maisy doesn't necessarily need to know what I'm doing if it helps her in the end.

"My own personal gray hat hero." Her eyes sparkle with amusement, and her beauty is almost blinding at this proximity.

The word "mine" echoes in my brain, and I don't know who moves first, but our lips crash together. I have her on her back on my bed in seconds. It's like we're picking up right where we left off last night, but we're behind closed doors this time. Fuck. I should lock the door. The number of times I walked in on Cash and Hollis making out means the universe has at least two more interruptions in store for me. But Maisy feels too good in my arms to tear myself away for something as trivial as a lock.

She moans into my mouth, so I slide my hand down her side then to the back of her thigh to pull her leg up so I can settle my suddenly aching cock between her legs. Her hand fists my tee at the back when I press against her while the fingers of her other hand spear through my hair and grab on tight.

Fuck, yes.

I grind into her again, and her hips lift to meet me, making me groan and stroke the bare skin of her thigh before traveling down until I can grab her ass in those tiny shorts. If I thought she had any doubts about what's going down, they're dispelled when she reaches for the hem of my tee and starts yanking it up. I'm not about to argue, so I help her pull it off, immediately bringing my mouth back to hers as soon as it's over my head.

Her taste is heady when combined with the sweet floral scent of her skin, and I'm soon letting my lips and tongue trail down her throat and settle along her collarbone where I take my time while she lets her fingertips skate across my bare back and shoulders.

She mewls my name, and I need to hear that sound a

hundred more times before I sleep tonight. My hands go to her waist, and I pull her shirt up until it settles above her tits. Then I rise to my elbows to get the full view. Rich caramel skin that pales as it approaches her black lace bra. Pert nipples visible through the lace as her breasts swell against the fabric with her quickened breaths.

I push the lace aside to reveal one creamy breast with a perfect brown nipple inviting me to feast on it. When I take it in my mouth, I'm rewarded with that sexy as fuck mewl again, so I swirl my tongue and suck before giving it the lightest of bites. Maisy's back arches right off the bed, making it impossible not to grind into her again.

"You're fantastic," I murmur over her nipple before switching to the other breast and pulling down the lace to give it the same attention.

"Oh, god." She fists a hand in my hair, and it has my dick going impossibly harder.

I need her to come, and I need it now. I need to see her face and hear her voice when she lets go. To that end, I sweep a hand over her belly and down to the waistband of her shorts. One twist of my fingers and the button comes undone, allowing my hand access.

"Is this okay?" I ask, and she nods her head so vigorously I'm afraid she might knock something loose. Lynn has been drilling it into my head that consent is everything, but I'm still shocked I had the headspace to remember to ask. I'm used to letting a girl's body do all the speaking, figuring she'll let me know if she wants to slow down. I like to think I've always been attuned, but the connection I have right now with Maisy tells me I was kidding myself before.

My fingers dip beneath the band of her panties and find heaven. A small patch of pubic hair lies above the promised land, and when my fingers find her, she's slick and hot. I swirl her clit with my middle finger and don't even get to her pussy before she's panting out her orgasm and coming on my hand. I pull up on an elbow to watch her—eyes squeezed shut, head thrown back, throat exposed, and lips parted on a silent cry. It's the hottest fucking thing I've ever seen. And the most beautiful.

If this is what being with Maisy is like, I'm putting everything I've got into making her mine for good.

CHAPTER TWENTY
INTENTIONS

MAISY

The entire percussion section is in my chest, and I'm unsure I'll ever fully catch my breath again. Miller's body lies warm and heavy on top of mine, and I want to wrap my arms around his torso and hold him to me until morning. But my limbs are jelly, and my chest is heaving too hard.

His lips meet mine, and we breathe each other's air for a silent minute before he slides his hand out of my shorts and nuzzles my neck.

"That was incredibly hot."

My lips start to curve at his comment when reality storms in like a flash flood to take over everything. My shoulders lock.

"Oh my god. Your mom and Bear are downstairs!"

"I'm pretty sure they're still outside." His lips don't stop brushing my skin, and my body erupts in goose bumps despite my mind screaming to leap out of bed.

"Get off!" I practically yell before slapping a hand over my own mouth when I realize how loud I'm being.

Miller chuckles into my neck. "She's got five grown kids. I promise it's no big deal."

"It's a big deal to me!" I whisper-hiss before shoving him in the chest and scrambling to right my bra. Ginny is going to take one look at us and know exactly what we were up to. I might luck out with Bear assuming we spontaneously decided to run a half marathon, but not Ginny.

When I finally get Miller off me, I rush to the bathroom mirror, my shirt grasped in one hand. It's worse than I thought. Not only does my face still carry the remnants of my crying jag earlier, but now it's overlayed with a glow that announced loud and clear I just had a fabulous, mind-bending orgasm. Crap, crap, crap!

Miller steps in behind me, casually pulling his T-shirt back over his head and grinning like the cat who got the canary. Darn it. I was so distracted by my orgasm, I forgot to inspect his tattoos! "I wasn't done with you, you know," he says to my reflection.

And while ninety percent of me really *really* wants to know what else he had planned—and all the ways I can reciprocate—the rational ten knows I need to get away from him and remind myself that I have nine hundred things on my plate, and the last thing I need is to get distracted by orgasms. Orgasms won't help Bear or get me an apartment. And Jamie may be my friend, but if we're married, there's no way he'll be okay with me having a boyfriend on the side!

Miller snakes his arms around my middle, and I sag back into him for a split second before forcing myself to straighten. "You can't touch me, or I'll forget what I'm supposed to be doing."

"You're supposed to be back in my room if my opinion matters." He kisses my shoulder, and there go the goose bumps again. I wonder how that tongue ring would feel if he went down on me. *No! Down, girl!*

"Miller." I lock eyes with him in the mirror. His are warm pools of liquid caramel, and his handsome features and mussed hair make me want to do whatever he suggests. "This is… a lot to take in. I didn't intend…" my voice trails off. I don't want him to think I regret it or didn't like it. I just need to be smart.

"Well, I very much intended…" he mimics my cadence and grins. But he must sense my panic because he releases me and steps aside to allow my escape to the hall.

I straighten my clothes and ponytail before jogging down the stairs in search of Bear. To my utter relief, he's still outside with Ginny. Their voices carry through the window as Ginny instructs him on where to dump his trowels full of soil. He'll definitely need a shower before bed.

Miller comes down a few minutes later, and I'm relieved when he drops onto the sofa and turns the TV on. I get over myself enough to settle on the couch next to him where I scroll apartment listings on my phone until Bear and Ginny come inside twenty minutes later.

"Shower and then bedtime," I tell him before following him up the stairs to get him settled in the bathroom. I'm yawning on the bed by the time he comes out, his wet hair sticking up in all directions and his boxers and T-shirt donned for sleep.

I'm reminded I need to do laundry, so I tuck him in and descend the stairs once more in search of Ginny, only to find that she's disappeared into her first-floor bedroom, leaving me alone with her hot progeny again. Oh, she's *good.*

When Miller sees my armful of dirty clothes, he correctly guesses my mission. "Laundry is in the garage. Follow me."

"So, is transportation the only barrier to staying here?" he asks as we cross the lawn to the detached garage. The heat has let up, and the stars are coming out as darkness settles.

"Well, I guess that depends." We enter the garage through a side door, and Miller pulls open the main one to create a cross breeze. The space is full of tools, boxes, bins, and machines I can't even begin to guess the purpose of. I head to the washer and toss our clothes in while Miller hands me the detergent.

"Jameson," he guesses correctly. "You said you're not into him, but you never said he's not into you."

Nothing gets by him. "That, and it's too much. I'm a stranger." Bear will be with Mom and Terry a lot, as usual, but even one extra person in the house will get old fast.

"Only if you choose to be," Miller responds, pretty much throwing down.

"You've known me for like two days."

He steps closer, and I take a step back, essentially blocking myself in between him and the washer. "So?"

"So?" I whisper back, my head getting light and my pussy remembering how much we like him.

He must be able to read my thoughts, his grin is so naughty. "Yeah, so?"

I want to say yes. I want to throw my arms around him, rip his shirt off, and trace his tattoos with my tongue.

But I can't. "I… can't." I barely get the word out.

Miller holds my eyes for long seconds, and I swear I

hear his heart beating. Then he steps back. But his expression doesn't close down as I expected. Instead, he switches to a casual grin and tone. "Okay."

"I don't regret what we did," I race to reassure him, my hands gripping the detergent bottle. "I just want to make sure we're on the same page." I hope I don't have to say more.

"And what page is that?"

Looks like I don't get my wish. "Well, this…" I let go with one hand, wagging a finger back and forth between us. "can't be a distraction from my end goal, whatever I decide about the concert or Jameson."

"But I like distracting you." He's being cheeky again.

"Yeah, that's clear. And I like being distracted." Way too much, in fact. "But I can't be."

He studies me for a few moments, his expression indiscernible. "Of course. I only do casual anyway; everybody knows that."

For some stupid reason, his words hurt. But they should make me happy, so I have no idea what tricks my mind is playing. I nod my head and reply, "Great." Then I start the washer.

CHAPTER TWENTY-ONE

SOCK IT TO ME

MILLER

Fuck.

I promised myself I would do whatever was best for Maisy, but I didn't know it would make me feel like this. There she was, looking all tousled and perfect, asking me not to pursue a relationship, and every cell in my body was ready to shout, "I want you to be mine!" But, instead, I told her what she wanted to hear—what anyone who knows me would assume is the truth. Miller Brooks isn't a serious person—not about women, work, or life.

Now I'm laying on my back in bed feeling anything but tired. I only have a short afternoon shift tomorrow, and I'd originally planned on picking up my new bike until the idea of a car to help Maisy's situation sounded smarter. But she'll be moving on soon, she's made that clear, so I'd be stupid not to go through with my plans.

Yeah, I'll pick up the bike, go to work, and then I'll still keep my promise to build the Bigfoot trap with Bear. I'll hang with Maisy and her brother—help them out any way

I can—until she gets her feet under her, probably by getting married. I won't delude myself into thinking she'll suddenly realize she wants me in the same way I want her.

However, none of this solves the immediate problem at hand: the giant boner in my boxers. And nothing says I can't use my imagination to have more of Maisy, so I take my cock in hand and start to stroke myself, imagining Maisy's pouty pink lips around me, her eyes looking up at me while she sucks me deep.

Years of practice has taught me how to be quiet, so I'm determined to take my time and live out this fantasy, making it last as long as I can. Behind my closed eyelids, Maisy adds a hand to the stroke of her lips and tongue, pumping at the base of my cock and making me tighten my jaw against the urge to groan loud and long.

I imagine her moaning as she creates a rhythm she likes, alternating suction with the laving of her tongue over the head of my cock. It's exquisite torture the longer it goes on. Finally, she squeezes the base, and I begin to tremble, knowing I don't have long. I should ease up, but I can't. The image of Maisy, her pretty pink tongue licking me and her full lips pulling me deep while her hair falls on my thighs has me stroking myself faster until I lose control.

I come all over my hand and stomach, my entire body jerking and every muscle stringing tight as my orgasm continues. Finally, I gasp in a breath, my shoulders falling back onto the bed, and a chill sweeping over my entire body as the cool air from the window unit hits the sheen of sweat that's risen to the surface of my skin.

And I lie there, sated, intermittently trembling from the after-effects, and wishing with everything in me that

Maisy was right beside me instead of across the hall or in my imagination.

"WHAT EXACTLY ARE WE LOOKING FOR?" Maisy's voice is a whisper as she crouches next to me a few yards away from the campfire. We're not *technically* supposed to camp here, but it's practically my own backyard, and it never stopped my dad from pitching a tent and piling us in when I was a kid.

There's an age spread among the Brooks kids that meant we rarely did activities as an entire family, but camping was one thing I remember doing together. Mama and Dad had Carter when she was barely nineteen and he was twenty-two. Cash came along three years later, and Denny three years after that. They figured they were done after him, but almost seven years later, I showed up, with Lynnie bringing up the rear a couple years after.

My older brothers did stuff with my dad that I was too young for, like brewing beer in the detached garage or trying their hands at bow hunting. At the time, I resented having to hang back with Mama and Lynn, but Dad paid attention, and he made sure to carve out time to do stuff with me—sometimes just the two of us biking on trails or playing basketball. Later, when my brothers were either working or had moved out, our shared love of horror movies was a surefire way to get some guy time alone. They scare the piss out of Mama and Lynn.

Maisy, I'm guessing, is not a fan of horror flicks either if her jumpy disposition since the sun went down is any indication.

"Something to make footprints with," I whisper back,

scanning the edge of the tiny clearing in the woods with my flashlight. We've already sprung the rudimentary Sasquatch trap, so now it's time for evidence.

Bear is passed out in the tent with a belly full of s'mores. Yeah, Maisy relented on the Sunday-night camping kibosh provided he abide by a ten o'clock bedtime—which he did. It probably didn't hurt that we tired him out with more hiking as well as hauling camping gear onto the trail. Now it's eleven, and I want to lay down some Bigfoot tracks for Bear to find in the morning before we have to take off.

I didn't end up getting my bike. Instead, I dropped Maisy and Bear at work and caught up with Dax before heading to work myself. Dax was acting strange and looking worse for wear again, but he insisted he was just tired. We smoked a joint and shot the shit, but I got nowhere on the job front before I left. If I thought he'd be reliable, I'd try getting him a job at Blue Bigfoot, but no way would Cash go for that. I'm not giving up, though.

My flashlight beam lands on a broken branch a couple inches in diameter, and I pull it free from the brush. "This'll do the trick."

Maisy laughs into her palm to muffle the sound when I start measuring out how far apart to make the prints. She clearly would be a disaster with this task if left on her own. You can't just randomly drop footprints and expect it to be convincing. It takes planning.

By the time I'm done, she's perched on a rock near the campfire, knees drawn up to her chest and nibbling on a graham cracker. She raises a brow at me. "You know you're only making it so he's going to beg you to camp with him all summer long, right?"

I shrug and drop down onto the dirt to sit next to her rock.

She turns to me, and I try to ignore the way the fire makes her skin glow. "Can I ask you a question?"

"Sock it to me, Gladys," I reply.

She shoves my shoulder. "Okie dokie, Morty."

"Morty? That's your best old man's name?" I mock her.

"Morty is totally an old man name. You got a better one?"

"I know lots of old men—Sunny's grandpa is Duke. Now that's a great name. Our neighbor is Winston. Classic. There's a guy at the senior center named Dudley and another one named Fuzzy. Those are all better than Morty."

"And they're all obviously taken, so Morty it is," she counters, crossing her long legs.

I shake my head slowly like I can't believe my disappointment, and she shoves my shoulder again.

"Anyway, what I was going to ask is why you don't tell your family about what you did with that doctor? I think they'd be proud of you."

My humor settles at the topic. "I'm not so sure."

"You should hear the way Ginny and Lynn talk about you. They adore you."

I'm about to say that comes with being a family member, but I stop myself since it's the opposite of Maisy's experience with family love. So, instead, I go with the honest truth. "I may have fucked up, and when I say that, I mean I may have put my family in danger. And that's not something I'm anxious to mention at the dinner table."

"What do you mean? Did he show up at the brewery again?"

I settle my elbows on my knees and drop my hands between my thighs while I watch the flames. "No."

"Then why? I think him showing up on Friday was random—you said yourself he left right after he caught sight of you."

"Could be, but I haven't told you everything. I'm thinking he knows it was someone in our family who set him up."

"Why? What haven't you told me?"

I turn and give it all to her, and I have no idea why. She doesn't want to be mine. But I can't help it. "A couple months after Driscoll got out, he started following me."

Her jaw drops, and the heels of her Converse hit the dirt below. "What?! Why didn't you tell me that last time?"

"Maisy, you have enough to worry about. You said so yourself." I'm not trying to make a dig; I'm just telling it straight like she did to me.

"I changed my mind." I know she's not talking about being together when she narrows her eyes at me. "Spill it."

I throw my hands up in surrender and do just that. "I noticed him following me and didn't recognize him at first. He'd gained weight and grew a beard, but I eventually figured out who he was. Then in a situation I'm thinking is not a coincidence, I got into a car crash while driving Carter's ride. And let's just say the car's brakes were working fine the day before, not so much when I had the brake pedal pressed to the floor at a red light but still sailed through the intersection and crashed into a fence."

CHAPTER TWENTY-TWO

PANTS ON FIRE

MAISY

"Oh my god! You could have been killed."

"I'm still here, aren't I? I just broke my arm and got banged up. Nobody else got hurt, but I'll say Carter wasn't pleased his car was totaled."

"Do the cops know? That has to be a parole violation, right?" Miller looks at me like I'm either crazy or stupid, so I amend my question, "I mean the following you part—obviously cutting someone's brake line wouldn't make a parole officer happy."

"It's tricky. If I told the cops, they'd want to know the whole story—including why I'd think he had a reason to target me or my family. It's really no more than a suspicion."

"What does your family have to say about all of this?"

"They don't know."

"Any of it?" When he shakes his head, I continue, "That's nuts. You need to tell them." His family is awesome, and they'd be pissed he's keeping this from them. They also wouldn't let Driscoll get away with it; that much I know already about the Brooks family.

"I'm already the family fuck-up. They don't need to know I fucked up again and put them in danger. And, despite what you think, they won't be happy hearing that my drug dealer best friend and I framed a guy and played with fire doing illegal shit to get him locked up. And I'm okay with that because I know my dad would think it was fucking righteous, so that's all that matters. Well, that, and making sure no other family has to go through what we did."

"You're not a fuck-up, Miller."

"That's nice of you to say, but as you've pointed out, you don't actually know me." God, he's so oblivious.

"I know enough. I know you love your family and would do anything for them. I know you're funny and kind and compassionate. And I know your mom and sister think the world of you, even if you don't think it of yourself." He's got to know all of this already if he's been paying any attention at all.

"This from the girl who's deciding between torture and marriage just to protect her brother."

I shrug. "Yeah, but I haven't gotten anyone arrested. Yet. Although I'm thinking Terry is the prime candidate if I get the urge."

"He do bad shit to Bear?" he asks in a whisper, like he's afraid of my answer.

"He yells and drinks, but apart from that he doesn't really *do* anything. That's the problem. But Bear isn't his child either. My mom is the one who needs to step up and get her act together."

She sent me another dozen texts today, pissed that I never brought Bear home. But I wasn't letting him miss the splash park with Jordan or the Bigfoot camping, so I somehow talked her into letting me keep him until after school tomorrow.

"You ever contact CPS about neglect?"

I groan. "There's a history there. He was in the system for six months a little over a year ago. Mom bitched and moaned that the social workers made shit up, but it's hard to convince anyone of that when your kid goes wandering to a neighbor for dinner because his mom and her boyfriend left him alone for the last twenty-four hours. That wasn't the first visit they got from CPS, but it was the final straw. Mom jumped through the hoops to get him back, but that's when she decided to take him to Puerto Rico. Terry's got some family there, and I swear the two of them think CPS doesn't exist outside the continental US."

"Which is worse, moving away or foster care?"

"Both. I know there are great foster families out there, but Bear didn't get one. He's terrified of going back, and I promised him I wouldn't let it happen." He got beaten up and bullied by another kid in the house, and the foster parents did nothing about it. He was scared of his own shadow by the time he came home.

"You know, I thought she'd actually be a better mom after he was taken away," I continue, "but she was up to the same old shit within weeks of getting him back." Leaving him alone overnight, sending him to school in dirty clothes when she remembered to send him at all, driving drunk with him in the car… the list goes on. "I take him whenever I can because then at least I know he's safe, getting regular meals, doing his homework, and getting to bed at a decent hour. I swear Mom and Terry are willfully oblivious."

"So now you need to keep your mom from moving until you can get custody."

"And I establish a good home situation for him. All I know is I'm not breaking my promise, and I'm keeping Bear safe."

"With how little attention they seem to pay him, I don't get why she won't just let you keep him." Miller looks at me with the same baffled expression I probably wear every time I'm around Mom.

"Because that would make me better than her, and she already says I think too highly of myself." You'd think I spat in her face instead of winning piano competitions.

"Sounds like it's justified if you ask me. You *are* better than her. Maybe you really do need to think about playing dirty to get what you want."

"I'm not sure I know how."

"Then it's a good thing you met me." He winks, returning to his playful—and sexy—self. I want to be friends with him. I really do. And I hope I don't mess it all up and drive him away, even if it might be the best thing for him.

I have to laugh, though, careful to keep it quiet for Bear's sake. "That's nice of you, but I think you've got enough to worry about. An ex-con stalker cutting the brake line on your car is a little more pressing than a custody situation."

"I'll figure it out." He shrugs, humor still lining his features.

"How can you be so casual about it?" I'd be flipping the fuck out if someone stalked me, or I thought they messed with my brakes.

"Because when I got hauled in for resisting arrest this last time, I was doing it while trespassing on Driscoll's property. I must have spooked him because, until Friday, I hadn't seen him since. And no bad shit has happened."

"Oh. Well, that sounds promising." Maybe it *will* be okay.

"I still don't like what him showing at the bar could mean, though. You don't walk into the business of a family you rendered fatherless. Ever. I don't care if it's to deliver a billion-dollar sweepstakes check. Anyone would know you don't do that shit."

"From what you've told me, it doesn't sound like this guy has the healthiest respect for boundaries—evidenced by him maybe trying to maim-slash-kill you or Carter." I can't believe I'm joking about this.

"You have a point." When he smiles again, I can't help my eye roll. I'm freaking out about playing the piano and fighting with my mom while he laughs off attempted murder and stalking.

"Miller, you—"

He cuts me off, his shoulders straightening. "What is that?"

"Haha. I'm not as big a sucker as you think I am, Miller Brooks." I refuse to look behind me where his eyes are directed at what I'm sure he's pretending is Bigfoot.

"I'm serious, Maisy. Is that… fire?"

I whip my head around as we both stand. And, sure enough, there's an orange glow in the distance, almost hidden among the leafy trees and evergreens.

"It's probably another camper?" I try, but Miller is moving now, so I follow.

When we stop, we have a much better view, and that is no campfire. It's a *fire* fire.

"Bear!" I race back to the tent and throw it open. "Bear, wake up! We have to go!"

His groggy voice mutters, "Did we catch Bigfoot?"

"No, buddy, we have to get going. There's a fire a little ways away, and it's not safe." I'm trying to keep the panic out of my voice, but I need him to move!

"Hey." Miller is at my side again. "Forget the camping stuff. Just grab your backpacks and let's go." His phone is to his ear, and I assume he's calling 9-1-1, but I'm proven wrong at his next words. "Mama! Look out the back window. There's a fire!"

He's silent for the next few moments, clearly listening to Ginny, and I realize the fire must be near their house. Given that we only hiked twenty minutes to get here, it shouldn't surprise me; I'd just lost my sense of direction. When I notice the fire looks brighter than before, I'm not sure if it's because it's grown or because Miller has doused our own campfire, and we've been left in darkness with only the light of his flashlight.

"Be there as soon as we can," another pause, "and we'll be careful." He hangs up and motions to Bear and me before grabbing his own backpack. "Come on. This way. I know these trails like the back of my hand."

He leads us by flashlight in the opposite direction from where we came, but I don't question him, instead focusing all my energy on keeping Bear calm.

Miller clearly reads my mind when he says, "The fire department is on the way, and they'll take care of it. I'm just taking us this way so we can avoid any smoke. Have you ever seen a fire truck up close, Bear?"

God, he's such a good guy. I want to ask how close to the house the fire is, but I need to let him decide how much he wants to share in front of Bear.

"I seen them on the street and when we drive by the stations, but I never been in one or anything."

"Well, tonight might be the night." Miller holds back a branch to let us through before it snaps back into place. "I'm also guessing you might be able to talk your sister into letting you sleep in tomorrow seeing as this hike is gonna take us till almost midnight."

"Midnight is technically tomorrow. Cool. It's like New Year's night—and nobody goes to school the day after that."

We continue following Miller along the rough trail, descending a steep rocky section where we each take one of Bear's hands to guide him. Relief sweeps through me when I hear sirens in the distance—it's a sound I've heard a million times and rarely paid any mind to, yet it's as hopeful as Beethoven's "Sonata No. 9" to my ears now.

"You hear that?" Miller asks over his shoulder.

"Fire trucks!" Bear exclaims, running ahead of us on the trail while Miller lights his way.

"Be careful!" I keep looking behind us, but the fire faded from sight five minutes after we left the campsite, and we haven't seen any trace of it since. I have no idea what direction we're headed, but I trust Miller to guide us.

By the time we make our way up another rocky section, I see lights ahead but don't know their source. "What's that?"

"It's the houses down the road from us. We'll cut through to the road and walk up the rest of the way."

I'm winded from all the hiking, which doesn't say a lot for my state of fitness. I need to start running or something before my lungs and muscles decide to shrivel up.

"I'm tired." Bear tugs on my arm as we emerge from the woods and onto the paved road that leads to Ginny's house. Miller was right; it's going on midnight, and this night is far from over, I'm guessing.

"Climb on," Miller instructs my brother, bending at the knees so Bear can reach his shoulders. Bear grabs on like a chimpanzee, and Miller stands, adjusting Bear's position on his back and forging ahead up the road.

I'm starting to doubt my resolve when it comes to Miller. I mean, I don't *have* to marry Jameson. But Miller said so himself he's not the kind of guy who does more than casual. I called it pretty much the moment I met him, so it shouldn't come as a surprise. But what if? I mean, really, how could a guy who does all this for a kid and a girl he doesn't know be anything but a positive addition to my life?

CHAPTER TWENTY-THREE

THE USUAL SUSPECTS

MILLER

We walk another fifteen minutes, watching plumes of smoke swell above the trees, and when we eventually round the last bend, it's to find a crowd of people gathered in the street behind a row of fire trucks. I've been doing my best to remain calm for Maisy and Bear's sake, but the sight of the people I love huddled together safe and sound has a lot of the tension in my body releasing.

"Mama!" I shout. She turns to us and jogs our way with the speed of a teenager.

"Oh, thank God you're all okay." She pulls me into a hug, drawing Bear with me out of necessity before moving on next to embrace Maisy.

"Is the fire out? Do they know what happened?" I ask, lowering Bear to the ground.

"I don't know anything yet." She attempts to tuck her brown curls behind her ears but they immediately bounce back in place. "They just managed to get it all out, so that's been our only focus. I was worried it would reach the house, so we shut off the gas and have every sprinkler on the street running."

My gaze takes in the Carmichael house to the left and Winston's house to the right. All look intact apart from the usual blemishes that Adrina likes to say give a house character. Of course, this is the same woman who has hosted raccoons in her house and likes to decorate with small taxidermied animals dressed and posed like humans.

We join the main group, Maisy taking Bear's hand to get a closer look at the firetrucks. The crowd consists of Mama, Lynn, Denny, Rosie, Adrina, Wes, Ari, her boyfriend, Jax, who must have gotten to town sometime today, and Winston. I'm encouraged to see Winston in a bathrobe as opposed to just his skivvies that he ordinarily walks about in. We've always figured that since the woods come right up to his house in the back, he assumes the trees give him more privacy than they actually do.

One of the firefighters approaches, and we all gather in. "Well, the good news is we got it under control before it got too out of hand. The bad news is we found accelerant. Which means you all need to stay here while we wait for the police and fire investigator to arrive."

There's a collective gasp at his announcement, and I'm almost surprised that all gazes don't gravitate my way. This is exactly the kind of nightmare I might have caused as a kid—breaking the rules and watching while shit went way out of control. But I ain't a kid anymore. The last time I played with fire, sure, I lit a dish towel up like a roman candle, but I was never *this* stupid.

Shit. A thought occurs to me, but it's too crazy to give

serious consideration. What if… no. Driscoll wouldn't take that big of a risk. Would he?

"Who would start a fire on purpose? Nobody comes up here!" Adrina exclaims, turning first to the firefighter and then Mama. "First your house gets broken into and now this? What's happening to the world these days?"

I hadn't even thought about the break-in. It happened a couple months ago and was the work of the same corrupt DC politicians Carter exposed. There's no definitive proof, but all the pieces fit, especially since nothing was taken; the place was just trashed because they were looking for something—and they were pissed on top of that. Carter really knows how to fuck with people. No wonder we're related.

But the fire is surely just a coincidence. Right? I glance over at Denny to find his eyes on me, hands propped on his hips like he's bracing. Crap. He's wondering the same thing.

"Has anyone called Cart?" I quickly add, "Or Cash?" to avert any suspicion of my thoughts.

"Denny did. They're on their way," Lynn answers, hugging herself with her arms across her chest like she's cold—despite the warm temperature.

The DC mess has mostly been dealt with. I mean, I guess there's former Senator Cody who's still hiding out in Iceland avoiding extradition. But he's got bigger problems to deal with than his former colleague's mom's house, surely. It's stupid when I think about it. I mean, with the break-in, they were looking for something, and Cart was living here at the time. A fire has no purpose, especially not now.

Unless Driscoll was either sending a message or hoping the fire would take the house. But I still don't know if he actually messed with the brakes or not, and aside from his brief appearance at the brewery, I haven't seen him in weeks.

The fire was probably just some high school kids causing trouble and running away when it grew out of control. Shit like that happens all the time, right?

"I got no enemies, so it can't be about me," Winston huffs in a deep, scratchy voice. It's maybe the third time in my life I've ever heard the man speak. He keeps himself to himself—always.

Adrina and Ari scowl at his insinuation, but Mama keeps the peace. "I'm sure it will all come clear in the end. It's got to be an accident."

The firefighter makes no more comment but stays close, telling me he's listening to everyone and filing anything interesting away. It's only five more minutes before the cop cars arrive.

Excellent. Just what I need. More face time with Asheville's finest. I already need to meet with my court-appointed lawyer this week to get my community service going. I hope like hell it's not picking up trash on the highway like last time. People throw some gnarly shit out car windows. Let's just say I haven't so much as sipped a bottle of Gatorade since then.

Carter and Sunny pull up at the same time, and after he checks on Mama, I pull Cart aside. Denny sidles up as well.

"Hey, do you think—"

I get nothing more out before Carter shakes his big head and cuts me off with, "Way ahead of you," followed by a chin lift to each of us and a quick, "Later."

"Who are the homeowners?" The first cop, an older

guy with gray hair and a comically large handlebar mustache, asks.

Wes, Mama, and Winston raise their hands. Adrina keeps hers down, probably because she's likely to snap at Winston and doesn't want to risk drawing attention to herself from the cops.

"We'll need to talk to everyone who was present at the time the fire was first observed," he says before he and a couple other uniformed officers listen and take notes as we all recount what we saw. When Carter stays silent, I take the cue and don't make any mention of his DC friends. I also stay quiet about Driscoll. Shit! I need to tell my family if there's any chance of him being involved.

Ari and Maisy take Bear into the Carmichael's house to try getting him to sleep while the rest of us hang around answering more questions and watching the firefighters clean up. Denny goes to chat with a few he knows from his work on the Water Rescue Team, but they can't offer any more information than the first guy.

By the time it's all done, the entire Brooks and Carmichael clans—including Cash, Hollis, and Luca—have gathered in the Carmichael house, and it's going on three o'clock in the morning. The mood is somber at best.

The fire got so close to our house, Mama doesn't feel safe having us stay there tonight. Despite the woods coming up to Winston's back door, however, he seemed to have no such fears and disappeared into his house a couple hours ago. Since Adrina and Wes's house is set farther from the forest, it's deemed the safest to hunker down.

In true Adrina fashion, she whips up a middle-of-the-night panini platter, and we all devour it within minutes. Bear sleeps through the entire thing, and Adrina insists

Maisy spend the night so as not to wake him to move. She bids us all goodnight and heads to Luca's old room where Bear is passed out. Lynn takes off to stay with Denny and Rosie while Mama takes Rosie's old room, and I grab the couch. Everyone else heads to their respective homes just before the sun starts peeking over the horizon.

CHAPTER TWENTY-FOUR

UNEXPECTED COMPANY

MILLER

Bear gets part of his wish when both he and Maisy sleep in until ten, but when Ari offers her car up to Maisy, he realizes he's not going to get away with missing the entire school day. I probably would have let him skip, but I ain't the one going for custody of the kid.

Despite staying up most of the night, half the household was up at their normal time for a Monday, meaning I was too since I was crashing on the couch. I might have transferred to an empty bed to get more shut-eye, but the sight of a taxidermied opossum tipping his top hat looming over my head the second I opened my eyes scared the ever-loving shit out of me and ensured I wouldn't be going back to sleep—maybe not even later tonight. So, I used the time to go retrieve our camping gear and tuck it away in the garage. Mama and Adrina took their coffees out to the swath of ash and black tree stumps that used to be part of our forested backyard.

Cart messaged asking all us brothers to come to Blue

Bigfoot at eleven to chat on the down-low—which means all three of my brothers are going to catch every kind of shit imaginable if their girlfriends ever hear about this. Let's just say none of them appreciates being left out of the loop.

I need to decide whether it's time to do some sharing with my brothers about Driscoll or not. That said, they'll undoubtedly put the women to shame with the amount of shit they'll aim my way once they find out the whole story. It'll be a gametime call.

Since Maisy and I are both headed into town, it's the three of us riding together once again, Bear grumbling in the backseat about school being "jacked" and how he's gonna use the summer to "get swole" like my brothers and me to "up his rizz." I doubt Amanda-the-hot-tutor would be impressed by his vocabulary, but I sure as hell am enjoying it.

Maisy turns to me, voice suddenly infused with excitement. "When are you picking up your bike?" She's obviously trying to distract me.

"Not sure yet," I answer. I'm off today, so there's no real reason not to, but this meet-up with my brothers could change my plans. My nerves are telling me to keep my options open.

Maisy has the day off as well, something I'd hoped to use to my advantage, but that's not in the cards. I'm dropping her at the café to get her scooter and have no clue what she's up to today. It's not a question a casual hookup asks. It wouldn't suck, though, to go pick her up later with my new bike and take her for a ride. Yeah, that wouldn't suck at all.

"You definitely should."

I only shrug and slide my tongue post along the roof of my mouth.

Bear forgets his grumpy mood and leans forward. "You getting a mountain bike?"

"No, I'm getting a motorcycle."

"Tight. Can I ride it?"

"You can ride on the *back* of it—if your sister says it's okay, that is." It's hard saying no to this kid.

"We'll see." Maisy tries to keep her tone stern but does a shit job of it.

"That means yes," Bear crows and pats her on the shoulder. "Don't worry, Mae, I'll wear my helmet."

Maisy rolls her eyes, and we pull up to the school where I wait while she walks Bear in. Fifteen minutes later, I'm turning into the parking lot behind Blue Bigfoot just as Denny and Cash pull in, both of them riding in Cash's piece-of-shit ride. For a business owner, he sure doesn't care much about his image.

"Whose car is that?" Cash asks as he unfolds from the driver's seat.

"Jealous?" I respond, twirling Ari's keyring on my index finger.

"I ain't bailing you out this time when you get busted for grand theft auto."

"Relax, moron, it's Ari's. She's coming down to hit a CBD shop with Jax this afternoon, and they're picking it up."

"Aren't you supposed to be buying a motorcycle so you can quit bumming rides, or was that a dream I had?" Denny joins in, looking to Cash for backup.

"Kinda hard to cart around his new girlfriend and her mini human on a motorcycle. Maybe he's rethinking,"

Cash offers on a smirk. I'm determined not to let him know I'd thought the same thing—before Maisy assigned us an expiration date. They'd have a field day with that one.

Carter pulls into the spot next to Cash and gets out.

"Now there's a man who respects his own reputation." I throw an arm out toward my oldest brother. "None of his car parts are attached with duct tape."

If I thought Cart would have my back, though, I'm mistaken when he grumbles, "I liked my old car better."

Right. Shit. That was the one I totaled—maybe now is a good time to tell them about Driscoll.

"Can we go inside, please? I'm roasting my nuts off out here." Denny gestures to the back door, and Cash gives him a chin lift as we all follow him, and he unlocks the place.

As soon as we step in, I can feel something's not right, and a glance at Cash and Carter says I'm not alone. The three of us rush down the hall toward the taproom, leaving a bewildered Denny behind.

"What the fuck?!" I exclaim, my brothers all echoing me.

Glass from the patio doors lies scattered across the taproom floor, shards catching the sunlight streaming in through the open frames. Both doors are destroyed, but nothing else looks disturbed. Tables and chairs are just as we left them, and the bar is tidy. Without speaking, we scatter in different directions. I race out the front door to see if anyone is hanging around or running away. Cash takes off down the hall toward the office, while Carter checks the brewhouse, and Denny pulls out his phone and calls 9-1-1.

Great, more cops.

There's no sign of anything unusual out front, and

Cash and Carter both emerge to report much the same while we continue scanning every inch of the place and wait for the police to arrive.

"This can't be a coincidence," Cash says with a growl, putting words to all of our thoughts. My stomach drops as I realize now is the time to tell them. I mean, Driscoll showed up three days ago out of the blue. It ain't a coincidence.

But before I can open my mouth, the front door opens. We all turn, expecting to see cops, but it's Carter's DC friend, Jeremy.

"What the fuck happened now?" He throws his hands out, staring at the shattered glass and our grim faces. He's dressed casually in jeans and a polo, but the quality of his clothes and the perfectly styled 'do keep his vibe the furthest thing from it. The guy dresses and acts like money, although the few times we've met he's been pretty cool. I mean, he even outdid me in giving Carter shit about his ugly-ass loaner car last time.

Carter goes to greet him with a handshake. "Thanks for coming, man." Well, the eleven o'clock meeting is now fully explained.

"I figured it was time for me to get over myself." Jeremy's half smile fades when he glances around again. "Trouble follows you guys around like a teenager after a short skirt. A fire last night and a break-in today? Do me a favor and tell me if you're betting on any teams this week. I'll choose the other guys."

"Hey," Cash barks, interrupting Jeremy's one-man show. "Where's Larry?"

Every pair of eyes snaps to the bar—specifically the spot beside the register where the Morton Frye carving of Larry calls home. But he's not there.

Cash rushes behind the bar to check, and the rest of us scan the floor of the taproom with no luck

Curses echo through the space, and I ask, "How much is it worth? Didn't you just have it appraised a couple months ago?" My eyes go to Cash but his go to Carter.

"A fuck of a lot." Carter frowns back at him while answering me.

It occurs to me that Driscoll wouldn't know about Larry, so maybe it's Carter's assholes after all.

"Larry's all over the website, right?" Denny asks. Shit, I've never even looked at the website. There goes my theory. "So it could be anybody. We don't know if it's your congress assholes."

Carter's gaze shifts to Jeremy.

"Word on the street is Clarence Cody is short on friends these days and keeping to himself in Iceland since you orchestrated the takedown of all takedowns." That was the congressman from Tennessee Carter busted—the ring-leader. Although Sunny and I did our part on the dark web convincing Cody's assistant to bust him so Carter's involvement wasn't so apparent. I'm still pretty proud of that one. I should get back in there and see if I can get some dirt on Maisy's mom or this Terry guy.

Carter brings a hand to the back of his neck. "About that..." He trails off, eyes dropping to the floor. Right. Jeremy's probably still irked at being left out—but Sunny must have been right that he was reaching out to Lynn in preparation to make peace.

As I thought, Jeremy shakes it off. "I know you were only trying to protect me by keeping it to yourself. Doesn't mean I still wasn't pissed." At the time everything went down, Jeremy was still working for one of the people Carter exposed, Congresswoman Grace Hopkins. Hell, he didn't even tell his own brothers until it was almost too late, so I can relate to Jeremy's resentment at being in the dark.

And it's the exact same shit I'm pulling with Driscoll. Time to prepare myself for an ass-kicking. I've made such a mess of this. My brothers will be livid we can't tell the cops without endangering Dax and me. I'll be putting them in such a shitty position. But I need to do it.

"I'm sorry, man," Carter says, and when Jeremy nods in acknowledgment, he continues, "Cody's always had a long reach, something I've learned from experience. How can we be sure he's not still coming after my family? And how's Hopkins been behaving? Anything suspicious there?"

But Jeremy shakes his head. "Cody's not a threat. The guy can't even afford a lawyer—no way can he pay for favors. And Hopkins has her tail tucked so far between her legs she's not even going to run for another term."

"Shit, man. I'm so sorry." Carter runs a hand through his mess of dark hair, and I realize this piece of news means Jeremy will soon be out of a job. "What are you going to do?"

"You know me. I always stay afloat." He lifts his chin, but it's obvious he's taking a hit and hiding it.

"Any reason you didn't tell Cart all this over the phone instead of driving all the way to Asheville?" Cash asks on a frown, clearly getting impatient.

Jeremy shrugs. "Beer?" When Cash's expression doesn't change, Jeremy looks back at Carter. "Just figured it was time to shake hands."

A knock on the door has us all turning that way again, this time to see two uniformed officers on the other side.

"Come on in," Denny yells.

The cops are gone an hour later, not having much to do besides take a statement and some photos. We put up a sign telling customers we're closed for the day, and Cash calls Oscar to tell him not to bother coming in. Denny borrows a truck from one of his buddies at work, and we pick up some plywood to board up the broken doors. By the time the last of the glass is swept up, it's past three, and my tongue is almost bloody from how hard I've been worrying the post in it.

We agreed not to tell Mama or Lynnie about this, considering both the fire and the sentimental value of Larry. And Cart and Denny don't plan on telling Sunny or Rosie because they'll only worry. But the plan all goes to hell when Ari and Jax show up to get her car, and she gets on the phone with Rosie.

Before we know it, everyone has descended on the place, and I've lost both my window to fess up about Driscoll and my chance to pick up the Triumph. Not my best day.

CHAPTER TWENTY-FIVE

DEMON SLAYING WITH STUART

MAISY

With an entire day off and no Bear, I decide to make the most of it. My attempt to cheer Miller up this morning didn't take, and I got the sense he wanted to be alone. But I worry he'll spend the entire day stewing about Driscoll. Or worse, doing something rash about it.

I promise myself to check in with him later as I ride to my first stop of the day, a piano store on Hendersonville Road on the way to Biltmore Forest. My conversation with Ginny from the other night has been on my mind, so I want to put myself in a room with pianos. I'm honestly not sure what will happen. I could conceivably break out in hives or throw myself on top of a baby grand and try to hump it. Either way, I fully expect to be kicked out of the store within minutes.

"Good morning," the slight, bespectacled man behind the dark wood desk greets me with a polite smile.

I paste on my own smile long enough to respond, "Morning." The air is still in here.

"Anything I can help you with?" I don't miss his perusal of my clothing. But there's little I can do about it since I only packed a few things when I left Mom and Terry's place. The rest of my meager belongings are either still there or in boxes in Dad's garage. I'm guessing the Piano Showcase doesn't get many solo twenty-year-old shoppers wearing cutoffs and Harley tanks.

"I'm just… looking," I try reassuring him by not using phrases like "trying not to faint or vomit" or "attempting to overcome childhood trauma."

He appears satisfied and returns his attention to the papers on his desk. My attention is pulled by the assortment of pianos in the room. They have everything from electronic keyboards in the back to uprights along the walls to digital Clavinovas and an assortment of grands in the center.

I trace my finger along the edge of a Queen Anne console, letting it drop to the keys to feel their coolness. But I don't press down. I'm on lap three before I even dare to sit on a stool.

The salesman must be bored because he asks from behind his desk. "Do you play?"

"I used to," I tell him.

"Ah, well. It is a commitment."

I want to laugh—the maniacal, off-kilter kind that gets people their own row of seats on the bus—but I manage to only nod and stupidly open my mouth to ask, "Do you mind if I?" I let the incomplete question hang in the air, and he quickly gestures for me to go on with it while he retreats to his desk.

I gingerly rotate to face the older model Steinway Grand. Here goes nothing. I don't know what I'm doing, and I'll probably make this poor guy's ears bleed with how rusty I am.

I begin by lightly dusting the pad of my middle finger from one end of the keyboard to the other and back again. Then I use my index finger and play a single lonely middle C. The hammer hits the string, and the note is amplified by the soundboard. I close my eyes until it all goes silent again.

Instead of wounding or frightening me, the sound brings a smile to my lips, so I do it again. Then I play simple scales, my fingers needing no direction from my brain. The sales guy must be rolling his eyes, but I don't care. This feels too fucking good.

Emboldened after several rounds, I take a chance and let muscle memory guide me into "Clare de Lune" since I associate it with a happy childhood memory of my old piano teacher. When I'm satisfied with that, I launch into Liszt's "Un sospiro," delighting in the bubbling arpeggios in the opening passage. My fingers float, and my feet automatically find the pedals as my body bends with the music. By the time I'm done, my vision is swimming with happy tears.

"You play excellently." The man at the desk has appeared at my side without my noticing, and I startle. "I'm so sorry," he apologizes.

"It's fine," I reassure him, careful to keep my teary eyes aimed down. I can't respond to his compliment because it makes me want to giggle. If my dad were here, he'd say I sound like a clumsy elephant, and he wouldn't be wrong. I'm nowhere near the level I was at before I quit. I wouldn't expect to be, and that's okay. It also proves my suspicion that it would take more time than I have in order to prepare for a performance anytime soon. Just as well.

"In case you're looking for... inspiration," the man says as he places a ream of sheet music on the music rack. Then he steps quietly away, leaving me with my old friends.

By the time I'm tired out, it's early afternoon, and I've not only made a new friend in Stuart, the sales guy, but I've secured an open invitation to come back and play whenever I want.

I take in my reflection in a shop window, noting that my cheeks are pink with exhilaration and my eyes bright. I hit Jameson's contact on my phone with giddy fingers as I suck Pepsi through the straw in my fast-food cup and lean my butt on my scooter.

"Are you calling to plan a kidnapping?" is his greeting.

"Um, no. But now I'm curious. Who are we kidnapping?"

"Me."

I drop my hand to rest the cold cup on my knee. "That bad?" He's been at his parents' house for probably two days now.

"Worse. My mother invited Liliana Hirschberger to dinner last night."

I gasp. "No!" Liliana is a nightmare cellist who's been after Jameson for years. She speaks only in the third person and has the pinchiest mouth I've ever seen. Which is no surprise since she only uses it to say vile things. Liliana once told a cellist I had a crush on that I carried a hidden colostomy bag and collected my own toenail clippings. Joanna, of course, adores her.

"Yes," Jamie confirms. "And she showed up with a good three-quarters of her left nipple actually peeking above the neckline of her dress. Joanna had to give her a heads up to adjust herself."

"Ew." My lip curls. Desperate twatwaffle. "You should come to Pete's tomorrow to escape. You can drown your sorrows in free macchiatos." I honestly don't know what he does with his time besides play.

"Invitation accepted," he replies. "But I'll need to make them Irish if I want to survive the next candidate in the parade of prospective brides. Joanna is on a mission."

Ugh. I hate this for him. And I could solve it with one word.

"Enough about me. Why did you call?" he asks.

But I don't feel right gushing about my day when he's stuck in his arranged nipple nightmare. It feels too much like rubbing it in. "Oh, no reason. Just check in for proof of life."

"Oh. Well, rest assured, I'm still breathing."

"That's good to know." I chuckle, but it's drowned out by a foursome of motorcycles roaring by on the street.

I hope Miller got his Triumph today. With all the stress he's under, he needs the distraction. I picture him as Ginny described, feeling the wind and wiping his mind clean, and the need to hear his voice suddenly balloons in my chest, so I say, "Hey, I've got to go, but I'll see you tomorrow, okay?"

I hardly even wait for his goodbye before I hang up and text Miller.

ME:

What are you up to?

His response is immediate.

MILLER:

I'm being suffocated

Wow. It seems the men in my life are magnets for disaster today.

ME:

Need a rescue?

MILLER:

Save yourself. Just promise not to let my memory die.

I laugh, and before I can type my response, he follows up with another text.

MILLER:

How's your day?

ME:

Pretty great, actually

MILLER:

Yeah? What happened, Gladys?

My grin threatens to split my lip.

ME:

I played a piano. It felt AMAZING

MILLER:

No shit? That's great! I'm happy for you

He's so sweet. And I'd love nothing more than to demonstrate exactly how sweet I think he is in person.

ME:

Where are you?

MILLER:

Work—wanna come over?

I text back an emoji of a scooter and chuck the rest of my Pepsi in the trash before hopping on my scooter to head north to Blue Bigfoot.

CHAPTER TWENTY-SIX

PANDEMONIUM AND OTHER FIFTY-DOLLAR WORDS

MAISY

The taproom at Blue Bigfoot is pure chaos. Which is particularly surprising considering the place is closed for business, and there are zero customers present.

"How have you boys not learned your lesson yet?" Rosie shouts at Denny.

"What did *I* do?" Denny throws his arms out at the same time Lynn shoves Cash's shoulder.

"What century do you think this is? First you guys try to tell me who I can talk to, and now you're keeping things from me again!" Her thick, dark braid whips the air as she turns to stomp away.

"It's *my* brewery, therefore, it's *my* break-in!" Cash yells after her as she retreats to a table where a man I haven't seen before sits. He looks to be in his thirties with carefully styled brown hair and an air of money I recognize from Jameson.

"It's been like this for thirty minutes," Miller says from my side. He's in another pair of ripped jeans today and a white T-shirt with an unbuttoned shirt over it. A black leather belt with a distressed silver buckle and some motorcycle boots complete the look.

"I didn't realize you guys were closed on Mondays. What's with all the yelling and the wood barricading the doors?"

Miller tells me about the break-in and theft, and my immediate response—after shock—is, "Driscoll."

Miller nods and pulls me to the back hall so we can hear each other over all the shouting. "That's what I'm assuming." He pauses and blows out a breath. "And the fire."

I gasp at that. "Seriously? I thought everyone agreed it was probably just some asshat teenagers."

"I was hoping," he responds, "but after this, I don't think so." There's strain on his face, and I want to smooth it away with a brush of my fingertips or maybe my lips. But this isn't the time, and I don't know if he would even welcome that kind of affection.

Instead, I say, "Ian Driscoll is one busy asshole." But my eyes widen as another thought occurs to me. "Do you think the fire was a distraction so he could be sure nobody was here when he broke in?"

Miller frowns and runs a tired hand through his gloriously messy hair. "Maybe?"

"You told your family and the police, right? Oh!" I grab his forearm. "Did they dust for prints?"

That makes him smile for some reason. "Uh, there have been about a hundred people using the doorknobs in this place in the last twenty-four hours alone."

"Oh, right." I bite my lip, and he looks at me like he wants to either laugh or kiss me. Let's go with kissing, please.

"And I'm going to tell my brothers—after this circus shuts down." He throws a thumb toward the noisy taproom, but I still scowl at him.

"*And* the police," I demand.

"Maisy…" he trails off. I remember his reasons, but I'm scared for him—and his family.

"I don't want you to get hurt." I force him to meet my eyes, and this time I don't stop myself from bringing my hand up to brush my thumb over his eyebrow, stopping at the metal barbell.

"I'll be okay." His voice is low and gravelly, making me want to press myself against his chest so I can feel the vibration in my own.

"You don't know that." I let my hand drop to his broad shoulder. I love touching him.

"Hey." He rubs my upper arms and waits until he secures my gaze again. "I promise I will." But he's clearly not satisfied with my expression because he adds, "I've got a lifetime of experience slipping out of tight spots, trust me."

I smile because I know it's what he wants. "Maybe you guys can set a trap and bust Driscoll in the act. Then you wouldn't have to tell the cops about you and Dax and Driscoll's motives." It would be hard, but this sudden escalation calls for all hands on deck.

Miller's grin goes lopsided, and his dimple comes out. "You know any mind readers or time travelers?"

"Damn, my usual guy just moved to Spain, but I'll let you know."

"Appreciate it. Now tell me about your playing. How did this happen?" he asks with a squeeze.

"Later." I pat his shoulder as I hear one of the women ask, "Where did Miller and Maisy go?"

"You guys scared her away!" another female voice accuses, so we grin at each other and return to the taproom.

Hollis rushes our way. She's a gorgeous blonde with black-framed glasses and an ass I would kill for. "I promise we're not usually this obnoxious," she reassures me.

"Yes, they are!" Cash counters, causing Hollis to spin on her heel and march back his way. He throws his palms out and laughs. These people are so freaking good-looking, it's like a casting call for *Love Island*, only everybody is dressed.

Almost the entire group from the fire last night is here—Ginny, Carter, Cash, Denny, Lynn, Rosie, Sunny, Hollis, Ari, her boyfriend Jax (a handsome older guy with spiky blond hair and a drawl that borders on mesmerizing), and this new guy. And everybody is still talking at once.

"I'm gonna need people to start wearing name tags," I tell Miller, making his lips quirk. "Who's that?" I ask, gesturing to the table where Lynn now sits with the new guy and glowers at her brothers from a distance.

"Jeremy. He's a buddy of Carter's from his old job in DC. Remember I told you about Sunny and me helping Cart bust a crooked politician?"

I frown. "He's not the politician, is he?"

"No." He laughs.

"Then why is Carter glaring at him?" It's true. Miller's oldest brother stands with his feet shoulder-width apart, hands frozen on his hips, and all of his focus centered on glaring daggers this Jeremy guy's way.

"Oh, because Jeremy's almost certainly been hitting on Lynn over text." I turn to blink at Miller, but he misinterprets my expression and attempts to reassure me. "But Lynn is too smart to fall for that shit."

Deciding to leave the caveman discussion for later, I ask, "Who was the politician?"

"Some dirtbag named Cody."

"Clarence Cody?" Clarence Cody is a congressman from Tennessee who fled the country to avoid charges for insider trading and some other corruption, I think. I remember it being a big deal a couple months ago. "I heard about that on the news. That was your brother?"

"Yup." Miller's grin turns smug.

"Wow." I survey the crowd again, seeing Sunny now trying to distract Carter, and Denny holding Rosie—crossed arms and all—in a bear hug while Cash leans in to say something in Hollis's ear. But Ginny's voice rings out above everyone's, announcing it's time to have a drink. "Your family's definitely not boring."

"You're not the first one to notice," Miller replies, leaning close enough that I can smell his skin.

Ginny gets everyone to at least sit down while they argue, and beers and sodas are passed around. I feel like this is a family matter, and I should excuse myself, but Ginny pulls me down next to her, effectively blocking my escape route. A lot of the talk is about the Larry statue, and I don't understand much of what's being discussed, so I start thinking about how they might be able to catch Driscoll. If somebody started following the guy again, they might learn something, at least. But he knows what all these people look like if he was stalking the family before like Miller said.

He doesn't, however, know what *I* look like.

Hmm.

After a while, Ginny rises from her chair. "The day's a

wastin', and there's not a whole lot more we can do about Larry but hope the police find him. I've got to get over to Madam Regina's to work on the *Dear Mona* column. Somebody's waiting for a response about the size of a man's member and how it relates to pleasure." While this statement is entirely inexplicable, it's somehow not all that surprising at the same time.

All the guys in the room either groan or wince—except Jeremy who throws his head back and laughs before declaring, "I'm going with Ginny."

A couple more people make moves to depart, and I stand to make my own excuses. But before I leave, I send Miller a meaningful look that says he needs to fess up and do it ASAP.

I, on the other hand, have my own plans for the rest of my day off.

CHAPTER TWENTY-SEVEN

IS SPANKING AN OPTION?

MILLER

It's only my brothers, Lynn, and Jeremy left in the taproom. Everyone else scattered over the last hour, having jobs and lives to get back to. Mama refused to take Jeremy along to Regina's—not because she doesn't like him, but because Regina runs a male escort business out of her Victorian in Montford and keeps visitors to a minimum. She did, however, say one of Regina's escorts is also a carpenter, and she'd see if he could fix our doors, so that's good news.

Cash pushes back from the table. "I'm going to the office to call the insurance guy. I'll let you know what they say," he tells Carter.

I worry my tongue post again with my teeth, trying to figure out how to get rid of at least Jeremy. If I have to confess in front of Lynn, so be it. She can keep a secret when it matters, and hell, she's the most likely to try and put a good word in for me. "You staying over?" I ask Jeremy. *Say no.*

"You can stay with Sunny and me," Carter offers before Jeremy can answer. Sunny officially lives with her grandfather, Duke, but I gather she and Cart do all their fornicating at Carter's place. I imagine having Duke walk in on you fucking his granddaughter would not end well.

"Nah," Jeremy refuses with a wave of his hand. Does that dude get manicures? "I'll grab a hotel."

Cart looks like he's gonna comment on that—probably to remind Jeremy he'll soon be unemployed—but instead, he says, "Come on back to the brewhouse. I've got a new brown ale I'm working on."

Jeremy doesn't need to be asked twice, and they both stand and grab their half-empty pint glasses to take with them, leaving only Denny, Lynn, and me.

"That's my cue," Denny says, "Gotta get my workout in," and I know it's now or never.

"Wait!" I shout. Everyone's eyes flash to me, some annoyed (Cash and Carter's), some curious (Lynn's), and the rest amused (the other fuckers). I open my mouth, having no clue how to start this conversation when my phone clatters on the table with an incoming call.

I pick it up to see Maisy's name on the screen.

"Well?" Denny asks from his spot nearby.

"What?" Cash demands from the mouth of the hall.

I glance at my brothers and sister and make a decision. "Never mind!" I'm sure there are groans and eye rolls, but I don't notice them because I stand from my chair and turn to the front door as I lift the phone to my ear. "Hey."

"Driscoll didn't do it!" Maisy shouts in my ear.

INSTEAD OF TAKING THE BUS, I steal Cash's keys and drive the four miles to meet Maisy in the parking lot of a shipping warehouse. When I pull up, she's leaning casually on her blue scooter, eyes to the phone in her hand, and lungs not breathing fire like mine are.

"What the hell, Maisy?!" I shout as I slam the door shut. The side mirror makes a groaning sound, but I ignore it as I stalk over to her.

She looks up from her phone and scowls at me. "Keep your voice down."

The only thing she'd tell me over the phone was that she followed Ian Driscoll. But that was enough.

"What is it you didn't understand when I said this guy is dangerous?" I grind out through gritted teeth.

She tilts her head, replying, "Well, technically, you never said that." She's trying to be cute, and I don't know whether to kiss her or strangle her.

I go with growling at her instead.

She steps forward and puts a palm on my chest. "Keep your pants on. I didn't talk to him." That's of some relief, but not much. Until her next words. "I talked to his wife."

Something explodes behind my eyes, and I only see white for several seconds. "You what?!" I never should have told her anything. I should have kept my shit to myself like I've been doing all along. This is how people get hurt—or worse. I'm no good for her, and now my stink has spread to not only her but her brother. What was I thinking being so selfish?

"Miller!" Both of her hands are on my chest now, but it feels like she's calling me from far away. "Breathe!"

Pain rips through my lungs, and it takes a few more seconds to realize I've stopped breathing. I blink and force my hands up to lay on the backs of Maisy's, and only when I feel the warmth of her skin do I snap out of it and draw in a deep swallow of oxygen.

"Miller," she says my name again, but this time it's spoken into my shirt because she's hugging me and burying her face in my chest. My arms come around her as I pull in quick breaths and exhale until I regain a steady rhythm. "It's okay." She burrows in and goes on tiptoe to place a kiss on the underside of my jaw.

I'm angry with her. I'm angrier with myself. And I don't know what to do with all that rage, so I do the only thing I can think of and drive my fingers into her hair to pull her head back so I can kiss her sweet fucking mouth.

I don't have gentle in me right now, so the kiss is almost violent. Our teeth clash, and our lips and tongues fight for dominance as our breathing grows heavy, and our fingers claw and search. Her mouth is hot and wet and her taste sweet as I pull her hair again to place her exactly how I want her for more of her mouth. She makes that mewling sound that drives me crazy, and I feel my cock thicken and grow heavy. One hand drops to her ass in those cutoffs, and I yank her into me so she can feel exactly what she's doing to me. She moans at the contact and drags her nails across my back. If it weren't for my shirt, she'd likely draw blood.

I squeeze her lush ass cheek again and move to slide my hand under her waistband to get skin-on-skin contact when a loud *honk* sounds, and Maisy jumps back. I release her, and we both turn to see a lady frowning at us through the windshield of her car where she's parked nearby. She rolls her window down and yells, "Some of us are trying to eat lunch!" in a snarky tone.

Maisy shoots her an apologetic wave while running her other hand over her hair to straighten the mess I've made.

I barely refrain from flipping the woman off and pull Maisy over to Cash's car where I hold the passenger door for her. When I get in on the other side, the feeble air conditioning does its best to keep pace while we both take a moment to calm down.

"I'm sorry," I finally say.

"For what?" Maisy replies, her tone almost amused. "That was hot."

I snap narrowed eyes at her to see that she's most definitely amused, which only gets my back up. "This isn't funny, Maisy. You don't know what kind of danger you've just put yourself in."

She shakes her head and drops the smile. "That's what you don't get, though. Driscoll didn't set the fire *or* steal Larry."

"Tell me you didn't ask his wife for his whereabouts." Sweet Jesus, is she *trying* to give me a heart attack at twenty-two?

"I didn't have to. As soon as I got near their house, I saw a guy with a beard leave the driveway in a red Kia." She waits for me to acknowledge that I know the car, so I nod because that's the exact car Driscoll drives. "So, I went to the door on the guise that I lost my dog and was canvassing the neighborhood looking for him. I even picked up a cheapo leash to make it more legit." She's looking pleased with herself, clearly not recognizing the lava threatening to overflow from the other side of the car.

"And," I prompt, taking pains to keep my tone friendly. I never really understood the whole spanking kink until right this very moment. Because everything in me wants to strip her shorts off, spank her pretty ass red, and then fuck her until she agrees to never do *anything* to put herself in danger like this again. Luckily, my voice doesn't betray my thoughts, or she'd be running for her scooter right now.

"Turns out the wife is chatty. And she's a dog person too, don't you know." She shifts in her seat, warming up to her story and facing me fully. I ignore the fabulous cleavage this new position provides. "In fact, she recently got a chocolate lab because she doesn't feel safe alone at night when her husband works from *eleven at night* to *seven in the morning* here at this warehouse!" She jabs a finger toward the windshield. "Including last night!"

My eyes go wide. That was not what I expected her to say. "For real?"

"For real." She throws her chin toward the warehouse this time. "I even verified with the guy at the front office that Driscoll was on last night."

When I send her a questioning look, she shrugs and looks down. "Boobs. They work every time."

I can only stare. And not at her tits this time. "So, he didn't have time to start the fire and get all the way across town to work, and if he took Larry, he would have had to shatter two glass doors right as the whole town was starting work."

"Yup."

"So this means… Driscoll might really be done with us."

Maisy nods, her lips curving in a gorgeous smile. "I'd bet on it." When I frown, she says, "But that's good, right?"

"Yeah, it's great." I stare out the windshield at the parking lot full of cars and the squat warehouse beyond. "But that also means this shit might have something to do with Clarence Cody after all."

She leans closer and grabs my hand in hers. "Or, more

likely, people are just assholes. You said yourself Cody has no resources—and the other congresswoman isn't involved. Not to mention the crimes don't fit."

She's right. "But it's still too much to be a coincidence."

"Miller." She waits until I meet her luminous dark eyes before continuing, "Bear has no father, was neglected by his mother, removed to a stranger's house to supposedly get better care, and was beaten up and traumatized before finally returning to plain old neglect again." She shakes my hand for emphasis. "Some people just get a shit deal. Other people sail through life never knowing hardship at all. It's the way it is, and you, my friend, got a shit deal. If I were you, I'd collect my insurance money, reopen the bar, and enjoy my front yard until the trees regrow in the back." She finishes with an emphatic nod like her words are truth itself, and I should believe every word.

I'm beginning to believe Maisy could make anything possible.

I look down where she holds my hand and lace our fingers together instead. "Do you know how amazing you are? I may have some bad luck, but you and Bear are the ones who got a shit deal." I bring our joined hands to my chest, leaning closer. "And here you are powering through and taking it all on your shoulders—not to mention taking time out to stalk *my* old stalker. And you do it all without complaining or feeling sorry for yourself." I close the space between us until my forehead rests on hers. "You're incredible, Maisy Romero."

Her cheeks rise with her smile. "You're not so bad yourself, Morty Brooks."

"Hey." I try to frown, but I can't. "That's Chester to you."

"Chester?" she asks with a laugh. "That makes you sound like a fat bloodhound."

"Alfred then."

"Hmm." She pretends to consider it.

I squeeze her hands again. "I meant what I said when I promised to help you keep Bear."

She nods, but it doesn't come with a smile, so I know she's forcing herself not to object.

"What do you say you let me take you out to dinner?" I venture.

"Like a date?" There's that sexy curve of her lips again.

"Yeah. That okay by you?"

She cups my cheek with her palm and studies my eyes before whispering, "Yeah."

CHAPTER TWENTY-EIGHT

IS IT CLOSING TIME YET?

MAISY

My date with Miller was hands down the best date I've ever been on in my life. Until I did the most idiotic thing and *fell asleep* before we got to the even better part. Luckily, I conked out in his arms, but still! I've been kicking myself since my alarm went off this morning, and I had to race to get ready for work. I'm on at Pete's in the morning and Jade's this afternoon, and then I should probably start crashing at their apartment or Grady and Kat's, since they're back from Atlanta. But it's the last thing I want to do. Sleeping in Miller's bed and getting to smell him and feel his warm skin was heaven. I could get lost in him.

Which is exactly why I should put some distance between us.

Of course, that's hard to do when I made him promise to drop by and see me today. I'm my own worst enemy —forget Mom!

Our date began like all the best ones do—with a kiss.

Then we dropped off Cash's car, which it turns out Miller did *not* have permission to take. This resulted in a hilarious ten-minute argument during which I learned a new insult (assbadger) and discovered that Miller's childhood nickname was Thumper. He assured me later it derived from his constant running up and down the stairs as a kid, but it's way too good not to use later.

Then I put my life in danger by letting Miller drive my scooter. I held on for dear life while he raced through town like a maniac until I took the keys back when we parked at Little Pigs BBQ. We ate until our bellies hurt, and I almost peed myself laughing at how big a mess he made of his face with all the BBQ sauce from his rib plate.

We ventured over to Battery Square Avenue in search of buskers by the Flat Iron statue and found a couple. One was a guitar player I knew from my days busking with Grady around town, and Miller and I leaned against a bike stand to listen while we sipped on sodas, and Miller quizzed me about my day at the Piano Showcase.

After last night's fire and the crazy day, neither of us wanted heavy talk, so we mostly told each other funny stories and talked about movies and music. It was perfect, and my cheeks hurt from smiling so much by the time he talked me into letting him drive the scooter home.

Lynn and Ginny were both gone, so we settled on the couch and watched *Into the Spider-Verse* for the one-millionth time for each of us. When Miller tucked me into his side, it felt so cozy and secure, I fell asleep before we even got to meet the badass that is Gwen Stacy.

I assume he carried me to his bed because I woke up in the middle of the night to find myself wrapped in his arms before the rhythm of his even breaths lulled me back to sleep.

I checked in with Bear during dinner last night, and he said Mom had to work but Terry was on the couch drinking beer and not looking like he planned on moving anytime soon. He promised to call if Terry changed his mind. Since I never heard from him, I assume all was okay, but I'll keep checking in until school is done for the year, and Mom will be tired of parenting. My bet is Thursday.

The bell on the door rings, and I look up from the espresso machine hoping to see Miller walking his fine ass in, but it's Jameson. I completely forgot about the promised macchiatos.

"Any interesting dinner guests last night?" I ask, adding fresh grinds to the portafilter.

He strolls to the counter in another pair of designer shoes, this time paired with slim-fitting navy pants. "Just the family, thank God. I still might need liquor in my macchiato, though."

Pete frowns at us from the milk jug he's wiping clean, and I roll my eyes. "I'm not serving liquor. Jameson will pour it himself from the flask he keeps strapped to his ankle at all times."

"Not a bad idea." Jamie shrugs. "How's Bear?"

"Crushing on a girl more than twice his age." I secure the portafilter in place and pause. "Do you know he actually said to me, 'Rosie's looking snatched'? At this rate, I'll be gray by twenty-five."

Jameson chuckles, but it's cut short by my dad bellowing, "Jamie!" as he walks through the door and into the café.

Shit. A headache immediately begins to form behind my eyes.

Dad takes care of himself, and I can admit that he's objectively a good-looking guy. I sort of lucked out by getting his deep brown eyes and golden skin tone. He swaggers into the café like a king into a great hall.

"Isn't this a sight for sore eyes." He lifts his arms to indicate Jameson and me.

I hold my palm out. "Dad—" I begin, but he cuts me off.

"Joanna tells me you're working on Rachmaninov's 'Sonata Number Two.' Excellent. One of Maisy's favorites." It's actually not; it's one of Dad's favorites. He turns to me, adding, "You should play it for the summer concert if Maryanne approves."

"Summer concert?" Jameson asks, his posture tightening.

"The Valley Symphony summer series. With Lee Joong-ki out, Maryanne is scrambling to replace him."

Jamie's eyes widen, and I know exactly what he's thinking. I also know Maryanne would never ask him to play, as much as any of us could wish it.

"I'm not doing the concert," I insist as much to Jameson as to my dad. The espresso machine spits beside me, but I ignore it.

"But Maryanne asked you?" Jamie's eyes are wounded. "Why didn't you say something?"

I throw my hands out. "Because it wasn't worth mentioning!" But instead of soothing his hurt, it only results in a wince. Dammit! "I didn't mean it like that," I try, but the damage is done. I've trivialized something Jameson would value like gold.

"That's why I stopped by," Dad says, oblivious to the mood change. "Maryanne is making it worth your while—ten thousand dollars for the honor of reintroducing Margarida Romero to the awaiting public. I wanted to tell you in person."

Jameson gasps, and I grit my teeth. Ten thousand dollars would be a dream, of course, but the universe is messing with me. I literally could not play a concert like this even if I wanted to in this short of timeframe. It's impossible, and despite the money, it would likely be soul-crushing.

"Dad!" My shout finally gets his attention, as well as that of the entire café, unfortunately.

"You okay, Maisy?" Pete asks from where he stands at a table by the window. I nod, but his eyes stay on me.

I lower my voice and lean closer, the edge of the counter biting into my middle, confessing, "I haven't touched a piano in two years. I'm not doing the concert, and that's final."

Dad's mouth drops open, and his face pales under his dark beard. "Two *years*?" The reality of my statement sinks in, and he looks lost. "But… why?"

My eyes well with tears, and I barely choke out the words, "Because it hurt too much."

He misunderstands, and I almost wonder if it's willful. "There are occupational therapists and drugs for that." This I know, of course, having dealt with joint pain and carpal tunnel on and off for years.

"That's not what I'm talking about," I croak.

"Nonsense!" He waves me off, then turns to Jameson. "Can't you talk some sense into her? Even if the summer series is out, this has gone on long enough!"

My tears spill over, and as I'm trying to decide between stabbing my father with a handful of drink stirrers or screaming bloody murder, a familiar voice enters the fray. "Somebody want to tell me what the hell is going on here?"

Miller rounds the counter, not so much as pausing at

the "Employees Only" sign and comes close. He turns me to him gently and brings both hands up to cradle my face, his thumbs wiping away my tears. "Baby, what happened?"

My belly goes liquid at the endearment, and relief floods my veins. It's the same endearment he used the other night when he saw my red nose and eyes. I did my best to ignore it then, but hearing it again makes me want him to call me only "Baby" for the rest of time. It feels like he's claiming me, cherishing me, and that's something I don't think I've ever felt in my entire life.

I'm too choked up to speak, so he turns angry eyes to Jameson and Dad. "What. Happened?" His voice is ice and fire at once, the storm in Tchaikovsky's "The Tempest Fantasia."

Dad blusters while Jameson demands, "Who are *you*?" His tone sounding too much like his father's.

"You didn't answer my question." More fire than ice from Miller this time.

I gather myself and lift my hands to Miller's torso. "This is Jameson and my dad." I turn my head, but not far enough that I lose Miller's touch. "This is Miller."

A flush rushes over Dad's face. "*This* is why you refused to marry Jameson?!"

Oh god. "Maisy?" Jamie looks even more devastated than he did before.

"You're choosing this… *derelict* over Jameson Newhouse? Over your career?"

Gross. I release my hold on Miller and lean over the counter, farther this time. "That's enough! You need to leave," I hiss at my dad, and he goes back on a heel at the venom in my voice.

"If you can't find the door on your own, I'm more than

happy to help you," Miller growls from behind me, his chest against my back for support.

"Sir." Pete appears at Dad's side and gestures to the door. "I think it's time for you to go." Of course Pete's manners prevent him from raising his voice or snarling like the beast behind me.

Dad scowls and turns to leave but stops halfway to the door, announcing, "You're throwing your entire life away, and I'm the only one who seems to care!" He shoves the door open and stalks down the sidewalk, leaving the rest of us in silence.

"I'm so sorry," I say to Pete, and when he waves off my apology, I switch my gaze to Jameson. "I'm so sorry."

Jamie studies me for a few moments, his jaw clenched tight and nostrils flaring before he treats Miller to the same. Without a word, he follows in my dad's footsteps, letting the door swing shut on an incoming customer's face.

Miller wraps his arms around my waist and drops a kiss on my hair as the customers return to their coffees and laptops, and the familiar hum fills the café again.

"Dax?" Miller says from behind me. I look up at him and follow his gaze to the customer Jamie almost concussed with the door. The guy is skinny with straggly blond hair down to his shoulders and a blank expression on his face, and I realize this is Miller's best friend—the one who helped him set up Driscoll.

I also realize something else. Dax is in some serious trouble.

CHAPTER TWENTY-NINE

NEVER NOBODY

MILLER

Fuck. Dax is doped to the gills, and I ain't talking weed. What the fuck is he doing? He only smokes Marlboros and herb.

"Yo!" He tries to lift his arm in greeting, but it sags back down to his side as he staggers into the café.

"Be right back," I tell Maisy with a squeeze before rushing out to the main floor to intercept my friend. "What are you on?" I get in his face.

His eyes come to mine, but they're unfocused, and his pupils are no more than tiny dots. "Nothin', man." He grins. "I'm here to meet your girl." I texted him earlier to meet me here so I could update him on Driscoll and introduce Maisy to my best friend. I told him to shower, not take a hit of smack.

"What's the matter with you? I'm not letting my girl anywhere near you like this." Okay, well, Maisy's not technically mine, but I might be gaining some ground.

He only smiles and pats me on the shoulder as he sways on his feet. "It's cool."

I grit my teeth. "It's not cool; it's fucked up. Tell me you're not dealing again."

His smile turns goofy. "You're startin' to sound like Cash, bro." Then he raises his voice. "Where's the beautiful Maisy?!"

I seize his arms in a tight grip and frog march him out to the sidewalk. "What did you take?" I demand again.

"It's no big deal," he slurs. "I got it under control." His breath smells like ass, and he's wearing the same clothes he had on two days ago.

"How'd you get here?" No way he could navigate the bus system in this state.

"Lester dropped me."

Goddammit! His old supplier. His name's not Lester—it's Leon—but he looks like a child molester, thus the nickname.

"Are you fucking dealing again, Dax?" I ask again, louder this time.

"Why do you want to know? You're killin' my buzz. I'm out." He turns and staggers down the sidewalk, and I know I have to go after him.

I glance back to the café to find Maisy watching through the window, her teeth caught on her lip and worried eyes aimed at me. "Hey." I gentle my voice when I go back in, getting close and scanning her face. "You okay?"

Her brow furrows. "Is *he* okay?"

"No." My jaw tightens.

"You need to go after him," she instructs, grabbing my arm to turn me back to the door. I resist.

"*You* need to tell me what that was with your dad and Jameson."

She shakes her head and tries shoving me again. "I'm here and next door all day. We can talk about my shit later. Go help your friend," she demands.

Knowing she's right, but still not wanting to leave her, I bring my hands up to the sides of her neck and kiss her. It's not chaste. It's hot and wet and full of promise. And I don't miss the steadying hand she throws at a chair when I release her and run after Dax.

DAX HAS DISAPPEARED.

For a guy as high as he was, I didn't expect him to get the slip on me, but he was nowhere to be seen when I got back out on the sidewalk. I ended up jogging around about ten different ways before giving up and checking his apartment. He didn't answer the door, so I broke in using some skills I learned back when we were asshole teens.

But there's no sign of my friend—or his stash. Yeah, I looked.

I'm late for work, so I grab a bus, text Dax for the fifth time, then check in with Maisy who assures me she's fine. In other words, she's lying. But there's not much I can do about it right now, so I ask her to hit Blue Bigfoot when she's done working. She says she's got a lead on an apartment and some errands to run, and I can't tell if she's avoiding me or being straight.

I close my eyes and drop my head back to the bus seat, worry buzzing through me.

I'm trying, Dad, but I could use a little help right about now.

"You're late. You're on john duty later," Cash barks at

me as soon as I pass the office, and I resist the urge to turn around and walk right back out the door. People behave like pigs in public restrooms, and drunk pigs are way worse.

My brothers have always liked Dax, but they essentially treat him like he stopped maturing in seventh grade —which arguably may be true. They're used to seeing him high and know he's been into stupid shit, but they don't know about the dealing. And I've always kept it that way.

So it ain't worth stopping in the office to have a heart-to-heart with Cash—or any of my family. That's if my brothers and I were capable of such a thing. I'm pretty sure the sincerest thing Cash has said to me in my life was, "Congrats, you didn't suck today," when I won a dirt bike race. It's just the way we are.

And there's no way in hell I'm talking to any of them about Maisy. I've dished out enough shit to all of them over their women, I'd be buried in seconds.

So I keep walking to the taproom, stopping only to grab my apron. There's a couple guys working on the patio doors, but other than that the place looks the same as always. I head right for a four-top that's just sat down and get to work.

I'm rounding up empties a couple hours before close when Maisy walks in looking a lot happier than the last time I saw her. She surprises me by walking right up into my space and going up on her toes to hit my lips with a kiss.

My smile is immediate. "Hello to you too." Since my hands are full, I can't pull her into me like I want, but it's still good just getting to look at her gorgeous face. Between yesterday and today, I get the feeling casual might be tossed out the window soon. But I need to follow her lead like I promised myself I would.

"I think I might have found an apartment." She rocks on the heels of her Converse, her smile getting wider. "It's technically a one-bedroom, but it has this alcove that would be easy to make private—it's way bigger than Bear's room at Mom's."

I'm conflicted, happy that she's excited but wanting her to stay at Mama's with me, as ridiculous as that sounds in my head. "That's great!" I say, keeping my thoughts to myself.

"Well, it won't be available for another three weeks, but Grady and Kat are back in town, and they have an extra bedroom for Bear and me until then. It's also close to the bus stop so I won't have to put Bear on the scooter or wake you up to drive me at the crack of dawn. Now I just have to figure out what to do with him when he's not at Mom's, and I'm working. He can't spend all that time at Pete's, and Jade does her best, but her patience with tiny humans is minimal," she rattles on as I fight a frown. Maybe I'm wrong about the change in casual status. "Oh!" She grabs my arm. "I told Grady and Kat about you guys looking for an act, and they said they'd love to chat with you guys. Isn't that great? You're going to love them. I also told them about me playing again, and they were super excited for me."

She's almost giddy, and after the episode with her dad and that Jameson guy, it's more than I could have hoped for. But she's moving out and putting distance between us.

"Give me their number, and I'll tell Cash." I force positivity into my voice.

A couple guys at another table flag me down, so Maisy finds herself a seat.

"Hey," Kelsie catches my attention when I go to the bar to place the order. When it's slow, I pour them myself, but we've got a decent crowd for a Tuesday night, so Kelsie's giving Oscar a hand. "Who's that?" She's pretending her question is idle chit-chat, but she can't hide her grin.

If it were any other girl, I'd say "nobody," but that's one word I could never use for Maisy. "Her name is Maisy."

"Oh yeah?" She watches Maisy swing her feet on her stool and sneak glances our way. Fuck, she's cute. Kelsie shifts her gaze to Oscar and yells, "Miller's takin' five. I'm getting his tables!"

I grin at her and give her the guys' order before heading back over to Maisy.

"I'm fine on my own. I know you have to work," she says as soon as I walk up.

"So, you're gonna hang out?" Maybe she *is* staying with me tonight after all.

Her mouth turns down. "Oh, well... only if you want me to." She bites her lip, looking uncertain.

And I decide to hell with it and go all in. She can always tell me to fuck off. I bend close and slide my hand around the side of her neck, bringing my voice low. "I always want you with me, Maisy."

She releases her lip, her eyes going liquid and her face softening. "Miller," she whispers. But it's not an objection.

So I continue with, "You're staying with me tonight," letting my thumb graze her jawline while I keep her eyes.

"Yes," she whispers again, and there's no doubt she gets my meaning.

I have no clue how I'm going to make it through the next two hours.

CHAPTER THIRTY

HOW'D THAT GET THERE?

MILLER

"I ain't your chauffeur, you know," Denny barks from the driver's seat two hours later, frowning at me in the rearview mirror. That's because as soon as he pulled up to the brewery, I opened the back door for Maisy and followed her in, leaving Denny in the front by himself.

But I did it out of necessity since it's hard to keep your hand on the bare thigh of a pretty girl in the backseat when you're stuck up front.

"What do you think, Gladys?" I turn to Maisy. "Is he a Jeeves or a Lloyd?"

She suppresses a laugh while Denny glances at her over his shoulder. "Sorry, Maisy, but I'm gonna have to throw your date out of a moving car." That has her letting her laugh go.

I like being her date, so I decide to shut my mouth and enjoy the ride. Denny is picking Rosie up at her parents' place, so he was headed up here anyway. Rosie's making the most of her time with Ari and Jax before they head back to Greensboro in a couple days.

The minute I get Maisy behind the closed door of the house, I back her into it and take her mouth. Her lips are soft and pliant, and I slide my tongue past them to get more of her taste—and to feel her responding moan. Her arms slip around my shoulders, and she lets me take the lead, moving her how I want and exploring her sweet mouth while my hands take on her curves.

I feel it the millisecond she freezes, but I'm ready for it. "She's asleep," I tell her, knowing she's worried about Mama walking in on us making out. I kiss her again, and when she doesn't immediately loosen, I say, "How can I know for sure? Because I checked that her light was out when we pulled up, and if she were awake, she'd be at the kitchen table right now. Kitchen's empty."

Maisy giggles this time when I go back in for a kiss, but her amusement fades when I slide my hand over her hip to her thigh and pull it up alongside me so she can feel my cock. As I grind into her, she responds by climbing me like a jungle gym, using my shoulders to pull herself up and straddle my hips with both thighs. I don't hesitate to grip her ass in both hands to hold her tight, never breaking our kiss as I turn and blindly take us to the stairs.

"Ow," Maisy says when her head hits the hallway wall, my lust-filled state having caused me to wander off course.

"Shit. Sorry," I pant, but she only pulls my lips back to hers.

Her mouth is incredible. Hot. Soft. Wet. Sweet. I can't get enough. And the little mewling sounds are back; I swear I could come from just hearing those alone. By the time I kick my bedroom door shut behind me, her tits and her hot pussy are straining against me, and she's clawing at my back.

She yelps in surprise when I drop her onto my unmade bed, but I swallow the sound when I follow her down for another taste of her lips. However, her lips aren't the only part of her I need to taste.

To that end, I rise to my knees and work the button of her shorts before unzipping them. She immediately assists by lifting her hips while I strip her shorts and panties off in one pull. A cute little bush sits above her pussy, and I skim my finger over its border, making her squirm with need.

I reach behind my back and pull my tee over my head, wanting to feel the bare skin of her thighs over my shoulders while I eat her. When I drag her to the edge of the bed and drop to my knees beside it, she yelps again, making me want to laugh. But my cock won't let me. He's in fuck mode which exhausts the effort of every thinking cell in my body.

Throwing her thighs over my shoulders, I can smell her before I taste her. Earthy and sweet. Dark pink folds barely hide her clit, and she's wet for me already.

"Soaked," I say, and when she squirms at my words, my grip tightens on her hips to hold her still.

I lean in for my first taste, drawing my tongue through her slick folds and up to circle around her clit before sucking it between my lips. She tastes even better than she smells, and I groan against her pussy as I take another swipe, this time delving my tongue inside. When the cold of my tongue post hits her clit, she moans, so I repeat the actions, returning to swirl her clit with the tip of my tongue before diving back in again. When she grinds herself into my mouth, I bring a hand around to stroke her clit with my thumb while I continue fucking her pussy with my tongue.

I pause only long enough to say, "Come on my tongue, Baby."

Almost immediately, the quivering of her muscles intensifies, and she comes in my mouth, her pussy clenching around my tongue as I feast on her. I don't let up until the last shudder runs through her and she's stopped panting my name.

My cock screams for me to stand and thrust into her relentlessly until I fill her with my cum, but I like to think I'm at least one step up from an animal, so instead, I kiss the inside of each thigh before rising up to drop my weight on her and kiss her chin.

"Holy shit," Maisy says, making me laugh.

"Glad you approve, Ms. Romero, but we're not done."

She circles me with her legs and arms, and I get to feel the wet heat of her against my lower belly while our breathing slows and evens.

"I knew you'd be distracting, but I didn't think you'd be *this* distracting." She smiles, intending her comment to be light. But I need her to know.

"I'm not a distraction, Maisy. I'm an ally. I'm on your team."

She studies my eyes and brings her hands up to cup my face. "You really mean that, don't you?" It's rhetorical, but I answer anyway.

"More than anything."

Then I lean in to kiss her again, allowing her to taste herself on my tongue until she's writhing under me again, and it's time to get naked. We shed the rest of our clothes in a flash, and I shift down to pay attention to her pretty tits.

Her tight brown nipples beg for my tongue, so I cover one with my mouth, sucking the peak in and tracing my tongue around it while I run my thumb over the other one. Maisy's fingers spear into my hair, and she arches her back while whispering my name. I respond by biting down gently on the hard bud, causing her to cry out, so I switched to the other breast and treat it to the same.

"I can't reach," she complains, squeezing me hard between her thighs, and I chuckle at her petulant tone.

"Can't reach what?" I tease against her breast.

"Little Morty."

I freeze and lift my head to catch her eyes sparkling with humor under the heavy need. "Don't *ever* say those words again."

She laughs, pushing at my shoulders and trying to roll me. I let her, happy to enjoy the view of her straddling me, her pert tits on display for my eyes and hands to feast. But I know she's got other plans when she shimmies down my body, letting her hot center slide over my hard cock on her way down.

When she halts, I know exactly why.

"You have…" she trails off.

"Hey, how'd that get there?" I tease, looking down my body at the ampallang piercing at the head of my hard cock.

Her initial hesitation fades as she inspects my dick like a pawn shop owner appraising a Rolex. Then she grins up at me with a look that has me simultaneously getting harder while dropping my head back to laugh.

She takes the opportunity to grip me in a hand and begin stroking. My laugh turns into a groan as she squeezes and slides, applying the exact right pressure to drive me insane. When she adds her tongue, I involuntarily flex my hips, thrusting into her mouth. She sucks me in, her tongue playing with my piercing.

I got the thing when I lost a bet with Dax, but the joke's on him because it not only drives women nuts, it enhances sex for me too. Like right now with Maisy's hot mouth and tongue over the head. It takes everything in me not to thrust hard down her throat. She continues to work me, stroking with her soft hands while she sucks and licks to the point where I have to pull away.

"Hey, I wasn't done." Her frown makes me need to fuck her even more than I already did, so I stretch over to my nightstand and pull a condom from the drawer.

I pull her up so she's beside me, then run my hand from her belly to the wetness between her legs. Two fingers slide in, and I begin to finger fuck her while my thumb tends to her clit. It's less than a minute before she begs for my cock.

"Please. I need you inside me."

I withdraw my hand to get the condom on and fit myself between her thighs. Smoothing her shiny hair back from her face so it splays over my bed, I slide in the first couple inches. She closes her eyes on a moan and arches her back, so I withdraw and thrust back in until I'm fully seated inside her soaked, hot pussy.

I lift to look down at her. Hair in a glorious mess on my sheets, lips swollen, and eyes so dark with lust they're almost all pupil, she's a fucking dream. And I'm making her mine. Her fingers flex on my biceps, and our breathing quickens while I establish a rhythm and her hips roll to match it. She mewls when I increase my pace, filling the air with her sounds accompanied by the coupling of our bodies.

My strokes get stronger, each one eliciting another

moan or mewl or whisper of my name until I can feel my control slipping. But no way am I coming until I feel the sweetness of her orgasm around my cock. When I pull out, Maisy gasps.

"What are you doing?"

I answer her by rolling us so her body's weight rests on top of me now.

"Ride me," I demand, and she doesn't hesitate to saddle up on a groan this time. Fuck, that's beautiful. Taking in the sight of her flushed skin and parted lips as she lowers herself back onto my cock, I memorize the moment, knowing I'll pull it from my memory often. I lose the visual when she bends to kiss my lips, her tongue sweeping my bottom one before she rises again and begins to ride me.

We watch each other as she establishes her own pace, tits bouncing with each drop and rise of her hips until I feel the familiar rush beginning. My thumb goes straight for her clit, circling the slick nub as the rhythm increases. I grit my teeth to hold back my orgasm, but when I start to feel her inner muscles quiver around my cock, I piston up from beneath her until she comes completely undone.

My own orgasm crashes over me as she rides the wave of hers, and I drive up into her like the wild animal I've been holding at bay. She claws at me and cries out my name until her body collapses on top of mine, and we both gasp for breath.

CHAPTER THIRTY-ONE
LIGHT AND DARK

MAISY

This guy might actually kill me. Aftershocks tremble through my body as I lie like a wet noodle on top of Miller and suck in all the air I can. He palms my butt and gives it a squeeze.

"I can't decide if I love your ass or your tits more."

"I definitely know which part of you I like the most," I tease on an exhale. His cock is a thing of beauty, and that piercing is the cherry on top. I've never slept with a guy who had a piercing, and now I kind of want to rent a billboard telling all men to man up and get one. "I think you've ruined me for all other men."

He squeezes again and grunts like a caveman, "No other men. Just me." And I've got to admit I don't hate the possessiveness in his tone. I've fought tooth and nail to be the master of my own fate and never let anyone exert control over me or make me beholden to them again. But everything in me now wants to belong to this man, just like I want him to belong to me. It just feels right.

Everything about Miller is fire and light, and when he turns all that energy and heat my way, I'm like a moth to the flame. But I know to my bones Miller would never burn me, despite what he may think of himself sometimes.

"I want you with me, Maisy," he murmurs in my ear, and a wave of intense relief and satisfaction washes over me at his words. Because I didn't realize until right now how alone I've been for so long and how that feeling of loneliness drained away almost the moment I met Miller Brooks.

He's so right; he's not a distraction. With him at my side, I can accomplish anything I set my mind to—including saving Bear.

"There's nowhere else I want to be," I confess, and he brings his arms up to encircle me, squeezing so hard I can't breathe properly. But I don't ask him to loosen his hold.

After a few minutes, we disentangle ourselves so he can take care of the condom. Then he flips the sheet back and we settle in, him pulling me to him so he's spooning me, and I fall asleep almost instantly, secure in the knowledge that everything will be all right.

I'M on afternoon shift the next day, so we sleep in until nine, and Miller tries calling Dax again with no luck. We come down to the kitchen to find banana muffins Ginny left for us with a note that says, "Good morning, sleepy heads. I'm off to run errands, but I'll be back by lunchtime. Carter is dropping Duke off this morning, FYI. Adrina can entertain him if you need to leave."

Miller groans, and I raise an eyebrow at him. "One of your old man friends?"

"Friend is putting it much too strongly. He's a cranky son-of-a-bitch." When I send him a quizzical look, he explains, "He's Sunny's grandpa, and he's got a lot of opinions. My advice? Ask him about Elvis and then pretend you believe everything he says. It'll get you on his good side."

"Noted." I pick up a muffin and realize they're still warm from the oven. It smells divine, and my stomach growls loud enough for Miller to hear it.

"You didn't tell me you were pregnant with a tiger cub."

I scowl at him, and he leans down to kiss me, distracting me from my breakfast for a few long minutes. We're interrupted by the ringing of the doorbell.

"Idiot forgot his keys," Miller says, dropping one last kiss on my lips before he heads to let Carter and Duke in.

I shove almost the entire muffin into my face and immediately know I'm going to gain ten pounds if I stay at Ginny's house much longer. My intention had been to crash at Grady and Kat's last night, but as soon as I saw Miller at Blue Bigfoot, my body got a mind of its own and velcroed itself to his front. Then he got all sexy and sweet and bossy on me, and I was toast.

I'm done fighting the pull he has on me. He makes me happy—simply sharing the same space as Miller had my awful encounter with Dad and Jameson yesterday fading away. I wasn't fighting a battle on my own; I had Miller in my corner, just like he said. Although I know I need to mend things with Jamie, it doesn't feel as hopeless or daunting as it might have. And my dad? After how rude he was to Miller, I almost don't care if we reconcile anymore.

"What part of 'not interested' don't you understand?" Miller's raised voice comes from the hall, and I wipe the crumbs from my lips to go investigate.

A woman in a sharp navy pencil skirt and a spotless white blouse stands on the other side of the threshold, visibly struggling to hold her temper down. "Is Mrs. Brooks here? Since she's the homeowner, I'd like to hear it from her, if you don't mind." Her light brown hair is pulled back from her face, allowing me to make out the tic in her jaw. What in the world is this?

"Well, she ain't home, but I can guaran-damn-tee you her answer will be the same one she's given your colleagues and everyone else." He slams the door in the poor woman's face and stalks back to the kitchen.

"What was that?"

He waves my question off and goes to the cupboard to grab two coffee mugs before sighing and turning around, the anger fading from his features. "Damn developers. They've been bugging all of us up here for years, wanting to buy the land. But there's only one way Mama or Winston or the Carmichael's are leaving this mountain, and that's in a coffin—hopefully a long-ass time from now. Although, I'm pretty sure Winston is three hundred years old."

"I didn't realize the land was so valuable." The houses are modest, and everything is surrounded by trees up here.

He chokes out a laugh and grabs the coffeepot to fill the mugs with our caffeine fixes. "It's not. The forest blocks all the good views people want when they buy property up in the mountains. Never keeps the vultures from pestering us, though."

Miller's rough edges don't bother me in the least. After all, he's a self-declared gray hat with not a lot of boundaries, but I'm about to suggest he didn't have to slam the door in that woman's face when my phone rings from the table. "Mom" appears on the screen, and I grab the device, saying, "It's my mom. Today is Bear's last day of school, so she probably wants me to come get him." I should add a car to my list of things I need but can't afford—because now that Miller and I have claimed each other, I need a better mode of transportation.

"Hey, Mom," I say into the phone, bracing for whatever mood she might throw at me.

"Nice of you to answer." What a surprise—rudeness.

I ignore her snarky tone and ask, "What's up?"

"What's up is we're selling the house and moving to San Juan. Got a buyer coming this afternoon, cash in hand, and as soon as we get it, we're buying plane tickets."

Every drop of blood drains from my face, and I blindly scramble for a chair before I faint. "What?" My voice is barely audible, but the expression on my face has Miller hurrying close.

"I figured you'd want to say goodbye, but don't get any ideas. You're not taking Bear out of my sight, you hear me? The last thing I need is you hiding the boy and making us miss our flight."

"Mom! Please don't do this!" I regain my voice and plead, "You've never even been out of the state!" Please don't condemn my brother to a life of neglect, abuse, and a home far from me.

Miller squeezes my shoulders, but I barely feel it.

Mom hangs up without a response or a goodbye, and my phone hand thuds to the table.

"When are they planning on leaving?" Miller asks, having deduced what the call was about.

"I don't know yet, but soon," I mumble, my mind racing for a way to prevent it. "I promised him," I say, finally looking up at the strained expression on Miller's face. "I promised him, Miller."

"I told you we'd figure it out, and we will. Might be time to play dirty." His voice is filled with conviction, but simply wishing for something doesn't make it happen—I learned that a long time ago.

I rise to my feet. "I need to go talk to her in person. Nothing's set in stone yet. They've supposedly got a buyer coming for the trailer later today."

"I'll come with you," he says, and that warm feeling of having him by my side starts flooding my chest. But I hold it at bay.

"No. It will only set her off." I know Miller won't rely on negotiation, and his tactics might backfire. "I need to try by myself first. I feel like we have time. Don't last-minute plane tickets cost a fortune?"

"Maisy," he objects. I love that he wants to help fight my battles, but this situation is too delicate right now.

"Just let me try on my own. If I don't get anywhere, we'll regroup."

"I smell bananas." A gruff voice comes from the hall.

"Shit," Miller curses through gritted teeth. "Duke."

A short older man with messy white hair and a pair of huge matching eyebrows wanders into the room, followed by Miller's oldest brother, Carter.

"Who's this?" Duke demands, pointing his cane at me, suspicion filling his eyes.

"Don't be rude," Carter scolds. "This is Maisy, Miller's girl." I guess we haven't been very subtle.

Duke narrows his eyes at me. "You don't *look* stupid. Couldn't you find someone without so many holes in his face?"

Carter laughs while Miller rolls his eyes, and I try not to think about the piercing I'm sure Duke doesn't know about. I need to focus, not spar with a stranger or talk about Elvis.

"You gonna be around for a while?" Carter asks his brother. "I've got some trees being delivered, but I gotta run back to the brewhouse for something. Figured we could plant a few today then finish up over the next couple days so Mama doesn't have to look at that mess back there." He gestures to the backyard where black ash and burnt tree skeletons stand out against the green.

Miller studies me before answering with a reluctant, "Yeah. If you can take Maisy with you. Her scooter's in the storage room."

I hug Miller tight and whisper, "Thank you. I'll call as soon as I can," into his ear before following Carter out the door.

I've got a fight on my hands and a promise to keep. No way am I backing down now.

CHAPTER THIRTY-TWO

MY NEW RIDE

MILLER

It's a struggle, but I keep my temper mostly in check as I pace the kitchen, and Duke settles into the den to watch TV.

"Where are the captions?" he bellows. "This show is in Dutch or something."

I go to the couch and grab the remote while turning to the TV. He's got an episode of *Sherlock* on. "That's not Dutch; it's English." Benedict Cumberbatch's voice comes from the TV in a perfectly normal British accent.

"I think I'd know if it was English. Just gimme that thing, and I'll do it." He snatches the remote from my hand, and I leave him to it.

All I can think about is Maisy's face yesterday when her dad was all over her—the same one I'm guessing she's wearing right now confronting her mom. I need to do *something* to help, even if I promised to give her time to try on her own.

"Shit!" I punch the door frame but only get split knuckles instead of any relief.

But the punch must have knocked something loose because an idea occurs to me. I pull out my phone to send a couple texts before stalking out the front door and through the lawn to Adrina and Wes's. Adrina answers the door with a smile and her usual Italian accent. I wonder if Duke thinks she's speaking Dutch whenever they talk. "Miller, hey. Come in, come in. Ari and I were just about to introduce Jax to telenovelas." Her smile is wide.

Christ, looks like I'm just in time. I follow her in to find Jax sitting on the couch with Ari, looking like he's just been introduced to his new cellmate and is about to become his bitch.

"Hey, Duke is over at our house, and I was wondering if somebody could go hang with him while I run a quick errand." I'm sure Duke is perfectly fine on his own; I'm honestly more concerned for Mango's sake. The old guy might beat him with his cane if nobody is around to remind him Mango's a pet.

Jax speaks up before I even finish. "Me! I'll go!"

"Who is Duke?" Ari asks.

Jax is off the couch and practically sprinting for the door. "I'll go find out."

"Sunny's grandpa," I explain to Ari before continuing, "I could also use a ride if it's not too much trouble. I'm going to pick up my new bike," I tell the women.

"Ooh! What kind?" Ari asks, straightening on the couch.

"A used Triumph Scrambler."

"I'll drop you if you promise to give me a ride later," she volunteers.

Adrina jumps in, "What about *Land of Desire*? We need

to find out if Aline chooses Caio or Daniel! You know I've been on team Daniel since the beginning."

"We'll watch when Jax and I get back."

I ask Adrina to keep an eye out for the tree delivery, and thankfully Ari doesn't waste time following me out the door. "How's Maisy?" she asks as soon as we pull out of the gravel driveway.

"Fine," I lie, not wanting to get into it. My knee bounces up and down as we round the first bend down the mountain.

"Did you catch Bear hitting on Rosie the other night? That was hilarious."

"No." I'm not trying to be rude—Ari is doing me a favor, after all. I'm just too keyed up for chit-chat. I should just ignore Maisy's wishes and storm over to the trailer park to have her back.

"He told her he was getting a new 'crib' with more room to entertain the 'babes.' Then he invited her over for chocolate milk."

I can't help cracking a smile at that. The kid is something else. "What did Denny have to say about that?" I manage to ask.

"He challenged Bear to a duel. Nerf guns at dawn."

I actually laugh at that, feeling the tension start to drain and getting control of my jimmy leg. I've got this. First, I need to show Maisy that I'm all in, and she doesn't need to do this alone. Then I'll make it so she doesn't lose Bear. I don't have a good plan for the latter yet, but I'm on my way to do the former.

Ari follows my directions to the seller's house in Black Mountain, and I thank her before closing the passenger door. Then I go ring the bell. When the guy answers, we walk over to his garage, and he pulls up the door to reveal my new ride—and the little something extra I texted him about.

Before long, I'm headed back home astride a growling Triumph Scrambler 900, barely resisting the urge to make a detour to the Redwood Mobile Home Oasis. But I agreed to hold off when Maisy asked me to earlier, and I can keep myself from reneging. At least for now.

An hour later, all three of my brothers stand staring at my new bike where I parked it on the lawn. Carter rounded them up to start on the trees before Blue Bigfoot opens, but nobody is paying even a little attention to anything but the Triumph.

"Shut the fuck up," I tell them, hands on my hips as I eye them.

Denny throws his palms up. "We didn't say anything." He tries and fails to keep humor from his voice.

"Shut. The fuck. Up," I repeat with more emphasis this time.

They all share glances and then lose their minds at the same time, laughing like a pack of hyenas at my expense. I close my eyes with a shake of my head. Assholes.

"I know we told you to get a ride of your own, but this is…" Cash guffaws and chokes out, "not what I expected."

"It's detachable!" I have to shout to be heard over their hilarity.

"Hey." Carter gets a hold of himself to speak. "I'd assume it was an impulse purchase, but I think our little brother actually thought this one through for once."

Of course I did. "It's for Bear, Maisy's brother," I explain unnecessarily as I shift my gaze to the Triumph with its attached sidecar. The seller had offered it to me before, but I'd turned him down flat, not having any use for it and not wanting to look like a douchebag riding around with it. When I texted earlier to ask if he still had it, I told him to tack it onto the price.

"Yeah, no shit," Denny says, still laughing.

"I never pegged Miller to be the first to venture into parenthood, but he's always been full of surprises," Cash offers, biting back more laughter.

"Very fucking funny." I flip them all off. "Are we planting trees or what?"

They finally let it go after a couple more jokes at my expense, and we get to work digging holes in the backyard under the blazing sun.

I've checked my phone every five minutes and sent Maisy a few texts—and Dax, for that matter—but it's been radio silence. So, I work out my mood with a shovel and rack my brain for ideas to help Maisy and Bear. Dax will have to wait. I've pretty much settled on blackmail by the time my phone finally rings. I just need to find out her mom's last name and Terry's, then find my way back to the dark web to start feeling things out.

"Hey," I say, gentling my voice and stepping away from my brothers. "You okay?"

"Yeah." She sighs. "Mom and Terry are home waiting for the buyer, and they haven't kicked me out yet, so that's a plus."

I swipe a gloved hand over my forehead to catch the drops of sweat before they get in my eyes. "Are you getting through to them? Need me to come down?"

"I don't know yet. Bear should be home in an hour—half day, so I'm sticking close. I don't want them telling him anything without me there."

"Good thinking." I prop a hand on my shovel and squint at the bright sky. "Hey, is your mom's last name Romero too? Her first name's Jackie, right?"

"Yeah, why?"

I don't tell her, instead asking, "What's Terry's last name?"

Her tone is wary. "Why do you want to know?"

"Just exploring options. I told you Bear's not going anywhere, and I meant it."

"Miller." Her tone turns from wary to willful. "Please don't do anything to get yourself in trouble."

"You gotta trust me, Baby," I urge. "What's his last name?"

"Fine. It's Barkowski. Now, what are you planning?"

"Nothing yet. You want me to come down?" I ask again. I'm anxious to show her the sidecar so she knows how serious I am about fixing her situation. There's no other option besides Bear staying put.

"Yo! Little brother! Stop slacking," Carter shouts my way. "The taproom opens in an hour." I wave them off while I wait for Maisy's answer.

"Not now." She pauses. "Don't you have to work today?"

"Don't worry about that," I respond. "If you need me, I'm there."

"You're a very sweet guy, Miller Brooks." She's said that before, although I have no clue why. When I don't say anything in return, she continues, "How about if I call you in a couple hours to update you?"

It'll have to do, so I agree, and we hang up. The boys and I get a total of six trees planted by the time we part ways to clean up and get to work. Mama comes home just as we're scattering, and she kisses each of us on the cheek, waving our concerns off when we tell her we're sweaty.

CHAPTER THIRTY-THREE

A PROMISE IS A PROMISE

MAISY

"Nice doin' business with you," Terry says as he shakes the buyer's hand in the doorway. I can't believe this is actually happening.

"You too," the guy says. "I can give you till Sunday to move out, but no longer than that. My old lady won't tolerate me a day longer." The buyer is chatty, having told us all about his wife catching him cheating and kicking him out—thus his need for alternate housing.

I tried several times to interject, sharing about the minuscule size of the second bedroom and how the heater doesn't work all that well in the winter. I even tried lying about shitty neighbors and an ant infestation, but Mom was all over me, making it hard to get two words in. She finally kicked me out so they could negotiate without my mouth getting in the way.

When the buyer drives off, Mom and Terry excitedly hug each other and chatter before Mom turns to me where

I stand near the bottom of the steps. "Now we can buy those tickets," she gloats.

My only hope now is that I was right and the ticket price will be higher than they anticipate. Not having the stomach to watch them celebrate, I trudge to the entrance of the park to wait for Bear's bus. I should take the scooter and just drive off with him. We could skip town and never look back. But that's not the life I want for Bear either. He needs security in addition to my undying love.

"Maisy!" he shouts when he hops off the last step of the bus. "Are we going to Miller's to try camping again? Miller said Bigfoot was probably scared off by the fire last time, so I'm pretty sure we can catch him when we try again. I already told Jordan, but he didn't believe me. He's gonna poop in his shorts when he finds out I ain't lying."

My chest constricts as I pull him into a hug and kiss the top of his warm head. "Not tonight, B. Mom wants you staying here." I release him and crouch down, forcing a smile. "But guess what? I'm staying the night with you guys." Mom said she wasn't letting Bear out of her sight? Well, she's not the only one.

"Can we have pretzel dogs for dinner?" He asks eagerly.

"Whatever you want."

I call Miller a while later and tell him I'm sticking close. While he's disappointed we won't be together tonight, he understands, and we plan to talk again when he gets off work. He makes no more mention of plans he may be hatching, and I'm completely torn on the idea. The reality is that he's been convicted of two crimes, and even if neither one was a felony, I'm guessing if he gets in trouble again, a judge might not be as lenient. I won't let him risk doing anything illegal to help my brother and me, but I'm a little afraid he might do it anyway. I decide to put my foot down when we talk tonight.

When I text Pete to tell him I won't be in for my afternoon shift, he asks if it has something to do with yesterday's drama. I lie and tell him I'm just not feeling well and don't want to spread the plague around the café.

On my fourth attempt to corner Mom late in the afternoon, she slams her bedroom door and locks it. Terry's out doing lord knows what, and I figure they'll switch when it's time for Mom to head to her shift at TJ's. I almost chew a hole through my lip as I sift through my options over and over. I could call CPS, but it would be a huge risk and one that could easily backfire. I also give consideration to lifting both of their wallets before moving on to tripping one of them so they break a leg and can't fly anytime soon. I even go as far as texting Jamie in case he's forgiven me enough to propose again. But even that won't help, so I just ask him to call me. I don't want to leave with things as they are between us right now.

When I do an internet search for flight prices, true panic sets in upon discovering that even last-minute flights from Charlotte to San Juan are less than $400. How can that be possible? I'm revisiting the option to go on the run when Mom emerges from her room to find Bear and me on the couch, him watching TV and me trying not to cry.

"Bear, shut the TV off. I got something to tell you," she says, and I brace.

"Hey, B, go into your room for a few minutes, okay?" I intervene, determined to talk sense into my mother. Maybe I can bribe her.

Bear stands to do as I asked, but Mom's not backing down. "No. Stay right where you are. I got big news to share." My brother's eyes go wide, and I imagine him anticipating some fabulous surprise—getting a gaming system or going to Disney World. When Mom says, "You, me, and Terry are moving to Puerto Rico," his little brow furrows.

"Where's that?" he asks me instead of Mom, but I can't tell him.

"It's a cool place with good food and beaches. Terry's stepdad lives there," Mom says.

Bear's panicked gaze darts from Mom to me and back again. "How far away is it? Is Maisy coming?"

"Far. We get to take a plane over the ocean." She's trying to make it sound like an adventure.

Bear stands, his back stiff and eyes wild. "Why are we moving?" He turns to me, and I swear I can hear his little heart break in his chest as he pleads, "Maisy?"

And I know right then what I have to do, so I take Bear by the shoulders and shore up every bit of courage to paste a smile on my face. "Don't worry, B. I'm coming too. It'll be great."

After all, a promise is a promise.

I don't call Miller like I told him I would. I can't talk to him because that will mean I have to tell him I'm leaving, and I'm not ready for that. Mom reluctantly gives me the flight information, and I'm horrified to find it's for Saturday, just three days from now. I use my for-emergencies-only credit card to book my ticket before playing a round of Sorry with Bear. He's moody and fidgety, not that I can blame him, so the best I can do is keep him distracted.

Terry rolls in as Mom is leaving for work in one of her child-sized shirts she swears get her bigger tips. I hear her tell Terry she's giving her notice tonight, and it's another nail in the coffin. I need to tell Pete and Jade in person that

I'm quitting and moving, so I decide to do it tomorrow when I show up for my shifts.

I make a to-do list, then run out to get pretzel dogs for Bear and me, and I even throw in some ice cream since everyone knows sad times call for sharing a pint with two spoons. I don't answer when Miller calls after dinner. And when he calls again after his shift, I only stare at his name on the screen while I lie on the couch in the dark and let my pillow soak up my tears.

Apart from having Mom change her mind, there's nothing I want more than to hear Miller's voice, but it's not smart. He'll only try to talk me out of going, and I need to be strong for Bear. Miller Brooks could probably talk me into just about anything—especially if he called me Baby—so I resist temptation and turn my phone off.

Twenty minutes later, the sound of motorcycle pipes startles me out of my daze. The loud noise abruptly stops just outside the trailer. So, I sit up, listening to the crunch of gravel under heavy footfalls approaching the front steps. The light knock on the door has me springing to my feet as my heart fights with my head about who we hope to find on the other side.

Bear is passed out in his room and Terry in his, and Mom is still at work. Still, I tiptoe to the door and slowly open it to avoid making too much noise. I'm both elated and scared when I see Miller standing on the top step in one of his black T-shirts and faded jeans with rips at the knees that I'd bet money were made the old-fashioned way.

His expression is one of frustration, placing creases between his brows and tension in his jaw. He opens his mouth to speak, but I quickly put a finger to my lips and step outside, forcing him down a step. Once I've closed the door, I put my hands to his shoulders and lead us away from the door.

But I stop short when I see what's got to be his new motorcycle parked a few feet away, and I cover my mouth with a hand so I don't wake the entire trailer park. Then I plow into Miller, wrapping my arms around him tight and wanting to stay right there forever. "You got a bike for three." My voice hitches on the last word.

CHAPTER THIRTY-FOUR

THE JIG IS UP

MILLER

I kiss the top of Maisy's head, strands of her silky hair catching in the scruff on my chin. My temper flamed on the drive here, just as it had been doing since this afternoon when she cut off contact. But now that her soft, warm body is pressed to mine, nothing but relief flows in my veins.

"If you're going all in for Bear, I'm going all in for you," I tell her, causing her arms to tighten around me. If I didn't know better, I'd think she was trying to choke me out. And I let her as the cooler night air swirls around us and the sound of a TV from a nearby trailer mixes with the chirp of crickets in the grass.

It's safe to say Maisy understands the meaning behind today's purchase, and I hope she lets me run with my plans to fix her situation. She's mine, which makes Bear mine, and I'm not letting anything happen to either one of them. It's how my dad would have played it, so that's how I know it's the right way to go.

When Maisy finally pulls back, her eyes are shining. "I can't believe how lucky I am to have met you." She smiles, but it's laced with sadness. I want to tell her I'm the lucky one, but she continues before I can speak, "You're an amazing person, and I don't want you to ever forget it."

"Maisy," I start, a strange sensation running up my spine. It almost sounds like she's saying… goodbye. But that makes no sense. "I have a plan."

Her smile wobbles in the dim light from her mom's porch, and she brings both hands up to my chest. "It's too late. They sold the trailer and bought their tickets."

Fuck! "It's not too late," I insist, my hands coming up to grasp her wrists. "I've got it all figured out. I already know how to navigate the dark web, and there's more than you can imagine on there. I can get dirt on Terry or your mom to give to the police, or we can figure out how to mess with them if that's a bust. I won't know the details until I get started. We just need a little time," I assure her. "When Sunny and I baited Clarence Cody's crooked assistant, it was a breeze." I wish I could offer her what Jameson can, but my reputation and lifestyle make that impossible. So, playing dirty is the only thing I've got.

She frowns then, a furrow etching deep into her brow. "Miller, there's no time left. And even if there was, CPS is not about to grant me custody. Not now, and probably not for a long time."

Okay, she might be right, but I can't imagine she's giving up. "We're obviously not just letting them take him, so if you don't like my plan, let's find another one."

"I already have one."

"Okay, shoot." Mine was kind of shit, I can admit, but we'll figure it out. Maybe I can even come up with something completely above board and respectable. Stranger things have happened, right? "I'm in, whatever it is."

Her voice drops to a whisper. "I'm going with them."

Oh. Okay, I reckon that could work. "And? Are you going to kidnap him and hope they don't bother with the hassle to get him back?" From what she's said, Terry is a lazy asshole, and her mom rates parenting just above death by fire on her list of activities she enjoys. "I've gotta say, though, I'm not all that excited for you to put yourself on the cops' radar like that." Me, fine, but not Maisy.

But she shakes her head and gazes up at me with only despair in her expression now. "No, you don't understand. I'm going with them to stay."

My breathing stops. "Wait, what?" She can't mean that.

"When I'm twenty-one, I can pursue custody there, just like here. I was reading about it today. His CPS file will just be transferred to an office in San Juan."

"No. You don't need to do that." My thoughts race. "I can steal their car so they miss their flight," I blurt. "Or…" What else could I do?

It's like she doesn't hear me, though. "You know I don't want to leave, but he's my brother. He has nobody but me to put him first, and I *have* to do it."

I let go of her wrists and pull her into my chest. "Maisy. There has to be another way." I realize the car thing won't work since they're obviously selling everything they can't take with them. But we'll come up with something better. The kidnapping thing might not be so bad. I can be the one to do it so she can stay out of harm's way.

"I can't even begin to tell you how happy I've been having you in my life, no matter how short the time. You're such a generous, kind, funny, incredible guy. Even if you don't see it, I do, and so does your huge, crazy extended family." She sucks in a breath, but I can't stop shaking my head. I don't want to hear her farewell speech. "Love isn't a given, even when it comes to family. But you've earned it, Miller."

I'm not even embarrassed by the croak in my voice when I respond, "What about you? You're unlike any person I've ever met, Maisy. You're the best person I know. You deserve love more than anybody."

"And I have it," she insists. "From Bear." I want to tell her she has it from me too, but she continues, "Our flight leaves Saturday afternoon from Charlotte. I think it's best to say goodbye now. It will only hurt more if we draw it out." She pulls away, taking her warmth and vitality with her.

But I hold on to her hand, not ready to let her go. "Maisy. Don't do this."

She goes for a smile, but it breaks just as she pulls her hand free. "Go have the wonderful life you deserve, Miller Brooks."

And she disappears inside before I can even tell her I've loved her since the second she jumped in my car in that ridiculous dress.

I fight with myself the entire ride home, determined to thwart her plans on one hand and to support her decision on the other. My mind races with questions. Why should Maisy have to give up everything? And why do I have to give her up? She just got here. Why do shitty people prevail? I'll never find anyone else as phenomenal as her. Maybe I should become a monk; they brew beer, right? Maybe I should move to San Juan too. Shit, I can't do that—I haven't even started my community service or paid my fine. Besides, Mama would come and drag my ass back the next day.

Although, she'd probably tag Maisy and Bear too, so it ain't the worst idea.

When I get home and try to crash, questions, options, and maybe a few revenge fantasies clutter my mind and keep sleep at bay. Around three in the morning, I rub my hands over my face and fix my eyes to the ceiling.

What do I do now, Dad?

But I already know his answer.

Put family first, before yourself. Always.

It's a tenet he lived by, and I know if I want him to be proud of me, I need to live by that same oath. Maisy is doing it for Bear, and I've vowed to do what's best for her. Making her feel shitty about it or trying to force my needs on her isn't putting her first. If she's sure me letting go is what she needs, I can be the one person in her life who thinks about what *she* wants, not what they want.

By the time I nod off, I've made the decision to support her. But if she thinks I'm staying away until she leaves, she's dead wrong.

"STOP FUCKING AROUND, and let's get this done! I have places I need to be before my shift," I snarl at Cash as I grab my shovel the next morning. He's throwing a tennis ball for Betty, but she clearly doesn't understand the rules. Every time he tries getting her to drop it so he can toss it again, she runs away so he'll chase her. I'm not sure who's the master and who's the dog in this relationship.

I'm tired as all hell and likely the crankiest I've ever been. It doesn't go unnoticed.

"If sex isn't putting you in a good mood, little brother, you're doing it wrong," Carter taunts from the grass by

Cash where he's drinking coffee from a travel mug. We're starting on the trees earlier today to knock it out and avoid the midday sun.

"Maybe he needs a diagram or something," Denny offers, and it takes effort to hold myself back from throwing a punch just to work my frustration out.

Cash finally wrests the ball from Betty's drooly mouth and hurls it across the yard. She runs after it. "Maybe Maisy dumped him. Still the longest relationship you've ever had, though, right, Miller?"

At the shit-eating grin on Cash's face, I lose my mind and go barreling headfirst into him, knocking his ass to the ground. He rolls and rights himself before coming after me and trying to pin my arms behind me. I spin and hook his leg, but before he falls again, he throws an arm around my neck and pulls me down with him, rolling us to pin me down on the dirt and grass. But I'm able to evade the pin and deliver a punch to his left cheek that has him roaring and charging me again.

Betty barks her head off, and I spot Lynn running from the house in my peripheral vision. "Why are you guys just standing there? Get them to stop!" she demands.

But Denny and Carter give us another minute before they eventually pull us apart. Betty runs circles around Cash, thinking this is all a game. We shake our brothers off, and I spit saliva and blood onto the ground from the shot Cash landed on my mouth. He sucks wind and shouts, "What the fuck was that about?!"

Hands on my hips, I pull in a few labored breaths before finally letting it all out, "Maisy's fucking leaving! She's moving to Puerto Rico with her family."

Lynn gasps and covers her mouth with her hand. "Oh, no!"

"Shit, man," Denny says.

But I'm on a roll. "And I have to let her go when what I really want to do is kidnap her—which I can't do for a whole shitload of reasons, one of which being my ass would end up in the clink for sure this time." I spike angry fingers through my hair, sending a cloud of dirt and dust into the air. "And, speaking of criminal behavior, Dax is smoking fucking heroin and avoiding me while somebody is still screwing with us, setting fires and stealing shit that feels way too personal to be random. So, this week has been kind of a lot, okay?!"

"Dax is hooked on smack?" Cash asks, absently rubbing Betty's head to settle her down.

I give him a curt nod. "And getting mixed up with the wrong people."

"That boy is his own worst enemy," Lynn says before switching gears. "Maisy didn't tell you she was moving before y'all hooked up?"

"It's complicated." I shake my head. "She's going along to keep Bear safe from her shitty mom and the maybe even shittier boyfriend. Everything was decided yesterday."

"Damn, sorry, Miller." Carter comes close and drops a hand on my shoulder. "Anything we can do?"

I draw in a deep breath and release it on a shake of my head. "Keep me from doing something stupid?" I suggest.

"That's kind of a tall order," Cash dares to taunt, holding both palms up to ward me off. But I'm too tired for a rematch.

Doing right by people you love isn't as fun as one might think, but while I'm at it, I may as well tackle everything at once and get it over with. So I look around at all my siblings and finally confess, "I've got something I need to tell you guys."

CHAPTER THIRTY-FIVE

DESPERATE TIMES AND ALL THAT

MAISY

"Seriously, Jade?" I snap my gaze from the door of Midnight Prints to my friend and employer. She only crosses her arms over her generous boobs and scowls at me as Grady and Kat waltz through the door wearing matching frowns.

"Look," I tell them all. "I've made up my mind, so nothing you say is going to change it." I should have known Jade would call Kat. The two of them are tight.

"Maisy," Grady ignores my statement, shoving his hands in the front pockets of his worn jeans. He and Miller could probably share a wardrobe now that I think about it. "There's got to be a way to keep your brother here," he repeats what's becoming an all-too-familiar phrase.

Kat, on the other hand, just walks up and folds me into a warm hug. She's all sweetness and light.

"Short of kidnapping, I don't see how," I tell Grady over Kat's shoulder.

As if the three of them ganging up on me wasn't

enough, Pete strides through the door connecting his café to the print shop, worry lining his forehead and turning his mouth down. "I came over as soon as I got the chance. What is this about you moving?"

I repeat the same explanation I gave Jade, to which Grady says, "As much as I hate the idea, maybe you should marry Jameson after all." The two of them get along, but I sense Grady knows Jameson's feelings run deeper than friendship when it comes to me.

"Excuse me," a woman in a tennis skirt and matching visor interrupts. "Does this come in any other colors?" she asks, holding up a child's shirt with an image of Bigfoot that says, "Hide and Seek World Champion" on it. As soon as I see it, I start to tear up. I'm in so much trouble. "My son loves—"

Jade cuts the woman off with a glare, "Can't you see we're in the middle of something here?"

The woman retreats to the other side of the store, and I start to worry Jade might go out of business if I leave her on her own.

"She's not marrying Jameson," Jade insists. "I said it before, and I'll say it again. He'd be in the next room every night jerking off to the nanny-cam footage from the adorable stuffed bear he'd gift her 'just because' on their wedding night." Okay, it seems Grady is not the only one who's caught the more-than-friends vibe from Jameson. Yikes.

I cringe at the thought and try to ignore her. "It's too late for that anyway. I'd have to fight for custody from a distance, and I promised Bear I'd never abandon him with Mom."

"I'm guessing your new boyfriend might also have something to say about you getting hitched," Pete offers.

"New boyfriend?" Jade, Grady, and Kat all chime in at once, and I glare at Pete. He throws his hands up.

I slept like absolute crap last night after Miller left. And since I have so many things to do in the next two days, I vowed not to think about Miller—it will only make me want to go see him, and I don't have time for the nervous breakdown that will cause. As you can guess, the not thinking isn't going well.

"He's exaggerating," I lie, and when I send daggers at Pete, he decides to help me out.

"My mistake. Must have been an old friend."

I nod, hoping they buy it.

"Are you gonna tell your dad you're leaving?" Grady switches gears, but my relief is short-lived. No doubt Grady hasn't forgotten the scene on the street with my dad two years back.

"I haven't decided yet," I admit. I'm so angry with my dad, it's probably best to just leave things as they are. Maybe one day, he'll see what he's done to drive me away, and he'll try to make amends. But he isn't my concern right now.

Since Mom appears to be serious about not leaving me alone with Bear, at least I didn't have to drag him into work with me this morning. Mom was up when I left, sorting through the trailer for anything of value to sell before Saturday, and I realized I'd also need to do something about my scooter and whatever else I can't take.

I sigh and face my friends. "Guys, this is something I have to do, so it would really help if you can stop trying to talk me out of it and just support my decision."

"You got it," Pete says. "What can we do to help?" Grady and Kat echo him, but Jade continues stewing.

Finally, she uncrosses her arms and comes forward to

hug me. "Fine." Then to Pete, she declares, "We're going to Puerto Rico for Christmas."

And like the smart man he is, he doesn't argue.

I KNOCK for the third time on the bedroom door, this time saying, "Jamie, I know you're in there. Please tell me I didn't just do battle with your mother for nothing."

Let's just say Joanna Newhouse wasn't too pleased to see me on her massive doorstep this afternoon. Unless I misread her greeting of, "Oh, it's you."

"I'm not speaking to you," Jameson finally declares. The door remains locked.

Well, looks like I'll have to do this through a door. "I'm moving to San Juan with Bear and Jackie."

The heavy wood door swings open so fast I'm surprised it doesn't blow Jameson's hair back.

"What?!"

Sitting on the damask sofa in his room—yes, in addition to the expected bedroom furniture, he has an entire living room's worth of furnishings in the cavernous space—I tell him the whole story, leaving any mention of Miller out of it.

Thankfully, he hears me out without interrupting. When I'm done, he stands and strides to his bedroom door. Not knowing what else to do, I scramble after him.

"Where are you going?"

"Mother!" he shouts, heading for the stairs with me trailing after.

"What are you doing?!" It occurs to me that he might be rounding up his mom to drag both of us to the courthouse. "Jamie, stop!" But it's like I'm not even speaking.

Joanna appears at the bottom of the stairs, finally causing Jamie to halt on the bottom step. She's wearing one of her sweater sets, despite the fact that it's eighty degrees out, and her hair is brushed out in its usual chestnut bob.

"What is all of this about?" she asks, frowning at both of us.

"I need your help," Jameson announces. "Maisy's mom is moving to Puerto Rico and taking Maisy's little brother with her. I need you to contact anyone you can think of to stop her."

"Really, Jameson, why is this any of my concern? She's the boy's mother."

Jamie's back straightens. "Because it's important to me, and I'm asking you to."

Joanna's gaze flashes back and forth between Jameson and me. "This sounds like a… *domestic* issue."

But Jamie doesn't give up. "Bear is nine years old, and he's already been in foster care for neglect. The kid has no shot without Maisy." Jamie draws in a calming breath and evens his tone. "So, I'm asking you to please do this. For me."

Joanna's lips purse as she studies her son until she finally says, "Very well. I'll see what I can do, but I'm not making any promises."

Relief floods my system, and I pull Jamie into a tight hug. I don't want to get my hopes up, but this might actually work. The Newhouses rub elbows with rich, influential people all over the state. Maybe, just maybe, someone can pull the right string.

We follow Joanna into the study and cross every appendage we can manage.

CHAPTER THIRTY-SIX

RECKONING

MILLER

"This is a stupid idea," Lynn hisses from behind me.

Denny turns to frown at her. "Nobody forced you to come."

"No way was I staying behind—again!" She scowls at him.

"Would you guys shut up?" Cash growls.

We all fall silent, listening to the extended chime of the doorbell as we stand crowded on the stoop. And we're just as silent ten seconds later when the door opens, and Ian Driscoll stands frozen, his hand gripping the doorknob and his eyes wide.

He looks like we just woke him up, which we probably did considering his work schedule. He also looks older now that I see him up close, deep wrinkles framing his eyes and lining his forehead. His beard and hair are peppered with gray.

Carter finally snaps out of it and speaks, "Dr. Driscoll, I'm—"

But Driscoll cuts him off. "I know who you are, Carter. And it's *Mr.* Driscoll, not doctor anymore."

Damn right it ain't! Denny mumbles something I can't make out, and Lynn makes what sounds like a dog's whine behind me.

"But Ian will do." When we don't say anything else, Driscoll lets go of the knob and sighs. "Would you like to come in?"

"We're good here," I speak for all of us, and he doesn't object, instead standing patiently waiting for us to explain our visit.

When I told my siblings about catching Driscoll following me and how I really got arrested trespassing on his property, they were understandably stunned. But the bigger shock came when I shared my suspicions about the car accident where the brakes gave out. "Who else would have done it? He was on my ass for weeks by that point."

"I thought you were bullshitting us when you said something was wrong with the car," Cash said. I knew they didn't believe me at the time, and my irresponsible reputation preceded me, so I hadn't pushed it.

"I couldn't figure out if you were bullshitting, or if Cody was targeting me and got you instead," Carter admitted, and I narrowed my eyes at him.

"You never told me that."

"You never told us Driscoll was following you!" he countered, his point not being entirely stupid.

"I don't get it," Lynn said. "Why would he follow you, and why after all these years? He's the one who did wrong."

So, it was finally time to tell them what I'd done to get Driscoll arrested. I tried to keep Dax out of it, but in the end, they guessed. It wasn't too far of a leap. It also turns out none of them had even known Driscoll was in jail the last five years, so they were ecstatic he hadn't been slicing other patients open all this time.

But as the possible implications of Driscoll's drug use while operating on Dad settled over my siblings, we all stood on the lawn in silence, apart from Betty's panting.

Denny lost it first. "Son-of-a-bitch!" His sharp voice startled Betty.

He was followed closely by a vein threatening to rupture in Cash's forehead as he shouted, "Fucking fuck!" and kicked at the ground. Carter remained silently simmering while Lynnie paced the lawn, rattling off a stream of cuss words, some of which even I'd never heard of before.

This lasted only a couple minutes before Carter abruptly closed the space between him and me and yanked me into a rough hug. "You did good, little brother," he said, his voice husky and his arms crushing my lungs. Lynn quickly joined the hug, followed by Denny and Cash, both of whom took turns ruffling my hair like I was six.

"Dad would be fuckin' proud," Cash grunted, and I felt something shift in my chest, like a jagged fault line sealing itself.

It was after I shared about Driscoll working during both the fire and the brewery break-in that my siblings got the crazy-ass idea to stop speculating about what Driscoll had and hadn't been up to since his release from prison and just go ask him face to face.

Lynn finds her voice first. "You want to tell us why you were following my brother?"

Driscoll doesn't appear the least bit anxious when he responds, "Which one?"

We all look at each other before I ask, "Are you saying I'm not the only one you followed, or you just don't know my name?"

"I know who you are, Miller. Just like I know Cash and Carter own Blue Bigfoot Beer, and Denny's doing his civic duty with the Water Rescue Unit, and Lynn is studying at App State." He gestures to each of us as he speaks.

"Do you have a problem?" Cash steps forward, voice threatening.

"Not at all." Ian Driscoll sighs and looks down at his shoes. "I spent some time in prison due to my drug addiction, and it gave me a lot of time to think. When I got out, I wanted to make sure you were all okay after… what I did."

"So you *stalked* us?" Lynn challenges.

He shakes his head, a ghost of a smile crossing his lips. "No. I tracked each of you down to see for myself you were okay. And, while I know your father's absence means nothing will ever truly be okay, I was heartened to see that you all appeared to have persevered."

"Except me," I say, finally understanding why he would have followed me and not my siblings.

"I was worried, yes. I figured the least I owed your father was to do what I could to keep you safe. When I saw you spending time with my former drug dealer, it concerned me, so I kept my eye on you."

Shit. He knows we got him busted.

"But when you started working with your brothers, it appeared you were keeping your head down and not doing anything to endanger yourself. When you came to my house, my wife thought you were a prowler and called the police. I told them it was a misunderstanding as soon as I saw it was you, but you ran. I knew then that you'd figured out I was following you, so I stopped. The last thing I wanted was to cause you more pain."

Denny scoffs, "I reckon you've done enough."

Driscoll's shoulders visibly sag, making him look even older. "I've thought about coming to see you a hundred times to apologize, but I resisted because, in the end, it would benefit me more than it would you. I had a weak moment just last week where I walked into your bar, but I knew immediately that it was a mistake, so I left."

Friday night.

"Look, this is all very touching, but none of it changes the fact that you killed our father," Cash bites out.

"You're absolutely right," Driscoll admits. "I will regret my actions for the rest of my life, but I don't expect that to be any solace to any of you. What I can say, however, is thank you."

"For *what*?" Lynn asks.

Driscoll's eyes find me. "The hospital had to protect itself, so I essentially escaped all responsibility. You getting me arrested was the best thing that ever happened to me. I'm confident I'd be dead right now if you hadn't made that happen."

Carter glances at all of us before responding, "I don't know that we're as happy with that outcome as you are."

"And that, I understand." Driscoll nods. "But my wife, my children, and I thank you nonetheless."

"So you didn't mess with the brakes on Carter's car while Miller was driving it?" Lynnie asks.

Driscoll's eyes widen in surprise. "God, no. Is that what happened that day?"

"You were tailing me? You saw that?" I'm kind of pissed I didn't spot him.

"Yes. I called the police and stayed with you until the ambulance came. You were unconscious."

I don't know how to feel about that.

"Did someone really disable your brakes?" Driscoll addresses Carter this time.

"We don't actually know for sure," my brother admits.

Driscoll frowns, the furrows in his brow deepening. "Is there anything I can do?"

Carter clears his throat. "I'm sure you can understand when I say the best thing you can do is to leave us be."

Driscoll's nod is emphatic. "I will. I promise. But can I just say one more thing?" When nobody objects, he continues, "I'd be proud to have kids as strong and devoted as all of you."

Had he said he knew Dad would be proud, I'd have punched him in the face, but I reckon I can live with what he did say.

We all turn to leave, and he doesn't move from the open doorway until we pile back into Carter's car and drive out of sight.

"We can probably still bring a new lawsuit against him," Denny says.

Lynn responds from the middle seat where she's pinned between Denny and me, "And what good would that do?"

Since the obvious answer is money or jail time, nobody bothers to respond. Because none of it can do the one thing that would make any difference at all—bringing our dad back.

Carter changes topics. "So, what do we think? Is Miller just a shitty driver, or did Cody actually try to off Carter?"

All four of them simultaneously answer, "Shitty driver."

"Fuck all of you. There was something wrong with that car—maybe nobody screwed with the brakes, and Carter was just too lazy to keep up with routine maintenance," I argue.

Cash turns to Carter with a sly grin. "Did Miller just call you lazy?"

"Says the guy who got fired from his landscaping job for sleeping in the truck with the A/C blasting," Carter replies as he turns out of Driscoll's neighborhood.

"It was a hundred degrees that day. I almost died of heatstroke!" I spend the rest of the car ride alternately shoving and insulting my siblings. Just as it should be.

CHAPTER THIRTY-SEVEN

GOODBYES SUCK

MILLER

The benefit of our visit to the Driscoll household is that it gave my mind something else to focus on besides Maisy. But as soon as I spot my bike in the driveway, it all crashes back in, and I retreat into silence.

"Hey, where were you guys?" Rosie jogs up to the car as we unfold ourselves from the tight quarters. "I thought we were doing a send-off at Blue Bigfoot for Ari and Jax before opening?"

"Shit. I forgot," Cash tells her. It's the first I've heard of it.

"How about if we make it lunch here instead?" Lynn asks. "I need to leave for work in an hour, and my boss is an ass. He's just waiting for a reason to fire me."

When I try to beg off, intent on getting to Maisy before I'm due at work, my siblings forcibly march me into Adrina and Wes's house for the impromptu farewell party. Almost the entire gang is here with only Hollis, Sunny, and Wes appearing to be missing. Don't these people have jobs?

"What's with Little Miss Sunshine here?" Ari asks when she sees my pissed-off expression.

"He's sad you guys are leaving," Lynn does a shitty job of covering for me before Denny throws me under the bus.

"Maisy is moving to Puerto Rico on Saturday, and he's not handling it well."

"No!" Mama appears at my side and puts an arm around me. There's no doubt in my mind she's pulled the entire story from Maisy over the course of this past week.

"We'll get some food in you to cheer you up." Adrina takes off for the kitchen, and Mama gives me another squeeze before going after Adrina, but the look she sends over her shoulder tells me we'll be talking about this later. She's followed by my brothers, all of whom would choose food over girl talk any day. Jax looks like he wishes he could follow, but Ari sits on his lap, effectively trapping him. Not that he's complaining.

"You owe me ten bucks," Rosie says to Ari.

Ari frowns. "No, you owe *me* ten bucks."

"Ari bet her ten bucks you'd screw things up with Maisy within a week. Rosie kept the faith, though," Luca explains while the women bicker. I'm so happy my misery could entertain everyone.

Now that the cat's out of the bag, Lynn wastes no time sharing the whole story with everyone, and Ari eventually agrees that I wasn't the one to fuck things up. I reckon I can die happy now. She hands the ten bucks over to Rosie who passes it directly to me.

"Sorry, Miller. I like her."

"Yeah, me too," I reply. Understatement of the millennium.

"She's pretty great, and her brother might be my new favorite person," Ari agrees and then turns to look at Jax. "We should get Ollie to do his magic and cancel their flight or something."

"Who's Ollie?" Luca asks.

"Nobody." Jax glares at Ari, but it bounces right off her.

"Jax's office manager. But he's a hacker on the side. I swear that dude can get past *anything*."

"I told you you're not using him for any more of your stunts," Jax growls, but Ari shuts him up with a kiss, and the rest of us turn away when they start taking things a little too far.

"I think I lost my appetite," Luca grumbles from beside me.

But I barely hear him because an idea just occurred to me that has me kicking myself for not thinking of it sooner.

"Ari, stop sucking face with your boyfriend. I need your help."

CHAPTER THIRTY-EIGHT
AT FIRST SIGHT

MAISY

It isn't until Friday night that I crack and text Miller.

He's texted me a half dozen times over the last day, and I've read them over and over, but I haven't responded until now.

ME:

Jameson's mom tried her best to help me keep Bear, so either the world is ending or she does not, in fact, have ice running through her veins.

He starts typing his reply immediately. I hold my breath while the ellipses dance, hoping he's not going to ask me to change my mind. But I shouldn't have worried. This is Miller; he's putting me first.

MILLER:

She didn't handcuff you to Jameson and take you back to the courthouse?

I smile as I respond.

ME:

Nope. She's got her sights set on a bitchy socialite now. I'm kind of disappointed to not have a reason to dislike her anymore. She used a ton of her contacts to go to bat for me.

Too bad none of it worked. I can't tell who's more upset about it: Jameson or me. We both cried when I said goodbye this afternoon.

MILLER:

How's Bear taking the news?

ME:

He's sad and anxious, but he's been talking about the pros and cons of long-distance relationships so he can decide if he wants to continue wooing Rosie from afar. In other words, he'll be okay.

It would be foolish to entertain the possibility of continuing my relationship with Miller over the distance, so I won't ever mention it. I know he won't either. Long distance is for people with money. And besides, we've only known each other for a week.

But I know I'm fooling myself on that last part because I've never felt like this about anyone I've dated before. I never knew I *could* feel this way about another person.

MILLER:

I'll tell Rosie to expect a love letter doused in Axe body spray in her mailbox.

I bark out a laugh, stunned that I'm capable of finding humor in anything right now.

MILLER:

What time is your flight tomorrow?

ME:

3:30. But we're taking the bus, so we leave in the morning for Charlotte.

MILLER:

I'm coming to the airport.

Panic sets in. If he comes to the airport, I might not be able to get on that plane. I shouldn't have texted him.

ME:

Please don't. I don't want to say goodbye like that.

MILLER:

I have a present for you and Bear, and I need to give it to you before you leave.

ME:

We don't need a present, Miller.

The memories of my time with him will do.

MILLER:

It's not up for debate. I promise you'll be glad to have it.

I chew my lip as I weigh exactly how stupid I'd be to cave and invite him over tonight. Colossally stupid is what I determine.

ME:

You can drop it off tonight.

My heart imitates a bass drum while I wait for his response. If I thought he'd jump at the chance to see me, though, I'm dead wrong.

MILLER:

It's not ready yet. Tomorrow.

I'm a bit dumbfounded by his response, and if I weren't so disappointed, I might be embarrassed about my eagerness. Maybe he's already over me. I thought him begging me to stay would make it harder, but this about-face is making it difficult to even breathe.

When I don't respond, Miller sends one final text.

MILLER:

Tomorrow.

"CAN I GET A PEPSI?" Bear asks as we sit with the luggage while Terry goes for one last smoke and Mom uses the restroom.

"Once we go through security," I tell him, my eyes scanning the crowd in the check-in area. Though I hate to admit it, I've been searching for Miller's face since the second we got off the bus and walked inside.

Mom strides our way in her high-heeled boots. "Everything is so frickin' expensive here. Can you believe they charge over two dollars for a donut?" she asks as she sinks her teeth into the overpriced treat.

Before Bear can ask if she got one for him, I whisper,

"I'll get you one with your Pepsi." This placates him, and he pulls a comic book from his backpack. I don't even care if I'm setting him up for a sugar crash on the plane. The kid wants a Pepsi and a donut? Done.

Mom puts her phone to her ear and talks into it with her mouth full. "Where are you? I wanna check in so we can get a drink where the planes are." I assume she means the terminal—and an airport bar. Yay, this should be a fun trip.

I keep my eyes on the various automatic doors spitting people in and out of the busy airport, and I see Terry wandering our way. My pulse jumps when Miller's face appears only a few paces behind him. Without any thought—or shame, apparently—I stand from my seat and sprint in his direction. At any other time, I might find the look on Terry's face hilarious as I run full tilt in his direction, but I only have eyes for Miller.

I crash into him at full speed and send him back on a foot as he grunts and catches me. "Sorry," I blurt as I wrap my arms around his strong back and press my face into the T-shirt over his firm chest. He smells like he always does, part woodsy, part spicy, and all Miller Brooks. Inhaling, I commit his scent to memory.

When he starts to disentangle us, I resist, not wanting to ever let him go.

"Maisy." He says, but I only shake my head. "Baby," he mutters with a laugh. "Let up for a sec."

Baby. My heart tears right down the middle while I commit that to memory too.

Knowing I can't exactly fuse myself to him and pretend we're conjoined twins who need to share a plane seat, I finally loosen my arms and take a small step back. And that's when I notice Miller isn't alone.

Two police officers stand to one side of him, and a man I've never met stands on the other. The man looks vaguely familiar, but I can't pinpoint how I know him.

"Where is he?" the man inexplicably asks, his tone eager. He's a natural baritone like Miller, but I'm guessing he likes to drop to a bass as well. Miller points to the row of seats where Mom, Terry, and Bear are sitting back and looking our way.

Terry appears bored, but as soon as Bear catches sight of Miller, he starts running toward us. It's only then I notice Mom's face has gone ashen.

And as I watch Bear pumping his little arms and smiling like a loon as he nears, it finally hits me how I know the strange man.

He's Bear, only thirty years older and with blond hair instead of sandy like Bear's.

I lose the powers of speech and motion as Miller intercepts my brother and lifts him in the air with ease. "Hey, B, how's it goin'?"

The man stares at Bear in wonder while the two police officers proceed to the seats, presumably to talk to Mom and Terry.

"Decent," Bear answers. "But I gotta dip. We're movin' somewhere. Sounds sus to me, but Mom says we gotta go."

Miller sets Bear down and turns him toward the man. I finally regain control of my muscles and circle Bear with my arms from behind, unable to stop taking inventory of the man's features.

"Bear, Maisy, this is Mason Langley." Being the smart guy he is, he leaves it at that. "Mason, this is Maisy." Miller pauses and ruffles my brother's hair. "And this is Bear."

At the look on Mason's face, my eyes immediately fill with tears, and it only gets worse when he crouches down to Bear's level and holds out his hand. "So nice to meet you, Bear."

My brother shakes his hand like a pro, saying, "You too." But that's as far as his nine-year-old manners take him, and he quickly turns back to Miller. "Did you get Bigfoot yet?"

"Not yet," Miller says. "Hey, can I talk to Maisy for a second while you hang with Mason?"

Bear glances from Miller to me and back again before a smirk plants itself on his face. "I got you, bro."

I manage to roll my eyes even through the threatening tears, and we step a few feet away—but not before I hear Bear start telling Mason about Jordan and his six-toed uncle. When I'm confident Bear won't overhear, I grasp Miller by his forearms and ask, "How? What? When?"

He grins at my stupefied word vomit. "June 2014 at a Marriott in Charlotte. A fuckload of men checked into a Marriott in Charlotte that month, but surprisingly few of them were named Jason or Mason. Got a pile of ID photos and knew him the second I saw him."

My mouth drops open. "I can't believe you remembered that."

"I remember everything when it comes to you." A corner of Miller's mouth lifts as he laces the fingers of both hands with mine.

I try not to swoon because I have so many questions. "But how?"

"I guess it's not that hard to get hotel records, at least that's what this Ollie guy said. He works for Jax. Took him ten minutes to get the records and another ten to download all the IDs. I had Ollie make sure Mason wasn't a serial killer, then I drove to his address in Boone. He remembered Jackie as soon as I mentioned her because it turns out she stole the money from his wallet and disappeared before he even woke up that day." Bear's dad has lived in Boone this entire time? That's less than two hours from Asheville.

"Always keeping it classy, my mom." Ugh.

"I told him what was up, and he requested an injunction to keep Jackie from taking Bear out of state pending a DNA test. Judge signed it this morning, and we came right here. That's what the police are telling her now." He shakes his head and grins, "Gotta admit we were sweating the timeline, though."

"So we're not going?" My voice is hesitant because this sounds too good to trust. The dice never fall my way—at least they didn't until I met Miller.

"If you try, I might resort to kidnapping after all." He releases my hands to cup the sides of my neck and smooth his thumbs along my jaw. I freaking love it when he does that.

"We're not going," I say, testing the words out.

"Nope." The dimple pops out as my man smiles and drops the sweetest of kisses on my lips.

I blink from my Miller daze, turning with a huge grin and yelling to Bear, "We're not going, Bear! We're staying here!" Half the eyes in the busy airport turn our way, but I don't care.

"Tight!" Bear yells back, holding up his fist for a bump from Mason—who obliges like Bear just offered him season tickets to the Panthers.

My eyes come back to Miller, and I shake my head. "I can't believe you did all this." Which isn't actually true. If anyone would go to these lengths for me, it would be

Miller Brooks, my gray hat hero on a motorcycle built for three.

He leans in so close I can see the ring of chocolate around his caramel irises. "I'd do anything for you, Maisy Romero. Besides, I told you I had a present."

I grin back at him and thread my fingers through his hair. "A present, huh. What were you going to give me if the injunction didn't come through in time?"

With a straight face, he immediately replies, "Chloroform. I hear it's handy for kidnapping."

I laugh and lift onto my tiptoes to plant another kiss on Miller's lips, hoping he can feel how grateful I am and maybe a hint of what I have in store as a thank-you gift.

"My babe lives in Asheville," we hear Bear inform Mason. "She's older, but that's how I like to roll."

Miller breaks our kiss to bury his face in my neck, and we both fight a laugh. Then we get back to the good stuff.

EPILOGUE

MILLER

One Year Later

"I'm told this one is for our friend, Miller Brooks," Grady says into the microphone where he, his girlfriend Kat, and Maisy all stand in the corner of the taproom like they do every Friday night.

I raise an eyebrow at Maisy from my spot behind the bar as they start playing the intro to some song I don't recognize. She laughs behind her keyboard.

"Here's your order—pretzel dog and an elk sausage." Kelsie appears beside me. "And Eden says we're officially sold out of pretzel dogs."

I give her a quick nod, my eyes still on Maisy. Grady strums his guitar, and Kat turns to smile at her before Grady starts in on the vocals. All I can do is shake my head at my girl when I finally realize the song is the Allman Brothers' "Midnight Rider."

Maisy laughs again at my expression, and I grab the

order Kelsie dropped off, walking it over to a table in the corner where Mason sits with Bear. I set the pretzel dog basket in front of Bear and hand the other to Mason.

"They're really good," Mason says, gesturing to the band. And he's not wrong.

Grady plays guitar and lead vocal, Kat does harmony and tambourine, and Maisy plays keyboard. But only on Fridays and only here at Blue Bigfoot—because my girlfriend is in high demand.

She teaches piano lessons six days a week, and she's got a waiting list a mile long. But she still makes time to play at the senior center once a month, and even Duke shows up to request songs and hear her play. She told me his latest request was "Hard Headed Woman" by Elvis, and he dedicated it to his sort-of girlfriend, Patty. We can't quite figure out if he loves her or hates her, but it's entertaining, nonetheless.

Mama says Maisy got her joy back when she started playing piano just for herself, and I reckon she's right about that. Mama has also unofficially adopted Maisy, giving her the mom she never had. The two of them chat on the phone so much, there are days I might never get my girlfriend's attention if she and I hadn't moved in together. We rent the one-bedroom with the alcove she found, allowing us both to save up for the future—whatever that might hold.

Her dad finally reached out, and we met him for lunch a couple months back. He wasn't a total asshole to her—or me—but there are still a lot of broken parts that need mending. He did drop by one Friday night and listened to the band, so I guess that's progress.

We sometimes hang out with Jameson, but I can tell he's still holding a torch for Maisy. I pulled him aside one night to make my position clear, and he's not crossed any boundaries since. Despite the parade of socialites his mom has brought in, he's resisted marriage, which I reckon has something to do with Maisy. But she insists he's decided to ditch his parents and their plans in favor of grad school. He'll be leaving in the fall.

"Maisy says I should learn an instrument, but I told her I'm gonna be a ball player instead," Bear informs us before taking a huge bite out of his pretzel dog.

"Oh yeah?" Mason gives him the side eye. "I thought you were going to join a motorcycle gang."

Bear only shrugs and chews before saying, "Both ball players and bikers get a lot of honeys, so I could do both."

Mason looks up at me for help, but I've got nothing. The kid is a regular Casanova. "What about Rosie?" I ask.

"I did a vibe check. She's dope and all, but I decided she's too old for me." Bear takes a sip of his soda and holds a palm up. "But don't worry. I let her down easy."

"Okay, Romeo. Let's let Miller get back to work." Mason ruffles his son's hair.

I head back to the bar and leave them to their meals, but I hear Bear's response as I walk away. "I ain't no Romeo, Dad. No babe is worth stabbin' yourself for."

I might need to have a talk with Bear someday about the crazy things love can do to a guy, but that can certainly wait. All he's interested in when he hangs with us is taking long rides in the sidecar, drinking smoothies at Pete's, and hunting for Bigfoot. We still haven't managed to catch him despite all our efforts.

Mason is dropping Bear off for the weekend, as he often does to give Maisy and me time with him. But Bear lives with his dad in Boone now. It took a while for everything to get officially sorted, but dad and son instantly clicked. Although we did buy Mason a slang dictionary to help him translate.

It turns out Mason is a widower, and he and his wife never had kids, despite trying. She died a year before he tied one on at a hotel bar in Charlotte and slept with Jackie. Not the best move, but also not one to regret since he got Bear out of the deal.

Since Jackie and Terry had sold their house, car, and pretty much everything else, they went ahead and took that flight to San Juan, hardly looking back. Don't let the door hit you on the way out, I say. Bear and Maisy stayed with us at Mama's while waiting on the DNA test—which was really just a formality since Mason and Bear are carbon copies of one another—and Maisy and Mason figured things out with a social worker's help. Bear slowly transitioned from staying with Maisy to moving for good to Boone.

While there were some tears from my girl, she knew it was the best thing for Bear, so it wasn't all that hard in the end. And when Bear goes back to Mason's after this weekend, he and his dad are flying to Chicago to spend the first full week of summer break with Mason's extended family. So, in the end, Bear not only got a dad, but a whole bunch of cousins, aunts and uncles, and grandparents.

When I get behind the bar, Cash is counting out change to a customer. He lets me tend bar a couple nights a week now, and I've officially graduated from bussing, thank God.

"You seen Lynnie?" he asks over the music and chatter.

"Nope," I lie. This ain't my first day.

"She was just here. Said she'd fill in for Jodi tonight if I needed, and we're getting slammed."

"Call Luca," I suggest. He's always up for hanging at

the bar, and he's filled in before. I reckon we've seen the last of Lynn for the night since I saw her out on the patio a half hour ago talking to one of the Asheville Arrows players. They looked like they were arguing, which tells me tonight's not the first time they've met.

She's home for the summer and working at the ballpark again, generally keeping herself to herself, not that I can blame her. When Jeremy was here last summer, he and Cart almost got into a fight over Jeremy hitting on Lynn. It was only resolved when Lynn decided they were both being assholes, and she took off on a beach vacation with her friends from school. She's no idiot.

Cash frowns at his phone and starts typing while I take the next customer's order and pour pints. Fifteen minutes later, Luca strolls in.

"Did you go see Dax today?" he asks as he ties a black apron on.

I wipe a puddle of spilled beer from the bar top and nod.

"He hangin' in there?"

"Best he can," I reply. "I told him you'd paint some more dirty pictures for me to bring him next time."

Dax's current address is the correctional center just north of town. He got busted for dealing about six months ago, and it was the best news I'd gotten in a long time. I couldn't help feeling like I'd failed him after he ghosted last summer. I'd only seen him once in the six months leading up to his arrest—he came to the taproom asking for money, and when I tried getting him to come back to the brewhouse to talk, he took off. But when he got arrested, he used his one phone call to dial my number, and Mama posted his bail before I could even check my bank balance. Dad always had a soft spot for Dax, so Mama wasn't about to let him rot.

He's been clean since he got busted, but we'll see if it sticks when he gets out. I go visit him a couple times a month and bring him shit my family comes up with that fits the short list of allowed items. Luca's naked lady paintings are a favorite.

"I'll get to work on that." Luca smirks and heads out to the floor.

"What can I get you?" I ask a bald guy wearing a golf shirt at the end of the bar by the register.

"You still got that Cryptid Chaos?"

I nod and grab a pint glass.

"Hey, what did you do with that Sasquatch that used to be here? Y'all called him Barry or something?"

I frown into the glass as it fills with dark beer. "Larry," I correct him. "Somebody stole him."

We never did get Larry back. The cops came up with nothing, so we took the insurance payout. But it's just sitting in the bank untouched in case by some miracle we ever get him back. It sucks to think about.

"No shit?" The guy picks up his beer from where I set it on the bar. "That sucks," he echoes my thoughts and hands me a tenner. "I saw one just like it in Raleigh at some gallery my wife dragged me to."

The hair on the back of my neck stands on end. As far as I know, Morton Frye didn't make two Larrys. Three more customers flag me, and I hold a finger up to them. "Hey, can I get your number? I want to find out more about this statue you saw."

"Sure." The guy jots down his number on a napkin, and I shove it in my back pocket. He's probably remembering it wrong—it's been a year since anyone saw Larry. But it's worth checking out anyway.

Just like with Larry, there were no good leads on the fire in our backyard either, but the trees we planted last summer are starting to come in, and we hardly notice it anymore. Mama's motto is to put things in the past and keep on living, so we've all decided not to dwell. It helps that no other catastrophes have fallen on the Brooks family since then—not even Ian Driscoll has raised his head.

I keep filling orders until Grady and Kat sing the last few lyrics of some song I don't know and announce they're taking a break—which means I'm on break too. I give Cash a shout and tag Maisy like I do every Friday during break time, dragging her to the storage room and closing the door behind us. It's become a ritual of sorts.

"Midnight Rider?" I ask, placing my hands on her hips. "I'll have you know I haven't been arrested in over a year."

She grins. "I thought it fit." She enjoys dedicating songs to me, and some I get but others are out of left field. When she picked "I Will Follow You into the Dark" by Death Cab for Cutie one week, I asked her if it was her way of telling me she'd been diagnosed with a terminal illness. She said she just thought the song was "cute." My woman is nuts.

"Did you see Lynn with Joey Martel earlier?" Her eyes light with interest.

Shit. "Whatever you do, don't tell my brothers. Now, can we stop talking about my sister and some ballplayer?"

I don't have to ask twice. Maisy snakes her arms around my neck and lets me feel her up while I kiss her. Summer means more of those short shorts she likes to wear, which makes it my favorite season of the year. I glide my hand down her bare thigh and back up again to grab her ass and pull her into me. She moans into my mouth, making me grind my hips into her and use my other hand to press against her back so we're flush against one another from hip to shoulder.

She jerks back on a gasp of pain, and I immediately loosen my hold. "Shit. Sorry, Baby."

She smiles, her lips swollen from our kisses and her cheeks heated. "It's okay."

"Lemme see." I twirl my finger to get her to turn around and then lift her shirt up to her neck so I can access the bandage just below her right shoulder. I peel it back to see the black piano keyboard tattoo she got yesterday. It still looks a bit angry, but it'll heal soon. "Looks okay," I say before replacing the bandage and dropping a careful kiss over it.

Maisy's pretty fond of my tattoos, especially the one I got for my dad—a pair of fiery angel wings over my heart. And when she said she'd always wanted one, I took her to the best artist I could find.

She told me choosing a piano is something she never would have done before she met me, but I don't think that's true. She's the one who worked through her complicated relationship with music. I was just there to listen.

"What are we doing with Bear this weekend?" She turns back around and looks up at me, those deep brown eyes and long lashes drawing me in like they always do.

"I figured we'd take him to get his own tattoo."

Maisy grins and puts her arms around me again. I return the favor. "Or how about we go riding?" She loves being on the back of my bike—she also likes swiping the keys and going for rides on her own. But her favorite is when we hitch up the sidecar and take Bear along with us.

"Whatever you want, Baby," I tell her.

"*Whatever* I want?" Her grin turns sly, and she slides a hand from my shoulder down my chest, only halting when she gets to my belt buckle.

I adjust my hold so her hips fit into mine again and dip my head to touch her lips. "Anything," I say against her soft skin. And I mean it.

My dad always said when you find what makes you happy, grab on to it with both hands and don't let go. I've always done my best to follow his advice, but it wasn't until I met Maisy that I understood he was talking about people, not things. So I'm holding on with both hands and giving it everything I've got, and the best part is knowing Maisy is doing the exact same thing for me in return. And that right there is surely making my old man smile, wherever he is.

Maisy sighs into my mouth, murmuring, "I've already got everything I need."

WE HOPE you enjoyed *Deja Brew All Over Again*. Up next is Lynn's story in ***Stout of My League***. What is she up to with Joey Martel?

SIGN up for Sylvie's VIP report for bonus content, freebies, and news on releases. You'll also get a **free book**, *Full-On Clinger* (Denny and Rosie's story!): www.sylviestewartauthor.com

. . .

WANT SOME SIDE CHARACTER TEA? Check out the ***Asheville Collection*** (Standalone Stories from the *Love on Tap* World). Catch Kat and Grady's story plus Pete and Jade's.

CURIOUS ABOUT ARI AND JAX? Hop on over to the *Carolina Connections* series for ***The Runaround***. Read on for an excerpt.

EXCERPT FROM THE RUNAROUND

CAROLINA CONNECTIONS, BOOK 6 (ARI AND JAX)

ARI: I've always said boyfriends are like martinis; they're lots of fun at first, but the longer you indulge the bigger headache they'll give you. With career goals to crush and more than a few balls in the air, there's no place in my life for the messy complications of love. Jax Crosby thinks he can tempt me to lose control and he's using his daughter to reel me in. He'd be dangerously easy to fall for, but there are more important things in life than love, aren't there?

JAX: I like to stay two steps ahead; that way, I'm never surprised. But even I didn't see this one coming. Congratulations to me—I'm a freakin' dad. Now I've got a teenage daughter who hates me, an ex who wants to cut things off my body I'm not ready to part with, and an attraction to a curvy songbird that couldn't have come at a worse time. But I've never met a situation I couldn't handle, and I've never let a female get the best of me. So why do I have the feeling Ariana Amante might be one more thing I never saw coming?

CHAPTER TWO
THE TROUBLE WITH WOMEN

JAX

"Don't even think about it, asshole," I muttered into my empty beer bottle before dropping it back to the bartop, completely disgusted with myself. She had me turned so inside out I was sucking on an empty beer, for Christ's sake. My eyes stayed on her full ass until she swung it around the corner and all I had was the sweet memory of it to keep me company.

Ariana Amante had a way of fucking with my mind, even when she didn't mean to. Not that I didn't see the clear delight in her eyes when she purposely challenged me—which was often. And, every damn time, it made me hard—something I should have remembered before I hunted her down tonight. My dick was gonna have zipper marks tattooed on it if I didn't get the hell out of here.

I flagged down the bartender, the same one who'd been sending Ariana puppy eyes all night, and asked for the check.

"I got hers. You can pay for yours," the kid said.

I gave him my best *no-fuckin'-way* glare and held up a twenty between my fingers before dropping it on the bar between us. "This'll cover both." Then I pushed back from the bar and walked off before he could respond. I couldn't blame the kid for panting after Ariana. She was every man's wet dream with her golden-bronze skin, long, silky hair and banging body with more curves than a Formula One circuit. But he didn't stand a chance in hell with a girl like her. She *played* with boys, this much I knew already.

I'd considered letting her try her game on me then showing her what it was like to date a *man* for a change, but that was before—before I'd gotten myself into a cluster the likes of which hadn't been seen since Pete Rose decided to give gambling a try.

And that right there was how I'd found my nearly forty-year-old self crashing a karaoke party at a shit bar downtown full of drunk kids and lovesick bartenders. Yeah, that was about on par for how things had been going lately for Jax Crosby.

Now, I pride myself on not letting shit get to me, but damn if God wasn't laughing like the devil himself at my ass lately. But I had a plan, as usual—one designed to return my life to its comfortable normal and rid myself of this unsettled feeling that had become my constant companion these last months. That meant regaining control and keeping complications to a minimum.

It also meant this wasn't the right moment to give the time or inclination to taking on an experiment like Ariana. Because that's what it would have been—an experiment. Nothing more.

No, I just needed her to do me this favor and then I could forget all about her again. Women came and went, just like everything else, and there was plenty of shit waiting on the other side of town and at my office that needed my time more than my dick needed to get laid. With that in mind, I steered my ass to the door, telling myself it was time to go.

Ariana's voice stopped me with my hand to the wood paneled door.

"Let's start this hour off with one of my favorites, shall we?" She teased the audience with her throaty laugh. "I'm sure you all know this one, so feel free to sing along."

The first few notes of Aretha Franklin's "Natural Woman" flowed from the speakers and I couldn't have stopped myself from turning around for anything.

Hardly a single person in the entire damn place uttered a sound as she launched into the first verse, her velvety tone hitting me in the gut like a sucker punch. I was captivated, standing there like a fool with my hand on the door and my head and nuts trying their best to bust out of me and jump on stage. How she was singing in a dive bar in Greensboro, North Carolina, instead of up on a stage at some packed stadium was beyond me.

I didn't know much about music, but I knew enough to be certain that Ariana Amante had something that didn't come along often. Her red painted lips slid into a sultry smile when she hit the chorus while one hand skimmed down over her waist and hip like a lover's touch, making my inner caveman clench his teeth and demand I march right up to the stage and carry her over my shoulder and out of this shithole. But to what end?

Yeah, I needed to stick to the plan and stay focused. And that meant getting my ass home.

Allowing myself one last drink of her lush body in that temptation of a black dress, I exhaled and pushed through the door. Her voice followed me for half a block until the street sounds drowned it out and I was back in my familiar world on my own. Hands shoved in my pockets, I bowed my head to the light spring drizzle and walked to my truck.

I'd have to steel myself before our next encounter.

There was no room for getting reeled in by her siren call. Not happening.

One thing was for sure, though. Lola hadn't been lying when she said Ariana was the best singer she'd ever heard. And, damn, if that wasn't inconvenient as hell.

Get your copy of ***The Runaround*** to continue reading Ari and Jax's story! www.sylviestewartauthor.com

Also available in audiobook

EXCERPT FROM ALE'S FAIR IN LOVE AND WAR

LOVE ON TAP, BOOK 1

Hollis Hayes is the worst neighbor in the entire history of neighbors.
She's also the hottest.
F.M.L.

I don't have time to fight with the dog groomer next door. There's a brewery to run, siblings to rein in, and a mom to look after. So if Hollis thinks I'll roll over and let her drive me out of business, she's not nearly as smart as she thinks she is.

Sure, I enjoy the little pranks we play on each other, and I don't hate watching her prance around in those tight leggings. But she's gone too far this time, even if she pretends to know nothing about it.

I'll do whatever it takes to save my business from going under, and if that means playing dirty with the girl I love to hate, game on.

CHAPTER ONE
VIRGIN SAYS WHAT?

CASH

"Blue Bigfoot Beer," I bark into the phone, tucking the receiver between my shoulder and ear. The customer across from me holds out his hand as I count his change from the drawer.

A breathy voice on the other end of the line has my hand freezing in midair.

"Is this Cash?" she purrs.

Hmm. Seems like my day might be about to turn around.

I drop the change into the customer's palm and toss him a chin lift.

"That's me. What can I do for you?" I have a few ideas if the voice matches the body.

She lets out a little giggle that has my dick twitching in my jeans. "I'm calling about your virginity."

My hearing must be going because it sounded like she just said I'm a virgin.

Turning away from the prying eyes of my brother a few feet down the bar, I take the receiver in hand and press it firmly to my ear this time. "Sorry, come again?"

"Your virginity," she repeats, her voice still filled with sex but carrying a tinge of amusement now. "I'm interested in relieving you of it."

I squint at my reflection in the mirror of the back bar, wondering if I always look this tired and trying to figure out which of my three brothers is fucking with me. I settle on Denver because that asshole has been way too jolly since he talked his girlfriend into moving in with him.

"Very funny, Rosie. Tell Denny I'm gonna kick his ass next time I see him." The phone drops back in its cradle with a heavy *clang*. I don't have time for jokes today. There's a brewery to run, a taproom to serve, a newbie to train, and a pale ale release tomorrow that I haven't promoted nearly enough.

I glance down the bar just in time to see Miller, my youngest brother, slosh water all over the floor mats as he drops a bus tub in the sink. The towel I throw hits him square in the face. "You *trying* to create a hazard, or does it just come naturally?"

He sends a glare over his shoulder, a new eyebrow piercing glinting at me as I brush past him to serve another customer. It's a regular named Smitty, so there's no need to ask for his order. I press a pint glass onto the glass rinser, then pull back the tap on *Squatch This*, a golden wheat with a crisp finish. It's one of our most popular beers.

The phone rings again, and I'm somewhat encouraged to see Miller answer it without any prompting while I get a card to start Smitty's tab.

"It's for you." My little brother thrusts the phone in my direction.

I gesture for him to make the rounds of the taproom as I grab the receiver. If I've got to work with him, I'm at least gonna train him right. Family can be a real pain in the ass sometimes.

"This is Cash."

"Oh, uh, hey." The masculine voice on the other end stumbles. I'd half expected it to be Denny cackling at his own stupid joke, but this voice doesn't belong to anyone I know. I wait another second for him to speak, but time is money.

"Who is this?" I demand, knowing I'm taking my busy day out on a stranger and hearing my mama's voice in my head urging me to be patient. It's never been my strong suit.

"Tom."

I rack my brain looking for any trace of a Tom but can't recall a soul apart from the guy who runs the smoke shop a couple spaces down. This is not that Tom, and I know this because that Tom is always high as an eagle's nuts and only refers to me as "Cool Money."

"Do I know you?" I glance out into the taproom to see Miller parked on his ass at a four-top of attractive brunettes. That little…

"Uh, no," Tom mutters.

Jesus, get to the point. "What can I do for you, Tom?" I repeat, impatience bleeding through.

"I was, uh, hoping *I* could do something for *you*."

For the love of Larry.

My eyelids drop closed as I brace a hip against the back bar. "Oh yeah? What exactly can you do for me, *Tom*?"

"Pop your cherry?"

When the receiver hits the phone's base this time, the clattering echoes through the entire taproom.

Someone is definitely fucking with me.

And I'm pretty sure I know who.

Recognizing the look on my face and the mood it signifies, Miller hauls ass back behind the bar, hiking his jeans up his hips as he goes. My little brother's contempt for belts is one of life's greater mysteries.

I take my agitation out on Larry, the Bigfoot statue that stands beside my register and watches over the patrons, scrubbing at some beer residue on its base with my towel. The ring of the phone has my molars gnashing, and I leave the receiver right where it is.

"Aren't you gonna get that?" Miller asks.

"Don't touch it!" I throw the towel onto my shoulder and stalk down the hall to the office.

If she wants to start something, I'll only bite back harder. My eyes narrow to slits as I attempt to bore a hole through the wall separating my brewery from the neighboring pet groomer.

Happy Tails Salon. The name is just as sickly sweet as her fake-ass smiles and fluttering eyelashes behind those misleadingly innocent glasses.

Miller's disembodied voice breaks through the speaker of the desk phone. "It's Mama, jackass. Line two."

Well, shit.

"Hey, Mama." I do my best to brush off my irritation. She doesn't need to know about any of my frustrations.

"Hello, darlin'. How are you?" Her concerned tone has me instantly wary. My eyes dart around the office, but I haven't one damn clue what I'm expecting to find.

"I'm great. How are you? Did you find Mango?" Mango is the love of her life, and everyone knows it.

She clucks her tongue. "You know, he showed up in the kitchen a few minutes after you left. I don't know what he got himself into, but he's here now, safe and sound. *Aren't you, my little sweetheart*?" she coos at the mongrel, and I realize I'm just being paranoid.

"That's good to hear." I glance at my watch. "Hey, aren't you late for work?" It's already halfway through the afternoon and I haven't gotten shit done.

"I'm leaving in a few. We're doing pizza and movie night," she replies. She works at the senior center coordinating activities and generally causing trouble. "I just wanted to call about your problem."

My butt drops into the desk chair, and I smile into the phone. "I wouldn't say he's *my* problem. I like to think of Miller as *all of our* problem."

"Oh hush, you. I'm not talkin' about your brother—although I am so glad you took my suggestion and hired him."

Took her suggestion? More like folded to her edict. Hiring Miller was not my idea at all, but the asshat crashed his bike and got fired from yet another job, so my hands were tied. Blue Bigfoot Beer is a family venture in many ways, but my oldest brother, Carter, and I are the only ones left holding the bag at the end of the day.

"Yeah, well." There wasn't much more to say than that. Mama always did teach us if you don't have something nice to say, don't say anything at all. "So, what problem are you talking about?"

"Your virginity, darlin'."

Fuck. My. Life.

Twenty minutes later, I'm staring at a Craigslist ad on my laptop that has both my name and Blue Bigfoot's phone number on it.

> *"Looking for someone gentle to break my guymen. I just haven't met the right person, and it's become a burden. Please be kind because I'm hideously ugly."*

"Dude, there are easier ways."

Miller's voice sends me jumping. The bastard is leaning over my shoulder reading the screen and breathing his nicotine dragon breath in my face. I give him a good shove.

"Fuck off. I didn't post this," I grunt. "And who's manning the bar?"

Hitching his jeans up again, he snickers, enjoying this way more than I'd like. "Relax. Oscar's got it covered."

I only glare in response. There's no way I'm telling him that Mama just offered the services of her buddy Regina to help me out with my so-called problem. The same Regina who runs an escort service catering to Asheville's elite and hard-up.

Of which I'm neither, thank you very much.

"Any idea who did it?" Miller flicks his tongue ring against his teeth, sending my already raw nerve endings buzzing.

There's only one person on this earth who can get this far under my skin and make me take my eye off the ball like this.

I grit my teeth around my growl of an answer. "*Hollis.*"

Find out what happens next in ***Ale's Fair in Love and War***
www.sylviestewartauthor.com

ALSO BY SYLVIE STEWART

Ale's Fair in Love and War, *Love on Tap,* Book 1

Smooth Hoperator, *Love on Tap,* Book 2

Asheville Collection, (Standalone Stories from the *Love on Tap* World)

Full-On Clinger, (*Love on Tap* Prequel - Denny and Rosie) *FREE ebook for a limited time at sylviestewartauthor.com*

* * *

Hot Flashes and Hockey Slashes, *Hot Flash Hookups,* Book 1

Mood Swings and Hockey Flings, *Hot Flash Hookups,* Book 2

Poppy & the Beast

* * *

Between a Rock and a Royal, *Kings of Carolina,* #1

Blue Bloods and Backroads, *Kings of Carolina,* #2

Stealing Kisses With a King, *Kings of Carolina,* #3

* * *

The Fix, *Carolina Connections,* Book 1

The Spark, *Carolina Connections,* Book 2

The Lucky One, *Carolina Connections,* Book 3

The Game, *Carolina Connections,* Book 4

The Way You Are, *Carolina Connections,* Book 5

The Runaround, *Carolina Connections,* Book 6

* * *

The Nerd Next Door, *Carolina Kisses,* Book 1

New Jerk in Town, *Carolina Kisses,* Book 2

The Last Good Liar, *Carolina Kisses,* Book 3

* * *

Then Again

Happy New You

Shorts and Novellas:

About That

Nuts About You

Booby Trapped

Crushing on Casanova

Playing by Heart

The Switch-Up

Taunted

ABOUT THE AUTHOR

USA Today bestselling author Sylvie Stewart loves dad jokes, hot HEAs, country music, and baby skunks—preferably all at the same time. Most of her steamy contemporary romances and romantic comedies take place in North Carolina, a.k.a. the best state ever, and she's a sucker for hugs from her kids and a good laugh with her hot-nerd hubby. She also cusses like a sailor and can't bring herself to feel bad about it. If you love smart Southern gals, hot blue-collar guys, and snort-laughing with characters who feel like your best friends, Sylvie's your gal.

facebook.com/SylvieStewartAuthor
x.com/sylvie_stewart_
instagram.com/sylvie.stewart.romance
bookbub.com/authors/sylvie-stewart
tiktok.com/@authorsylviestewart
pinterest.com/sylviestewartauthor
youtube.com/@sylviestewartauthor

Made in the USA
Coppell, TX
10 June 2024

33324086R00184